The wave of shock was almost tangible as it rippled around the table

On the silver tray in the middle of the table Lady Juliana reposed in all her nude and provocative glory. Slivers of grape, strawberry and melon were strewn strategically around her nakedness. Her whole body was dusted with icing sugar and shone in the pale candlelight like a statue carved from ice, an untouchable snow maiden. But there was nothing maidenly about the expression in her narrowed green eyes as she invited the men to eat....

Lady Juliana turned her head and her gaze fell on a gentleman, his face unreadable in the shadowed room. Juliana felt a curious sense of recognition. She smiled at him. "Come along, darling. Don't be shy."

The gentleman looked up, his green-blue eyes appraising her with complete indifference. "I thank you, ma'am, but I have never liked dessert."

* * *

Wayward Widow
Harlequin Historical #700—April 2004

Praise for Nicola Cornick's latest books

The Notorious Marriage

"This is a delightful Regency romp of manners,
mores and misunderstandings. Cornick's characters
come to life in this well-written story."
—*Romantic Times*

Lady Allerton's Wager

"A charming, enjoyable read."
—*Romantic Times*

"Ms. Cornick has managed to pack a whole lot
of mystery and humor in this highly romantic
and fast-paced story and is nothing short of a
pure delight to read."
—*Writers Unlimited*

"The Rake's Bride" in The Love Match

"Through vivid detail, the author firmly establishes
time and place for her rollicking tug-of-war."
—*Publishers Weekly*

The Virtuous Cyprian

"This delightful tale of a masquerade gone awry
will delight ardent Regency readers."
—*Romantic Times*

Nicola Cornick

WAYWARD WIDOW

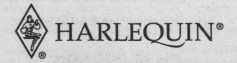

HARLEQUIN®

TORONTO • NEW YORK • LONDON
AMSTERDAM • PARIS • SYDNEY • HAMBURG
STOCKHOLM • ATHENS • TOKYO • MILAN • MADRID
PRAGUE • WARSAW • BUDAPEST • AUCKLAND

3 3113 02276 9634

ISBN 0-373-29300-3

WAYWARD WIDOW

Copyright © 2003 by Nicola Cornick

First North American Publication 2004

Visit us at www.eHarlequin.com

Printed in U.S.A.

Please address questions and book requests to:
Harlequin Reader Service
U.S.: 3010 Walden Ave., P.O. Box 1325, Buffalo, NY 14269
Canadian: P.O. Box 609, Fort Erie, Ont. L2A 5X3

To the girls.
Thank you.
This one is for you.

Prologue

1802

Lady Juliana Tallant had no memory of her mother. She had been only four years old when the Marchioness had run off with a lover and the Marquis of Tallant had banished his errant wife's portrait from the blue saloon. These days it lay swathed in sheets in the attic, gathering a layer of dust and dead spiders. The Marchioness's warmth and vitality, captured so accurately by the young artist who had been another of her lovers, was quenched by the shadows.

When matters in the house were particularly grim, Juliana would creep up to the attic and pull back the sheet that covered her mother's disgrace, and stand for hours staring at that pretty, painted face. There was an old spotted mirror in the corner of the attic and she would pose before it in her too-small gowns, her slippered feet stirring the dust as she tried to trace the resemblance between her own features and those on the canvas. The eyes were the same, emerald green with specks of gold, and the small nose and the generous mouth, too wide for true beauty.

The shape of Juliana's face was different and she had what she thought of as the Tallant auburn hair, although she had heard her father say that she was none of his begetting and so it was hard to see how she could have inherited his hair.

'It is difficult for the girl to be without her mother,' Juliana had once heard her aunt Beatrix say to the Marquis, but Bevil Tallant had given his sister a look that said she was a simpleton and told her that the child had the servants and a governess, and what more could she want?

On that particular summer's afternoon, Juliana had grown bored with the French lessons that Miss Bertie had been trying to drum into her and had begged and begged to be released into the sunshine. In the end the beleaguered governess had agreed and Juliana had skipped downstairs, ignoring Miss Bertie's instructions to take a parasol and behave with decorum. Young ladies always wore bonnets; young ladies did not run through the wildflower meadow, young ladies never spoke to a gentleman without first being introduced… Even at fourteen, Juliana knew that being a young lady could be a tiresome business. Even at fourteen, she was a rebel.

The door of the blue saloon was ajar and she could hear her father's voice above the clink of the teacups. Aunt Beatrix was making one of her infrequent visits to Ashby Tallant.

'I found Marianne living in Rome with Count Calzioni,' Juliana heard her spinster aunt say, in answer to a question from the Marquis. 'She asked after the children, Bevil.'

The Marquis grunted.

'I do believe that she would like to return to England to see them, but it is impossible, of course.'

The Marquis grunted again. There was a pause.

'I hear that Joss does very well at Oxford,' Beatrix said brightly. 'I am surprised that you do not send Juliana away to school as well. I am sure that she would blossom this time. You know she is eager to please you.'

'I'd be glad to send her away but it is all a waste of damned time,' the Marquis said. 'Did as you suggested last time and look what happened, Trix! The girl's wild to a fault, just like her mother.'

Beatrix tutted. 'I do not believe that one can condemn Juliana so harshly, Bevil. The incident at the school was unfortunate—'

'Unfortunate? Reading French pornography? Outrageous, more like. I ask you, Beatrix—'

'It was scarcely pornography,' Beatrix said calmly. 'Some naughty cartoons smuggled in by one of the other girls... Besides, if Juliana wished to read that sort of book, she need look no further than your own library, Bevil!'

The Marquis grunted a third time in a very bad-tempered way. Juliana checked that there were no servants lurking, then leaned more closely towards the half-open door so that she could hear more clearly.

'There is always marriage,' Beatrix was saying thoughtfully. 'She is a trifle young yet, but in a couple of years...'

'As soon as she is seventeen,' the Marquis said crossly. 'Married off and an end to it.'

'Let us hope so,' Beatrix said drily. 'It was not an end for Marianne, was it, Bevil?'

'Marianne was a wanton,' Bevil Tallant said coldly of his estranged wife. 'She lost count of her own lovers. Aye, and the child is cut from the same cloth, Trix. You mark my words. She will come to a bad end.'

The voices continued, but Juliana turned away and traipsed across the black-and-white marbled entrance hall and down the wide stone steps at the front of Ashby Tallant House. The heat struck her as soon as she was out of the shadow of the portico, bouncing up from the white stones and burning her face. She had forgotten her bonnet. And her parasol. There would be more freckles tomorrow.

She walked across the drive, taking the path that ran between the lime trees and away across the meadow towards the river. Her footsteps were slow and her thoughts dragged as well. She did not understand why her father always wanted to send her away. Every day he would endure a painful quarter-hour with her when she told him what she had learned at lessons that day, but with a child's instinct she knew that he was not really interested. When the clock chimed he would send her away without a backward look. On a larger scale, he had been pleased to pack her off to school at Miss Evering's Seminary and was awesomely angry when she had made her unscheduled return. Now it seemed that if she wanted to please him, she would have to marry as soon as possible. Juliana thought that she could probably do that. She knew that she was pretty. All the same, a little voice told her that she might do that and more, and her father would never be pleased with her. He would never love her.

Juliana took the path through the reed bed that bordered the river. Here the water flowed sluggishly in a series of bends as it approached the village of Ashby Tallant, and there was a big pool by the willow trees where the ducks preened and the fish sunbathed in the shallows. Juliana pushed the willow curtain aside and slipped into the golden darkness.

Somebody was already there. As her eyes adjusted to the dim light, Juliana saw a boy scramble hastily to his feet, rubbing the palms of his hands on his breeches. He was tall and gangling, with straw-coloured hair and a face pitted with the cruel spots of adolescence. Juliana stopped dead and stared at him. He looked like a farmer's son, or perhaps a blacksmith's boy. For all that he was the taller of the two, she still looked down her nose at him.

'Who are you?' She spoke with the cut-glass condescension she had heard in Beatrix's voice when she addressed the servants, and she expected it to have the same effect.

However, the boy—or perhaps he could more accurately be described as a young man since he must be at least fifteen years old—merely grinned at her tone. Juliana noticed that he had very white, even teeth. He sketched a clumsy bow that looked incongruous with his grass-stained shirt and ancient breeches.

'Martin Davencourt, at your service, ma'am. And you are—?'

'Lady Juliana Tallant of Ashby Tallant,' Juliana said.

The boy smiled again. He had a most engaging smile. It made two deep creases appear in his cheeks. It drew attention away from the disfiguring spots and made Juliana think of the brightness of sunlight on water.

'The lady of the manor herself!' he said. He gestured to a jumble of stones, the remnants of an old mill, which were scattered in the long grass. 'Will you take a seat with me, my lady?'

It was only when Juliana looked down at the grass that she saw the book lying there, its pages riffled by the slight breeze. There were diagrams and pictures, and beside it lay some paper and a pencil, where Martin Davencourt had evidently made sketches of his own. Bits of wood, string and nails were scattered in the long grass between the stones.

Juliana stared. She had evidently been embarrassingly

wide of the mark when assessing his social status and now she felt at a disadvantage.

'You are not from the village!' she said accusingly.

Martin Davencourt's eyes widened. They were beautiful eyes, Juliana thought, greeny-blue, with thick dark lashes.

'Did I say that I was? I am staying at Ashby Hall. Sir Henry Lees is my godfather.'

Juliana came forward slowly. 'Why are you not at school?'

Martin smiled apologetically. 'I have been ill, I am afraid. I go back at the end of the summer.'

'To Eton?'

'Harrow.'

Juliana sat down in the grass and picked up one of the oddly shaped pieces of wood, turning it over in her fingers.

'I am trying to build a fortification,' Martin said, 'but I cannot get the angle of the wall quite correct. Mathematics is not my strong point—'

Juliana yawned. 'Lud, mathematics! My brother Joss was the same as you, always playing with his toy soldiers or building battlements. It quite bores me to death!'

Martin squatted beside her. 'What sort of games do you enjoy then, Lady Juliana?'

'I am too old to play games,' Juliana said scornfully. 'I am fourteen years of age. I shall be going to Town in a few years to catch myself a husband.'

'I beg your pardon,' Martin said, his eyes twinkling. 'All the same, it seems melancholy not to play any games. How do you spend your time?'

'Oh, in dancing and playing the piano, and needlework and…' Juliana's voice faded. It sounded quite paltry when she listed it like that. 'There is only me, you see,' she added quietly, 'so I must amuse myself.'

'In playing truant by the river when the sun is shining?'

Juliana smiled. 'Sometimes.'

She stayed for the rest of the afternoon, sitting in the grass whilst Martin struggled to fit together the pieces of wood to form a drawbridge, with frequent recourse to the book and a certain amount of mild swearing under his breath. When the sun dipped behind the trees she bade him farewell, but Martin barely looked up from his calculations and Juliana smiled as she walked home, imagining him sitting in the willow tent until darkness fell and he missed his supper.

To her surprise, he was there the next afternoon, and the next. They met on most fine afternoons throughout the following fortnight. Martin would have some peculiar military model that he was working on, or he would bring a book to read—philosophy or poetry or literature. Juliana would prattle and he would answer in monosyllables, barely raising his head from the pages. Sometimes she chided him for his lack of attention to her, but mainly they were both content. Juliana chattered and Martin studied quietly, and it suited them both.

It was on a late August afternoon, with the first hint of autumn in the air, that Juliana threw herself down in the grass and moodily complained that it was foolish for her to go up to London to catch a husband, for no one would ever want to marry her, never ever. She was ugly and unaccomplished and all her gowns were too short for her. No matter that it was another two years before she would be able to visit the capital. Matters would get worse rather than better.

Martin, who was idly sketching two ducks that were

flirting in the shallow pool, agreed solemnly that her dresses would be much shorter in two years' time if she carried on growing. Juliana threw one of his books at him. He fielded it deftly and put it aside, picking up his pencil again.

'Martin…' Juliana said.

'Hmm?'

'Do you think me pretty?'

'Yes.' Martin did not look up. A lock of fair hair fell across his forehead. His brows were dark and strongly marked, and they were drawn together a little in concentration.

'But I have freckles.'

'You do. They are pretty, too.'

'Papa says that I will never get a husband because I am a hoyden.' Juliana plucked at the blades of grass, head bent. 'Papa says that I am wild just like my mama and that I will come to a bad end. I do not remember my mama,' she added a little sadly, 'but I am sure she cannot be as bad as everyone says.'

The pencil stilled in Martin's hand. Looking up, Juliana saw a flash of what looked like anger on his face.

'Your papa should not say such things to you,' he said gruffly. 'Was he the one who told you that you are ugly and unaccomplished?'

'I expect that he is right,' Juliana said.

Martin said something very rude and to the point that fortunately Juliana did not understand. There was a silence, whilst they looked at each other for a long moment, then Martin said, 'If you are still in want of a husband when you are thirty years of age I shall be glad to marry you myself.' His voice was husky and there was shyness in his eyes.

Juliana stared, then she burst out laughing. 'You? Oh, Martin!'

Martin turned away and picked up his book of philosophy. Juliana watched as a wave of colour started up his neck and engulfed his face to the roots of his hair. He did not look at her again, concentrating fiercely on the book.

'Thirty is a very great age,' Juliana said, calming down. 'I dare say that I shall have been married for years and years by then.'

'Very likely,' Martin said, still without looking up.

A slightly awkward silence fell. Juliana fidgeted with the hem of her dress and looked at Martin from under her lashes. He seemed engrossed in his book, even though she could swear that he had read the same page time and time again.

'It was a very handsome offer,' she said, putting a tentative hand out to touch the back of his. His skin felt warm and smooth beneath her fingers. Still he did not look at her, but he did not shake her off either.

'If I am unmarried at thirty I would be happy to accept your offer,' Juliana added, in a small voice. 'Thank you, Martin.'

Martin looked up at last. His eyes were smiling and his fingers closed around hers tightly. Juliana felt a strange warmth in her heart as she looked at him.

'You are very welcome, Juliana,' he said.

They sat for a little while holding hands until Juliana started to feel chilled with the breeze off the water and said that she must go home. The next day it rained, and the next. After that, Martin was no longer to be found in the pavilion beneath the willow trees. When Juliana asked, the servants said that Sir Henry Lees's godson had gone home.

It was almost sixteen years until Juliana Tallant and Martin Davencourt met one another again and, by then, Juliana was well on the way to the fate that her father had predicted for her.

Chapter One

1818

Mrs Emma Wren was commonly held to host the most dashing and daring parties in the *ton* and invitations were eagerly sought by that raffish group of fast matrons and bachelor rakes whose exploits were loudly denounced by the more staid elements of society.

On a hot night in June, Mrs Wren was holding a very special and select supper party to celebrate the forthcoming nuptials of one of her circle, that shocking womaniser Lord Andrew Brookes. The menu for this event had been hotly debated between Mrs Wren and her cook, who had almost resigned on the spot when appraised of the plans for the dessert. Eventually a compromise was reached when a French chef was hired especially for the occasion and the cook retired to his corner of the kitchen, muttering that no doubt Carème, the Prince Regent's chef, would have been the best choice, being far more accustomed to this sort of immorality than he was.

The hour was late and the dining-room air was thick with candle smoke and wine fumes when the dessert was brought in. The guests, predominantly gentlemen, were lounging back in their chairs, well fed, pleasantly inebriated and entertained by the ladies of the *demi-monde* whom Mrs Wren had daringly placed amongst her acquaintance. One of these Cyprians was perched on the bridegroom's knee, feeding him grapes from the silver dish in the centre of the table and whispering provocatively in his ear. His hand was already inside her bodice, fondling her absent-mindedly as his face flushed a deeper puce from drink and lust.

As the double doors were thrown open and the footmen staggered in, Mrs Wren clapped her hands for silence.

'Ladies and gentlemen…' her voice dipped provocatively '…pray welcome your dessert, a most special creation to mark this sad occasion…'

There were murmurs and laughter.

'I am sure that Andrew will not be lost to us,' Mrs Wren continued sweetly, glancing meaningfully at Brookes, who had an overflowing brandy glass in one hand and the lightskirt in the other. 'It takes more than *marriage* to come between a man and his friends… Andrew, this is our gift to you.'

There was a smattering of applause. Mrs Wren drew back and gestured to the footmen to place their huge tray in the centre of the table. They stood back and the liveried butler whipped off the silver lid.

There was a silence. The wave of shock was almost tangible as it rippled around the table. Several of the rakes sat up straighter in their chairs, their mouths hanging open in amazement. Brookes went quite still, the girl sliding unnoticed from his knee.

On the silver tray in the middle of the table Lady Juliana Myfleet reposed in all her nude and provocative glory. Her auburn hair was fastened up in a dazzling diamond tiara. There was a jewelled garter about her right thigh and a thin silver chain about her neck. There was a grape in her navel, curlicues of cream placed strategically about her body, and slivers of grape, strawberry and melon strewn artfully across her nakedness. Her whole body was dusted with icing sugar and shone in the pale candlelight like a statue carved from ice, an untouchable snow maiden. But there was nothing remotely maidenly about the expression in her narrowed green eyes. She held out a silver spoon to Brookes with a little catlike smile.

'You have first dip, darling…'

Brookes obliged with alacrity, scooping up some fruit and cream with such enthusiasm that his hand shook and he almost spilled it on the floor. The other men pressed close with catcalls and cheers.

Sir Jasper Colling, one of Lady Juliana's most persistent admirers, pushed to the front. 'I want to get my spoon into that pudding—'

He was pushed back again by Brookes. 'You'll have to wait your turn, old chap. This is *my* party and *my* pudding. Damned if I won't be licking it up in a minute.'

The *demi-mondaine* looked extremely put out to be upstaged.

Lady Juliana turned her head lazily and her gaze fell on a gentleman she had not seen before at Emma's soirées. He was tall and fair, and though he was of a slim build he had broad shoulders and a durable air. With his strong, bronzed face and the ruthless line to his jaw, he looked as though he would be a useful ally in any altercation. He was sitting back in his chair as though scorning the eager blades who circled the table, and his gaze was dark and unreadable in the shadowed room.

Juliana felt a curious sense of recognition. She smiled

at him, her come-hither smile. 'Come along, darling. Don't be shy.'

The gentleman looked up. His eyes were a very dark greeny-blue and they appraised her with complete indifference. 'I thank you, ma'am, but I have never liked dessert.'

Juliana was not accustomed to being rejected. She gave him back level stare for level stare. He looked close to her own age of twenty-nine, or perhaps a little older. There was a certain world-weary look in his eyes, as though he had seen all this and more many times before. A faint, cynical smile curved his lips as he held Juliana's gaze.

A strange wave of feeling swept over Juliana. Just for a second she felt very young and very confused, as though the whole tawdry tableau was some dreadful mistake that she had stumbled into by accident. The predatory smiles, the grasping hands... For a moment she almost slid off the salver and ran, shaken by the cool challenge in the man's eyes. Her smile faltered, yet she could not tear her gaze away from him.

Then he turned away to gesture to a footman to fill his wineglass and the strange feeling passed. Juliana turned one shimmering shoulder and bent a smile on the youngest and most excited of the gentleman there.

'Simon, my pet, why do you not lick the cream off... just there...?'

Juliana arched her body briefly to the scavenging hands, then stood up, scattering the fruit on the tiled floor, and beckoned to a maid to pass her her wrap. There were groans of disappointment from the men, but already the more enterprising of the Cyprians and the more daring of the ladies were moving in to take up where Juliana had left off, spooning the fruit and cream from the salver and feeding the gentlemen. Juliana, casting a quick look over her shoulder, saw that the evening was already set fair to descend into one of Emma's famous orgies.

A footman, scarlet to the ears, held the dining room door open for Juliana to exit. She swept through in her bare feet, spilling the last remaining bits of food across the polished tiles of the marble entrance hall. The cream was sticking to her wrap and the icing sugar was starting to itch. She hoped that Emma had remembered to tell the maid to draw a bath for her.

The dining-room door closed behind her and Juliana could hear the roar of conversation swell to a new, excited level as everyone started to pick over her latest, outrageous exploit. A little smile curved her lips. That would give them something to talk about in the clubs! No matter how tasteful the wedding on the morrow, Drookes's marriage would be remembered for the disgraceful exploits the night before. Once again, society matrons would exclaim over the shocking behaviour of Lady Juliana Myfleet, the Marquis of Tallant's daughter, who had once been one of their own and had fallen from grace so spectacularly.

'This way, my lady.' The maid was gesturing her towards the curved staircase. She was very young and she looked plain. Juliana reflected that Emma always chose plain maids, being unable to stand any competition. The girl ushered Juliana through a doorway on the landing and into the room that Juliana had used earlier when she changed out of her clothes. Another door led into a smaller room, where another maid was pouring steaming water into the bathtub. She looked up as Juliana came in and her perspiring face flushed a deeper red. She emptied her jug of water, dropped Juliana a flustered curtsy and fled, as though just being in the same room as the *ton*'s most wicked widow might put her in danger.

Juliana turned her bewitching smile on the first girl, slipped off her wrap, bent to remove the garter from her leg and stepped into the water.

'Thank you. You may leave me now.'

The maid gave her a tight-lipped smile in return and took the soiled robe in her hand. She too dropped a curtsy, disapproving and not over-awed, and left the room. Juliana laughed.

The icing sugar was turning sticky in the water and Juliana reached for the long, wooden-handled brush to give her skin a good scrub. She preferred to do it for herself. The thought of some ham-fisted maid attacking her tender flesh made her wince. The remains of the cream were floating on the top of the water like some unpleasant scum and there was a sliver of apple swirling around in the brew. Juliana grimaced. The after-effects of her outrageous behaviour were proving a deal less pleasant than the trick itself. At this rate she would require a second bath to wash away the residue of the first.

She lay back and closed her eyes, recapturing the moment when the footmen had whipped the lid off the silver salver and exposed her in all her glory. To cause such an uproar had been such fun. The women had looked furious and the men had looked like little boys in a sweetshop. Juliana smiled with satisfaction. It was so very pleasant to be able to arouse such emotions. Admiration, desire…and contempt.

She sat up abruptly, remembering the expression on the face of the fair-haired stranger.

'I thank you, ma'am, but I have never liked dessert.'

Infernal impudence! How dared he be so disdainful? It had only been a joke. And what was such a puritan doing at one of Emma's debauched suppers anyway? Perhaps he had been looking for a church meeting and had taken the wrong turning.

For a moment Juliana remembered the look in the man's blue eyes and felt disturbed all over again. She had been so certain that she knew him, with a bone deep recognition that she had never felt before. Yet it seemed that she was wrong.

She stood up, slopping water over the side of the bath on to the floor, and reached for the towel. The diamond tiara snagged on the material as she drew it about her shoulders and with a quick impatient movement Juliana pulled it from her hair and cast it on the dressing table. Suddenly she was anxious to be gone. She padded across the bedroom, leaving a trail of wet footprints on the carpet. Her clothes were all laid out on the bed. She need only ring the bell to summon the disapproving little maid to help her dress, but she did not want to wait. She had left Hattie, her own maid, at home in Portman Square. Hattie invariably disapproved too, to the point where Juliana's friends enquired why she did not find herself a new maid rather than tolerate Hattie's censure. Juliana never answered. The truth was that she rather liked having a strict maid. It made up in part for the mother she could not remember.

On impulse Juliana started to dress herself, getting into a tangle as she tried to fasten her silk stockings to her garters, casting her stays aside and slipping into her chemise. The evening dress she had chosen was deceptively simple, a wrap of aquamarine gauze. Even so, she found it surprisingly difficult to fasten it without help. The diaphanous material was intended to cling and drape seductively and it was almost transparent. Juliana frowned at her reflection. The dress was gaping inelegantly like that of a blowsy, drunken trollop and looked not so much seductive as ridiculous. Clearly there was more to this business of dressing oneself than met the eye. She would not try it again. She could not bear to look unkempt.

She sat down at the dressing table and studied her reflection. She had not the first idea of what to do with her hair, which, now that the tiara was removed, tumbled down her back in auburn profusion. To have her hair loose about her face softened the breathtaking angles of her cheekbones and made her look younger. The sprinkling of freckles across the bridge of her nose only added to the youthful impression. Those freckles had withstood years of forceful scrubbing and all her attempts at removal with Dr Jinks's Lemon Ointment. Juliana leaned closer. There was a hint of vulnerability in her eyes that she did not wish to acknowledge. It made her feel strange, just as she had when the unknown man had looked at her.

The door opened and Emma Wren rustled in. Juliana could immediately tell that Emma was a little the worse for drink. Her colour was high, the rouge on her cheeks smeared, and her hairpiece slightly askew.

'Juliana, my dear!' Emma was high with excitement. 'You were utterly magnificent! Why, the gentlemen can talk of little else! They are all waiting for you, my dear. Are you ready to go down?'

Juliana turned back to the mirror. She was aware of making excuses. 'Not quite. I need some help with my gown and my hair.'

Emma tutted. 'You should have called my maid. Dessie will fix it in a trice. Although…' she stood back and considered Juliana's appearance '…you do look quite charmingly rumpled and wanton like that, my dear. I am sure the gentlemen will appreciate it. Tumbled curls are quite the thing, you know, and make you look so young and innocent.' She gave a peal of laughter. 'You will quite sweep them away!'

Not for the first time, Juliana reflected that Emma was wasted as the wife of a junior government minister and would have been most successful as the madam of a bawdy house. There was, in fact, very little difference between Mrs Wren's elegantly appointed town house and a Covent Garden bordello. Or a rookery in a less salubrious part of Town, for that matter. Juliana turned her shoulder. She might connive at some of Emma's more outrageous games for her own amusement, but she had no intention of playing to someone else's rules. The trick played on Brookes had alleviated her boredom for at least an hour, but now she did not propose to go downstairs and act the harlot.

'Sir Jasper Colling is asking for you,' Emma said meaningfully, putting her painted face close to Juliana's, so that Juliana could smell the stale wine on her breath. 'And Simon Armitage. He is a sweet boy, Ju—and so very young and eager. Think what fun it might be to initiate him…'

Juliana felt a wave of repulsion. There *was* something sweet about Simon Armitage's untried adoration and it would be a gross betrayal to take that adoration and use it for her own gratification. She was hardly so steeped in dissipation, whatever the gossips might say. She was determined to refuse Emma's blandishments, but before she disappointed her hostess's expectations and drew her ire, there was something that she wanted to know. She tried to make her voice sound casual.

'That gentleman, Emma—the one who looks like a rake but behaves like a priest—who is he?'

Emma's expression cleared. 'Oh, I see! You prefer someone new! There is nothing so intriguing as a stranger, is there, my dear?' She frowned. 'A few hours ago I should have said that you could not have chosen better, but now I am not so sure…' She flung herself down on the end of the bed. 'That is Martin Davencourt. One of the Somersetshire Davencourts, you know. No title, but rich as Croesus and connected to half the families in the land. He is back in London following the death of his father last year.'

'Davencourt,' Juliana repeated. The name rang a very faint bell, but the memory escaped her.

Emma's voice had taken on a petulant note. 'Yes, Martin Davencourt. I was told that he was amusing—indeed, he *should* be amusing, for he has knocked about the capitals of Europe for several years.' Juliana, watching in the mirror, saw her pull a face. 'I invited him because I thought he would be fun, but he seems the most prosy bore. Perhaps it is because he wants to be a Member of Parliament now and seems to take himself so seriously. Some MPs do, you know. Or perhaps it is having those seven tiresome half-brothers and half-sisters to care for. Whatever the case, he declines to enter into the spirit of things tonight, but perhaps you could change his mind for him.'

'Martin Davencourt…' Juliana frowned. 'The name is familiar, but I do not believe we have met. I am sure I would have remembered him. I could almost swear that we *had* met, yet I cannot think when…'

Emma arched a knowing eyebrow. 'I believe his diplomatic work has kept him out of the country for a good while. Still, even if you do not really know him, you can always pretend. Come downstairs and persuade him to renew old acquaintance, Ju.'

Juliana hesitated, then shook her head. She stood up,

scooping her cloak from the bed where it rested beside Mrs Wren's elaborate coiffure.

'I do not think so, Emma. Mr Davencourt is proof against my charms. And I fear I must decline your offer of entertainment tonight. I have the headache and think I will have an early night.'

Emma sprang to her feet, looking affronted.

'But, Juliana, the gentlemen are waiting. They are all expecting you! I promised them—'

'What?' Juliana stared. There had been a note of panic in Emma Wren's voice and with a sudden insight she realised what had happened. She had been promised as part of the entertainment—not simply offered on a tray, as it were, but to be thrown to the guests afterwards at the orgy, along with the Haymarket ware that Emma had imported for the occasion. The thought made her furious. Emma knew perfectly well that Juliana might indulge in risqué tricks to entertain herself and her friends, but to promise her services to the guests was another matter.

'I am not going downstairs to play the Cyprian for Simon Armitage, Jasper Colling or indeed anyone else,' she said, as calmly as she could. 'I am tired and I wish to go home.'

Mrs Wren's painted mouth thinned to an obstinate line. There was a knowledge in her eyes that was as old as the hills and it made Juliana, for all her experience, feel very naïve.

'I fail to see why titillating their appetites by appearing naked on a tray is more acceptable than spending a little time with my gentleman—'

'It is not merely my time you wish me to give,' Juliana said stiffly. She could feel her colour mounting as she stared at Emma's contemptuous face. She knew there was an element of truth in her erstwhile friend's assertion. She had deliberately set out to shock and provoke and now she wanted to retreat from the consequences of her actions. She took a breath.

'I agreed to play the trick on Brookes because it was fun, a joke to tease and shock your guests! Anything else is out of the question.'

Emma made a noise of disgust. 'At least the lightskirts are honest in what they do!'

Juliana flushed. 'They are doing their job. As for me, I have no taste for masculine company tonight.'

'You seldom do.' Emma's eyes had narrowed to a glare. 'You think that I have not observed that? How you flirt and flaunt and tease, yet never deliver on what you promise? I do believe, my dear—' she thrust her face in Juliana's, reaching up, for she did not have Juliana's height '—that your reputation for wickedness is nothing but a sham!'

Juliana laughed. It was best to ignore Emma when she was in her cups, for if she answered in kind their friendship would be lost. Juliana needed that friendship.

'And I believe that you are a little castaway, Emma. Perhaps you should return to your guests. I will see you tomorrow at the wedding.'

'I'll see you in hell!' Emma shrieked, picking the silver-backed hairbrush from the dressing table and throwing it inaccurately at Juliana's departing back. 'You're nothing but a milk-and-water miss who hasn't the stomach for the games you play. Run away, little girl! I'll never forgive you for spoiling my party.'

'You will forgive me soon enough when you want to take money off me at whist,' Juliana said coldly.

She hurried down the curving staircase. Behind her she could hear the crash of objects bouncing off the walls as Emma devastated the bedroom. She had always known that Emma had a bad temper, had seen it turned against luckless servants and shopkeepers, but it had never been directed at her before. For a second, the image of her father rose before her. She could well imagine his disapproving expression, his cold, cutting words: *'You count this woman your friend, Juliana? An ill-bred fishwife who has neither taste nor quality? Upon my word, how did you come to this?'*

Juliana shivered violently. It was no secret that the Marquis of Tallant disapproved heartily of his only daughter—no secret that he doubted she was actually his child and deplored the fact that she had apparently followed in her mother's immoral footsteps. Whilst he sat in cold judgement in his house at Ashby Tallant, Juliana ran riot in town, playing for high stakes and keeping low company. Since her brother Joss's marriage two years before, she had inherited the mantle of family black sheep and had played up to it with a vengeance.

The entrance hall was in darkness but for one tall stand of candles by the front door. From the dining room came the sounds of masculine laughter, the tinkle of music and roars of encouragement. Evidently one of the Cyprians—or perhaps one of Emma's guests—was performing the dance of the seven veils. Juliana reflected that the party was progressing well without either its hostess or herself to add to the entertainment.

She espied a footman standing like a sentinel by one of the pillars and beckoned him over. She wondered if it was one of the men who had carried her into the dining room earlier. Certainly he was avoiding her eyes, as though he had not quite recovered from gazing at other parts of her anatomy.

'Summon my carriage, if you please,' Juliana said imperiously. It would do no harm to show some authority.

'Certainly, my lady.' The man shot away like a scalded cat and Juliana turned towards the door. Her coachman knew better than to keep her waiting. In a few minutes she would be free of this house and an evening turned sour. All the fun that she had derived from the trick on Brookes had evaporated with Emma's tantrum. Juliana sighed. She should have known better, known that her friend's licentiousness went far beyond the playing of a simple joke, known that there would have been another side to the evening.

She had reached the steps up to the main entrance and was looking around for the butler to open the door for her when a man stepped from the candlelit shadows.

'Running away, Lady Juliana? Are you not intending to finish what you started?'

The deep voice made Juliana jump. She had not seen the figure until the last minute and his sudden appearance had startled her. He was dressed for the outdoors and was drawing on his gloves, and now he gave her a glimmer of a smile that for some strange reason set her pulse awry. Juliana recognised Martin Davencourt and felt an unfamiliar lack of self-assurance. He was watching her steadily and there was something in his gaze that made her feel vulnerable. Something about this man made her sophistication feel parchment thin. Juliana would have said that her brother Joss was the only one who knew her well, was the only one who was allowed close to her, yet she had the strangest feeling that Martin Davencourt's searching blue gaze saw far more than she wanted him to see. She raised her chin, instinctively on the defensive.

'I am going home.' She allowed her gaze to scan him from head to foot. 'It seems that the entertainment is not to your taste either, Mr Davencourt.'

'Indeed, it is not.' There was a note of grim amusement

in Martin Davencourt's voice. 'I am cousin to Eustacia Havard, Lady Juliana—the lady who is marrying Lord Andrew tomorrow. I had not realised that this was his...' he paused, finishing ironically '...his bachelor swansong, I suppose it could be called.'

Juliana smiled sweetly. Cold disapproval was something that she could easily deal with. She had encountered it often enough.

'I see that you do not approve of our little entertainments, Mr Davencourt,' she said. 'Perhaps you should try Almack's, or the débutante balls in future. I hear that they even serve lemonade there. That might be more to your taste if this is too stimulating for you.'

'Perhaps I shall take your advice,' Martin Davencourt said slowly. He was watching her thoughtfully and now he gestured towards the closed door of the dining room. 'I am surprised to see you leave so prematurely, Lady Juliana. The party is only just starting, and after your performance earlier I would have thought that you had plenty to contribute to the rest of the evening.'

Juliana laughed. No matter how dull Martin Davencourt's tastes, his wit was still sharp. She was enjoying crossing swords with such a man.

'I apologise for confounding your expectations, Mr Davencourt,' she said. 'Emma's entertainments are not to my taste tonight.' She narrowed her gaze on him thoughtfully. 'Though if you were inclined to join me I might be persuaded to change my mind.'

Martin Davencourt gave her a smile—and a look from those sleepy dark blue eyes that made her feel hot and very bothered. He spoke gently.

'Are you always this persistent, Lady Juliana? I would have thought that one refusal would be enough for you.'

Juliana raised a haughty brow. 'I am not accustomed to rejection.'

'Ah. Well, it happens to us all at some point.' Martin Davencourt gave her a rueful smile. 'Accept it.'

Juliana felt a hot rush of annoyance, mainly with herself for inviting a rebuff a second time. It had been her pride that had spoken—she had wanted Martin Davencourt to regret his previous indifference towards her. She had wanted him to want her, and then she could have played her usual game, leading him on a little but not too much, his admiration balm to her soul. She had played the game so often, first encouraging a suitor and then dropping him before his attentions became too pressing. She was an expert at the art. Except that Martin Davencourt did not want to play her games...

Juliana ran her fingers over the wooden edge of the doorframe and looked at him thoughtfully from under her lashes. He gave her back look for look, direct and clear. Juliana thought she could distinguish a flicker of cool amusement in that blue gaze.

'I had heard that you were a man of experience, Mr Davencourt,' she said coldly, 'yet you behave more like an Evangelical. You are sadly out of place in this house.'

She saw him frown and felt a skip of excitement, like a naughty child provoking the adults. She imagined that it might be exciting to provoke Martin Davencourt and to see how deep that calm self-control actually went. Or perhaps not. There was something about him that suggested it might actually be rather dangerous to push him too far.

He smiled at her gently. 'I realise that I am in the wrong place,' he said, 'but perhaps you are, too. Take my advice, Lady Juliana, and cut loose of all this. Everyone has to grow up some time. Even a lady rakehell, such as you profess to be.'

Juliana laughed. 'Is that what you think me? That I am a rake?'

'The role is not necessarily confined to the male of the species. Is it not the reputation that you cultivate?'

Juliana shrugged. 'Reputations may be exaggerated.'

Martin Davencourt inclined his head. 'True. They may also be encouraged.'

A crash from upstairs made both of them jump. Emma Wren's voice rose to a crescendo. The door to the servants' quarters thudded open and a couple of frightened-looking maids scurried up the stairs.

'Time to leave,' Juliana said. 'I fear that Emma is cross with me tonight. A refusal to join in the game so often offends, does it not?' She smiled. 'But I do not need to tell *you* that, do I, Mr Davencourt? You strike me as a man quite happy to cause offence by refusing to conform.'

'I play by my own rules,' Martin Davencourt said. 'One cannot allow someone else to dictate the game.' He threw her an appraising glance. 'In that sense I do believe we are two of a kind, Lady Juliana.'

Juliana laughed. 'If that is so, then I think it must be the only thing we have in common, sir.'

Martin Davencourt tilted his head enquiringly. 'Are you sure of that?'

Juliana raised her brows. 'How could it be otherwise? You are staid and orthodox and ever so slightly shocked at the company you find yourself in.'

Martin laughed. 'You have divined a great deal about me in a short acquaintance.'

Juliana shrugged. 'I can read a man at thirty paces.'

'I see. And yourself? You were about to make some observation about your own character, I infer.'

'Oh, well, I am unorthodox and rebellious and—'

'Wild?' There was an ironic inflection in Martin Davencourt's voice, as if such qualities were scarcely admirable. Juliana shrugged carelessly.

'We are chalk and cheese, Mr Davencourt. No, on second thoughts, not. Cheese can be quite delicious. Wine and water? You remind me of flat champagne. So much potential wasted.'

She heard Martin take a careful breath. She could not see him clearly but she could hear the repressed amusement in his voice.

'Lady Juliana, are you always so rude to chance acquaintances?'

'Invariably,' Juliana said. 'But this is nothing to how I can be, I assure you. I am being nice to you.'

'I believe you.' Martin's tone changed. 'You should think twice before you indulge in these games, Lady Juliana. One day you will take on more than you can deal with.'

There was a pause.

'I do not think so,' Juliana said coldly. 'I can take care of myself.'

She saw a smile touch the corner of Martin Davencourt's mouth. His gaze swept over her slowly, thoughtfully, from head to toe. It lingered on the tumbled auburn curls that framed her face and on the freckles across the bridge of her nose. It considered the curve of her waist and the dainty slippers that peeped from under the hem of her gown. He did not make any move towards her and yet Juliana felt strangely vulnerable. A deep, disturbing sense of awareness swept over her, leaving her breathless. She wrapped the cloak closer about her, her fingers clenching at her neck in an attempt to conceal the flimsy aquamarine dress. Ridiculous, when Martin Davencourt and many others had seen her stark naked only an hour before, and yet she suddenly had an intense desire to shroud herself in as many layers as possible.

'Are you sure?' Martin Davencourt spoke softly and his searching blue gaze held hers relentlessly. 'Are you sure you can take care of yourself?'

Juliana cleared her throat, her fingers tightening unconsciously on the cloak. 'Of course I am sure! I live alone and do as I please, and have been doing so since I was three and twenty.'

Martin Davencourt straightened up. He was smiling. 'That sounds like a mantra, Lady Juliana. The sort of thing that if you repeat it often enough you start to believe it. So if it is true that you are a…hardened lady rakehell, it is strange that on occasion you should look like a frightened schoolgirl.'

Juliana felt a shiver go through her. She did not like his observation. It accorded too closely with what she had seen earlier in the mirror. 'It is a very useful accomplishment, I assure you,' she said flippantly. 'The gentlemen find it fascinating that I am able to play the innocent. Many a Cyprian has asked me how I manage it. I believe they charge a great deal for false virtue.'

She saw the expression in Martin's eyes harden. 'You are very cool, I will say that for you, Lady Juliana. Nevertheless, I am offering a word of advice. If you proposition a gentleman, be sure that you are prepared to deliver on your promise. Otherwise it brands you a cheat.'

Once again Juliana felt a rush of annoyance. 'Two pieces of advice in one evening,' she said, in honeyed tones. 'You should charge for your opinions, Mr Davencourt. You might make a fortune. Then again…' she pulled a face '…perhaps not. You are not very interesting.'

Martin Davencourt laughed. 'You used to be such a sweet girl, Lady Juliana. Whatever happened to you?'

Juliana paused, looking at him through narrowed eyes. 'Are you trying to claim a previous acquaintance with me, Mr Davencourt?'

She saw the flash of Martin Davencourt's teeth in the darkness as he laughed. 'I am not trying to claim anything, Lady Juliana. I suppose you do not remember our previous meeting. Let me remind you. We met at Ashby Tallant, by the pool under the willows on those long hot summer days. You were fourteen years old and a very sweet and unspoilt child. Whatever happened to change that?'

Juliana turned away. 'I expect I grew up, Mr Davencourt. I would like to say that I remember you, too, but I do not.' She raised a brow. 'I wonder why that would be?'

Martin Davencourt held her gaze for a long moment and Juliana found herself fidgeting under his scrutiny, her cheeks growing hot. She was about to burst into speech, any speech, to ease the discomfort of that moment, when she heard the sound of the clatter of hooves on the cobbles as the coach was brought round. Seldom had she felt so relieved to escape a situation.

'Oh! My carriage, I think.'

Martin smiled. 'How timely. Enabling you to run away yet again, Lady Juliana.' He held the door open for her courteously. 'Goodnight.'

He followed her out through the door and with a negligent wave of the hand he strolled away down the street.

Juliana paused, staring after him into the darkness, her foot poised on the carriage step. She was used to people trying to scrape an acquaintance—they were usually gentlemen—but Martin Davencourt hardly struck her as the

type. He had made it plain that he did not admire her. Yet
if they had really met as children it might explain that
peculiar sense of recognition that possessed her whenever
he was nearby.

The touch of raindrops on her face recalled her to the
present and she climbed up into the coach, leaning forward to draw the curtains against the dark. As she did so
a movement across the other side of the square caught her
eye. A man was standing in the shadows and now he
stepped forward into the pool of light thrown by the
lamps. Juliana stared. Her heart started to race. He was
staring directly at her and the tilt of his head and the set
of his shoulders was oddly familiar. It looked like her late,
unlamented husband, Clive Massingham. Except that
Massingham was dead, knifed in a brawl in an Italian jail.

The coach started with a jolt and the curtain fell back
into place and Juliana relaxed back against the seat. It had
been a trick of the light, that was all. That, and her memory playing tricks. There was no cause for alarm.

As for Martin Davencourt, it would be better to stop
thinking about him and his stern disapproval. Except that
Juliana had the strangest feeling that forgetting Martin
Davencourt would not be easy at all.

Martin Davencourt breathed in the fresh night air with
a sense of relief. The atmosphere in Emma Wren's house
had been stifling in more ways than one. He squared his
shoulders, shaking off the niggling sense of irritation that
had pursued him throughout the evening. It had been his
own fault for thinking that Mrs Wren's supposedly so-
phisticated supper would be a place for stimulating discussion. Clearly he had been out of London for too long.
Either that, or he was getting too old.

The cheap lasciviousness of the whole evening had dis-

gusted him. Martin shook his head. God knew, he was no
plaster saint himself, but the pointless immorality of
Emma Wren's guests had been more depressing than anything else. Most depressing of all was that Andrew
Brookes was marrying his cousin on the morrow. Martin
did not know Eustacia Havard well—he had been out of
the country for several years and had an affectionate but
distant relationship with his aunt and her family—but nevertheless he did not like to think of his cousin marrying
such a loose fish as Brookes. He had disliked Brookes on
sight and he did not rate Eustacia's prospects of marital
bliss as any better than those of the Prince Regent.

He turned into Portman Square. The night was dark
with an edge of rain on the breeze. It smelled fresh, like
the country. A sudden, fierce ache to visit Davencourt
possessed him. Once the Season was over, perhaps... It
would be impossible to leave Town just now for, in addition to his work, his younger half-sisters were enjoying
the novelty of their visit and would complain if he brought
it to a premature end. It would also be unfair to their older
siblings, especially Clara, whose début had already been
delayed for a year because of their father's death. She had
caused quite a stir in society and might well make a dazzling match in her first season if only she could be persuaded to stay awake long enough to offer one of her
suitors some encouragement.

If he could see her settled, and find a husband for Kitty
as well... But Kitty was far more of an intractable problem.

Martin frowned. Kitty had shown no interest in any of
the entertainments that London had to offer, other than
the opportunity to lose endless sums of money at the gambling tables. Martin was aware that a deep unhappiness
was driving his half-sister's behaviour, but she would not

speak to him about it. It was hardly surprising, for he was a good ten years older than she and they did not yet know each other well. And in the meantime, Kitty was gambling recklessly and people were talking.

Thinking of gamblers made Martin's thoughts turn to Lady Juliana Myfleet. Juliana, trailing two marriages and a string of lovers behind her like a gaudy comet. He had heard much of her exploits—who had not—but it had been almost sixteen years since they had met. No wonder she had forgotten.

In the intervening time he had met plenty of women like Juliana Myfleet; bored wives whose beauty had hardened into dissatisfaction or widows who had the jaded shell of the society sophisticate. Martin pulled a face. The only difference between Juliana Myfleet and a whole host of other women was that she frequently went too far. He thought she did it deliberately, to test and provoke, a spoiled child grown into a spoiled woman.

Except that when their eyes had met for the first time that night, all he had seen was a vulnerable girl acting a part that was too grown-up for her, like a child in adult's clothing. The impression had hit him with the force of a blow to the stomach, contrasting as it did with the provocative shamelessness of her pose on the silver salver. Whilst all the others had been burning with lascivious excitement he had been possessed by an astonishing urge to protect and cherish her, whilst at the same time feeling a sick disappointment to see what she had become. No doubt youthful infatuations always ended in disappointment.

Perhaps he had been mistaken in thinking her vulnerable. Martin's steps quickened. Later she had shown nothing but the brittle boredom he would have expected, plus a malice that betrayed a certain unhappiness. At any rate, it was none of his business. *She* was none of his business. And he had too many other things to worry about.

He turned into Laverstock Gardens and went up the steps of his town house. All the lights were blazing, despite the fact that it was just past two. Martin recognised this as a bad sign.

Liddington, the butler, opened the door with an expression so blank that Martin's heart sank even further.

'That bad, Liddington?' he murmured, as he divested himself of his coat.

'Yes, sir.' The butler was matter of fact. 'Mrs Lane is awaiting you in the library. I did try to suggest that she should leave the matter until the morning, but she was most insistent—'

'Mr Davencourt!' The library door opened and Mrs Lane swept out in a swirl of draperies. She was a large woman with greying hair and a perpetually agonised expression. When Martin had first met her he had wondered if she was plagued by some medical complaint that kept her constantly in pain. These days he realised that it was apparently the effort of chaperoning his sisters that caused her misery.

'Mr Davencourt, I simply must speak with you! That girl is quite hopeless, and does nothing that I tell her! You must speak to her. She is fit for Bedlam.'

'I assume you refer to Miss Clara, Mrs Lane?' Martin asked, catching the matron's arm and steering her back into the library and away from the servants' stifled amusement. 'I know that she can be a trifle indolent—'

'Indolent! The girl is a minx.' Mrs Lane pulled her arm away huffily. 'She pretends to fall asleep so that she may ignore her suitors! It is no wonder that she has yet to attract an offer from a gentleman. You *must* speak with her, Mr Davencourt.'

'I shall do so, of course,' Martin said. The last time he had tried to talk to Clara about her behaviour he had felt as though he was wrestling with a very slippery fish. She had looked innocent and puzzled and told him that she tried very hard to show an interest but she found the Season dreadfully fatiguing. There had been a stubborn look in her eyes and Martin had been uncomfortably aware that his half-sister was trying to hoodwink him, but he had not even scratched the surface of the reasons for her behaviour.

'As for Miss Kitty…' Mrs Lane swelled wrathfully. 'That girl is getting into bad company, sir. How is she to catch a husband when she spends all her time at play? Gambling away her allowance, I have no doubt, though the chit will tell me nothing.'

'I shall speak with Kitty as well,' Martin said. He felt in desperate need of a drink. 'May I offer you a glass of ratafia, Mrs Lane?'

'No, *thank* you, Mr Davencourt,' Mrs Lane said, as though Martin had suggested something unspeakably vulgar. 'I never take spirits after eleven. It upsets my constitution.' She billowed to her feet. 'I merely wish to add that if Miss Davencourt and Miss Clara do not reform—and quickly!—I shall be taking my services elsewhere. There are plenty of young ladies who would be glad to have my chaperonage and would not cause me one moment's anxiety. I am much in demand, you know!'

Martin felt panic and irritation stirring in equal measure. The thought of losing Mrs Lane, humourless as she was, was terrifying. He would never find another reputable lady willing to chaperon Kitty and Clara about town, not in the middle of the Season when the girls had a reputation for being so difficult. His sister Araminta had had to work very hard to persuade Mrs Lane in the first place. The chaperon had implied that a house with seven children and lacking the steadying hand of a mistress must surely be a hotbed of wickedness, and now his half-sisters were proving precisely that. Martin ran his hand through his hair.

'Please do not leave us, Mrs Lane. You have done such a splendid job so far.' He could hear the insincerity in his own voice.

'I will think about it,' the chaperon said graciously. 'Of course, if you think that I have done such a splendid job, Mr Davencourt, you might consider reflecting that fact in my fee…'

Martin could feel the screws of blackmail turning. Only the previous week he had been obliged to increase the wages he paid to his younger brother's tutor to prevent him from handing in his notice. Then the governess had threatened to leave after his younger sisters filled her bed with stewed apple. It only required the nursemaid to re-sign and he would have a full house.

He held the door open for Mrs Lane. 'I shall see what I can do, madam. In the meantime, be assured that I will speak to both Kitty and Clara—'

'Martin!' A plaintive voice floated down from the stair-case. Daisy was sitting halfway up the stair, swinging her feet through the delicate iron tracery of the banisters. She was clutching her teddy bear and looked tiny and dishev-elled. Daisy was five years old and a late child, the result of Mr and Mrs Davencourt's last, ill-fated attempt at rec-onciliation. Martin hurried up the stairs to scoop her up into his arms, and felt the fierce heat of her tears against his shirt.

'I had a bad dream, Martin,' his youngest sister hic-cupped. 'I dreamed that you went away and left us for ever and ever—'

Martin smoothed his hand over her hair. 'Hush, sweet-heart. I am here now and I promise never to go away—'

The nursemaid came hurrying along the landing, a can-dle clutched in her hand, a wrap thrown hastily over the nightdress. Her eyes were full of sleep and anxiety. She held her arms out.

'Now then, Miss Elizabeth, what's going on here? Come back to bed.'

Daisy clung to Martin with the tenacity of a limpet, winding her fat little arms about his neck. 'I want Martin to put me to bed and tell me a story!'

Martin thought longingly of the huge glass of brandy as yet unpoured in the library and the pristine newspaper he had not even unfolded. But the nursemaid's look was pleading.

'If you would be so good, sir… Miss Elizabeth has been having so many nightmares lately and I am sure she will sleep better if you tuck her up.'

Down in the hall Mrs Lane was still watching him with a look of cupidity in her sharp grey eyes. Her expression reminded Martin of a hunting cat closing in on the kill. He felt anger and helplessness in equal measure. He turned away deliberately, pressing a kiss on Daisy's tum-bled fair curls.

'Come along then, sweetheart. I will tell you the story about the Princess and the Pea.'

Daisy snuggled up to him. Her warmth comforted him. When the terrible news of their parents' death had reached him the previous year, he had been stunned and appalled. The late Mr and Mrs Davencourt lived for most of the time in a state of armed neutrality towards each other, barely spending any time together. It had been ironic in the extreme that they had died together in a fire at their London house. Philip Davencourt had been a staunch

Tory who had deplored his son's Whiggish tendencies, but for all their political disagreements, father and son had had a healthy respect for each other and Martin knew that his father had been proud of him when he had been appointed to Castlereagh's delegation at the Congress of Vienna. The only thing that his father had disapproved of was Martin's failure to marry.

Perhaps his father had had a point, Martin thought ruefully, as he carried Daisy back to the nursery. A man who had seven younger half-brothers and half-sisters to care for needed help and a far more permanent relationship than the transient affairs that he had been accustomed to in the past. Not only that, but in future he would need a wife to act as political hostess as well.

He held Daisy close. His sister Araminta, the only other child of his father's first marriage, had argued that the younger girls should go to live with her when their parents had died. Martin had been tempted, but in the end he had decided against it. He might only be thirty-one years old, he might have no wife to support him, but that was as nothing compared to the powerful sympathy he felt towards his younger siblings. They had endured enough misery over the death of their parents and he would not be responsible for separating them now. They stayed with him and he did the best he could for them. But he needed a wife.

Juliana lay in her huge canopied bed and watched the play of shadows across the wall. The house was completely silent. Even in the daytime there were no children to spoil the peace and nothing to disrupt the almost sepulchral silence. Juliana lived entirely alone, with no companion to give her countenance and to quell the tongues of the gossips. She had chosen it that way, declaring that to live with some tedious poor relation would make her run mad.

Juliana rolled over on to her side and pressed her cheek against the cool pillow. She felt hot with the effort of repressing her tears and angry because she did not understand why she wanted to cry, except that it had something to do with Martin Davencourt. She thumped her pillow. How maudlin could a person be? She had everything she could possibly want, so there was no reason to be sad.

Remembering a game she had played when she was a child, Juliana tried to enumerate the reasons why she should be happy.

One. She had money—enough money to buy anything she wanted and to gamble the rest away. Her father, whilst deploring her behaviour, was quick enough to spare her financial embarrassment, so she need never worry that she would go without.

Two. Tomorrow Andrew Brookes was marrying Eustacia Havard and she was invited to the wedding. That gave her a purpose, something to do, a reason to get out of bed. She would not be bored tomorrow. She would not even be lonely, for she would be surrounded by people. Juliana felt slightly better at the thought. Her misery receded slightly. This was a good game.

Three. She was beautiful and she could have any man that she wanted. Juliana frowned. Instead of making her feel better, the thought engendered a slight chill. Firstly she had not met any man that she genuinely wanted. Armitage, Brookes, Colling…they were at her beck and call, as were countless others. But the truth was that she did not want to call them. Since the end of her disastrous marriage to Clive Massingham, she had been wary of love. She would not let it make a fool of her again.

Then there was Martin Davencourt. His stern face was

before her still. Severe, upright, steady. She was not sure why she had wanted him. She did not even like him. He was everything that she usually dismissed in a man. Perhaps that was why she had decided to try to attract him. She had wanted to see if he was really as sternly honourable as he seemed. She had wanted to see if she could corrupt virtue.

Juliana rolled over on to her stomach and propped herself up on her elbows. She hoped that that was the reason. God forbid that she should suddenly and inexplicably be attracted to an honest man. That would ruin her bad reputation once and for all.

'We met at Ashby Tallant, by the pool under the willows on those long hot summer days. You were fourteen years old and a very sweet and unspoilt child…'

Martin Davencourt's words had struck a vague chord of memory. Generally Juliana tried not to remember her childhood because it had not been a particularly happy time. Now, however, she deliberately tried to recall that summer. There *had* been a pool under the willows, where she would sometimes run away and hide from her governess when the days glowed with sunlight and the schoolroom was intolerably stuffy. She had lain in the long grass and watched the sky through the shifting branches of the trees, and listened to the splash of the ducks on the still water. It had been her secret place, but one day—one summer when she had been about fourteen or so—there had been someone else there; a boy, all straw-coloured hair and gangling limbs, reading some dry tome of philosophy…

Juliana sat bolt upright. Martin Davencourt. Of course. He always seemed to have his nose in a book, or to be fiddling with some sort of mechanical invention. He had had no interest in her girlish chatter about the Season and balls and parties and the eligible gentlemen that she would meet when she made her debut…

They had made some childish pact that summer. Juliana wrinkled up her nose, trying to remember. She had been fretting that she would never meet a man to marry and Martin had looked up from trying to fix the arm of a catapult or some such tiresome invention, and had said that he would marry her himself if they were both still unwed at thirty. She had laughed at him and his chivalrous impulses.

Juliana had laughed then and she laughed now. It had been very sweet of Martin, but of course she had gone to London and had fallen head over heels in love with Edwin Myfleet and had married him instead. She had not seen Martin Davencourt from that day to this.

Juliana pulled her knees up to her chest and sat there, curled against her pillows. It had been a sunlit summer even though Martin, with his bumbling ways and obsession with his books, had been a bit of a bore. She smiled. Some things did not change. He had been dull then and he was dreary now. His looks had improved considerably, but that was the best thing that she could say for him.

Juliana paused. She knew that that was not strictly true. Somehow—and Juliana was not quite sure how it had happened—Martin Davencourt had managed to get under her skin like a sharp thorn. His observations were acute, his gaze far too perceptive. There was something decidedly disturbing about him, and about the treacherous sense of familiarity she felt in his company.

Juliana realised that Martin would be at Andrew Brookes's wedding on the following day and her heart missed a beat with a mixture of anticipation and something approaching shame. She felt vaguely embarrassed about confronting him again after their encounter that evening. She did not understand why. Her exploits at Emma's party had only been in jest and it was not for Martin Davencourt to approve or disapprove.

Juliana lay down, and then sat up in bed again. She knew she would not sleep, for her mind was too active. But if she did not sleep, she would look like a hag at the wedding and no one would admire her. That was inconceivable. She reached over to light her candle, then trod barefoot across to the wooden chest in the corner of the room. The box of pills was at the back of the top drawer, beneath her silk stockings. She took two laudanum tablets quickly, washing them down with a draught of water from the jug on the nightstand. That was better. She could almost feel the tiredness creeping up on her already. Now she would sleep and when she woke it would be the morning and there would be things to do and people to see, and everything would be well. Within five minutes she was asleep.

Chapter Two

'We are *relying* on you, Martin.' Davinia Havard, mother of the bride, fixed her nephew with a menacing look. Over her shoulder, Martin could see his sister Araminta, pulling an apologetic face at him. Now Araminta was gesturing widely to indicate that she had tried to calm their aunt, but to no avail. Martin grinned back sympathetically. He and Araminta had always been close. The only children of Philip Davencourt's first marriage, they had been natural allies, and Martin was grateful for Araminta's uncomplicated support and affection.

They were in church and there were only ten minutes to go before Eustacia's wedding service began. The conversation was therefore being conducted in discreet hisses from Mrs Havard and polite whispers from Martin in reply. Mrs Havard had penned her nephew in a pew and was leaning over him, keeping him in his place by her sheer bulk and force of personality. Martin shifted, crossing one leg over the other in an assumption of ease and wishing his aunt would back away a little. She smelled very strongly of camphor and it always made his nose itch.

'I am at your service, of course, Aunt Davinia,' he

whispered politely, 'but I am a little at a loss. Precisely what task do you wish me to perform?'

Davinia Havard gave a long sigh. 'I am *depending* on you, Martin—' she stabbed him in the chest with one stubby finger in emphasis '—*depending* on you to prevent that appalling woman Juliana Myfleet from *ruining* Eustacia's wedding. I knew it was a mistake to permit her to attend! Lady Lestrange has just told me what she did last night at the dinner given for Andrew Brookes. Have you heard?'

'Heard?' Martin murmured. He gave her a rueful smile. 'I fear I *saw* what happened rather than merely heard about it!'

There was a sharp intake of breath from both his listeners. Araminta, his staunch supporter, looked both reproachful and amused. She leaned forward and added her own hissing whisper to the conversation.

'Martin! Surely you were not at one of Emma Wren's orgies? How could you have had such poor taste?'

'I left before the actual orgy,' Martin whispered, giving his sister the ghost of a grin. 'I merely stayed for the *hors d'oeuvres*. I made the mistake of thinking that "stimulating", when applied to Mrs Wren's dinners, meant that the conversation would be good.'

Araminta stifled a laugh. Davinia Havard looked disgusted. Martin immediately regretted the impulse that had led him to joke. Unlike Araminta, their aunt had no sense of humour.

'Then you know what that Myfleet creature is capable of, Martin! I am sure that she will do something unspeakably vulgar and my poor little Eustacia will be humiliated on her wedding day!'

Martin grimaced. To his surprise he felt a strong surge of irritation to hear Juliana referred to as 'that Myfleet creature' in so disparaging a way. He struggled with his annoyance.

'I am sure that you are letting your imagination run away with you, Aunt Davinia,' he said coolly. 'I am persuaded Lady Juliana intends no such thing.'

His aunt gave him a darkling look. 'I will remind you of that when she disrupts the proceedings and makes us a laughing-stock! Martin…' Her voice dropped even further in an attempt at conciliation. 'Perhaps it is fortunate that you are a man of the world. I know I can rely on you to deal with the creature, should anything untoward arise.'

By now almost every member of the congregation was studying them with ill-concealed curiosity as they craned their necks to try and eavesdrop the conversation. Andrew Brookes was sitting across the aisle, looking thoroughly sick and jaded, and Martin felt a sharp stab of anger followed by resignation. At least the man had turned up for the wedding, even if he was still warm from a courtesan's bed.

Martin took his aunt's arm and shepherded her firmly into her own pew. He bent close to her ear.

'It may be that your fears are all for nothing, Aunt Davinia, for I do not see Lady Juliana amongst the congregation. Nevertheless, should the situation arise, I shall do what I can.'

Mrs Havard collapsed nervelessly into her seat. 'Thank you, Martin dear. There is so much to worry about at a time like this.'

Martin pressed her hand, feeling a rush of affection. 'Do not worry. Eustacia will be here in a moment and then everything will progress smoothly, I have no doubt.'

Mrs Havard groped in her reticule for her smelling salts. Somewhere in the congregation, someone tittered at the sight of the mother of the bride in such a state. Martin, deploring the fashionable and malicious crowd who had gathered to see his cousin wed, made a mental note that if and when he married, it would be in the most private ceremony imaginable. This public show was a sick mockery. Most of the people there cared little for Eustacia's happiness and were only present for the entertainment. He strode back to his sister's side, a heavy frown on his face.

'I cannot believe that any of Aunt Davinia's fears are like to materialise, Minta,' he complained.

Araminta put a soothing hand on his arm. 'Martin, surely you know that with Aunt Davinia, it is simply easier to agree? Then, in the unlikely event of Lady Juliana Myfleet…um…*unveiling* herself in the church, we shall all be confident that you will handle the situation!'

Martin groaned, resisting the temptation to put his head in his hands and garner even more public attention. For a moment, his mind boggled at the thought of Lady Juliana Myfleet slowly peeling off her clothes before the altar. He boggled even more at the idea of physically grappling with a nude woman in a place of worship. If she chose to display herself as she had done the previous night, the entire congregation would be riveted…

'Martin!' Araminta said sharply.

Martin sighed. 'Minta, I have four children here to keep an eye on. It is asking too much to expect me to act as nursemaid to Lady Juliana Myfleet as well. I do not know why she was even invited if she is Andrew Brookes's mistress. It seems the most shocking insult to Eustacia.'

Araminta sighed and edged closer to him along the pew. 'I suspect that tells us what sort of a man Andrew Brookes is.'

'Surely you knew that already!'

'I knew, but Aunt Davinia did not.' Araminta sighed again. 'For all her bluster she is quite naïve in the ways of the world, Martin. Apparently Brookes put forward the names of his guests and Aunt Davinia accepted them at face value. She almost had an apoplexy when she discovered the truth!'

Martin shook his head. 'If they had not had the folly to marry Eustacia off to Brookes in the first place...'

'I know.' Araminta made a slight gesture. 'He is sadly unsteady, but he is the son of a Marquis and Eustacia cares for him.'

'And which of those factors weighed most heavily with Havard when he was agreeing the match?' Martin asked sarcastically. He had little time for his uncle, who was an inveterate social climber. Martin had always believed that Justin Havard had married into the Davencourt family to further his social ambitions and now he was selling his daughter off in the same manner. A fortune here, a title there...it was the manner in which a man like Havard might make himself influential.

Araminta was looking at him with resignation. 'You are too principled, Martin.'

'I beg your pardon. I was not aware that that was possible.'

Araminta gave an exasperated sigh. 'Everyone has to bend a little. As a future Member of Parliament, you should know that.'

Martin did know. He just did not like it. He heaved a sigh.

'In the unlikely event of Lady Juliana Myfleet causing a disturbance, I promise to carry her bodily from the church. But in return, you must promise to keep an eye on Daisy.'

Araminta bent over to kiss his cheek. 'And Maria and all the rest of the brood. I promise. Thank you, Martin! You are truly kind.'

'Let us hope I am not called upon to fulfil my pledge,' her brother said darkly.

Lady Juliana Myfleet slid into a pew at the back of the church and bent a brilliant smile on the young groomsman who had offered his escort. She was not sitting at the back in order to be discreet but simply because she was late. The decision of what to wear, demure green or shocking scarlet, had been a difficult one. In the end she had chosen the low-cut scarlet, embellished by the silver crescent moon necklace that she always wore and a matching silver bracelet.

Her obscure position at the back of the church did not prevent her from being recognised by her acquaintance. She had chosen to sit alone, but there were people she knew in the congregation, both friendly faces and those less so. She could see her brother Joss and his wife Amy sitting next to Adam Ashwick, his new wife Annis and his brother Edward. Edward Ashwick smiled at her and sketched a bow. Juliana felt her heart unfreeze a little. Dearest Ned. He was always so kind to her, despite the fact that he was a vicar and she was such a fallen angel.

Other members of her acquaintance were less kind. Already several heads were turning and bonnets nodding as the members of the *ton* passed on the delicious gossip about her activities at the party the previous night. Juliana smiled slightly. No doubt the tale had grown as it was whispered around the clubs and passed from there to the houses of the nobility. It was amazing how quickly a story could travel. Now the staid dowagers would have another reason to tut when she passed by, another story to add to the shocking list. Her father had heard of them all—the outrageous tricks, the extravagant gambles, the parade of supposed lovers. There were many who thought that Juliana and Andrew Brookes had had a love affair, but Juliana knew better. He had squired her about town for a few months, but there had been nothing more to it than convenience and entertainment. It meant that she had an escort and Brookes had a beautiful woman on his arm, and neither of them saw any reason to complain at that.

Juliana found it amusing that Brookes now looked supremely uncomfortable as he waited for his bride. His fair, florid face was flushed, as though he had imbibed too freely to give him the Dutch courage to go through with the wedding. He was running a finger around the inside of his neck cloth as though he found its constricting folds stifling. Juliana cynically reflected that Brookes probably found the whole idea of marriage oppressive, even with a fortune of fifty thousand pounds to sweeten the pill. Still, the marriage bed would not be cold before he was returning to his latest *inamorata*.

As Juliana settled the skirts of her exquisite scarlet silk dress about her and tilted her bonnet to a demure angle, she reflected that money would never be enough to hold a man of Brookes's stamp. She almost felt sorry for Miss Havard. A small, sneaking feeling of sympathy touched Juliana's heart, then fled as swiftly as it had come. One made one's bed—and then one lay in it. There was no place for sentiment in modern marriage.

A man was watching her. He was standing in the shadow of the open door, where the sun cast a blinding arc of light on to the flagstone floor. Juliana was attuned to male admiration and she could tell that this man was studying her intently. She flicked him a glance from under the brim of her hat, then felt her stomach drop. It was Martin Davencourt.

She met his eyes. They were very dark blue and contained a look of cold dislike as they swept over her from the feather in her hat to the tips of her bright red pumps. It was easy to read his thoughts. He was deploring her deliberate choice of scarlet and the attention she was drawing to herself. Juliana conceded that it had not been subtle, but then she had not intended it so. It was only now, confronted with Martin Davencourt's disgust, that she wished she had chosen the green and faded into the background.

For a frozen moment they stared at each other and then Juliana dragged her gaze away with a little jerk and fixed it on the carved angel high on the organ screen. She was trembling with surprise and anger, and she knew that her colour had risen. She was blushing. That rarely happened to her. How dared he have that effect on her? Normally disapproval only made her behave all the more outrageously.

The bride had arrived, a winsome little girl with blonde curls. Juliana grimaced. She hated these milk-and-water misses. The Season was full of them these days, with their simpering manners and their giggles and their innocence. The bride was dressed simply in white muslin, with a white shawl over her gown. The hem of the gown and the edge of the shawl were embossed with white satin flowers and the shawl was shot through with primrose yellow thread. She looked pretty and excited. Six small bridesmaids in white dresses with white ribbons on their straw bonnets, jostled and milled about in the doorway. Out of the corner of her eye—for she was certainly not looking at him—Juliana saw Martin Davencourt bend down with a smile and touch the cheek of the smallest bridesmaid. She remembered that Emma had said he had several younger sisters. Juliana gave a small, unconscious sigh.

The bride began her progress up the aisle and Juliana admired the look of pure terror that came and went on

Andrew Brookes's face. This is it, she thought. Brookes is caught in parson's mousetrap at last. It happened to all the eligible rakes eventually. There was only Joss's friend Sebastian Fleet left, if one discounted utterly ineligible libertines like Jasper Colling. Soon she would have no one to escort her about town. At least Brookes had made no bones about the fact that he was marrying for money. Both Joss and Adam had been odiously mawkish and had actually fallen in love with their brides. Juliana had no time for such sentiment. She had tried that and found it wanting.

She shifted a little on the pew, wishing that she had not come. It was one thing to cause a stir by attending the wedding of a supposed lover, but it was quite another to be obliged to sit quietly during the tedious proceedings. No one was looking at her now, for their attention was on the bride and groom. Juliana tried not to sneeze. For several minutes she had been aware of a large urn full of lilies that was placed on a plinth to her right. The lolling stamens were loaded with rich, orange pollen and looked vulgarly fecund. Juliana wondered if Eustacia would prove similarly blessed. Brookes had never wanted children. He had said that they were a tedious interruption to pleasure. Juliana had agreed with him, but when she had seen Martin's tiny sister she had felt a pang…

Juliana sneezed and buried her nose in her handkerchief. Her throat felt thick with the pollen and her eyes had started to water. It was undignified. She was afraid that she would start to look ugly soon. She sneezed again, twice. Several people turned to hush her. The vicar was droning on about the reasons for marriage. Juliana's memory suddenly presented her with the image of herself standing before the altar, a young débutante of eighteen, fathoms deep in love. Edwin had gripped her hand in his so tightly and she had smiled at him with a radiance that paled the sun. Eleven years ago... If only he had not left her...

The obstruction in Juliana's throat suddenly seemed like a huge lump of stone and her eyes were streaming so much that she could not see properly. She knew that she had to escape.

She got to her feet and started to edge out of the pew towards the main door, treading on peoples' toes as she went. She could not really see where she was going, and when she tripped over the end of the pew and someone caught her arm and steadied her, she was grateful.

'This way, Lady Juliana,' a low voice said in her ear. Her arm was seized in a firm grip and she was guided towards the door.

'Thank you, sir,' Juliana said.

She knew that she was outside when she felt the sun on her face and a soft breeze caressing her skin. Her eyes were still streaming and she was tolerably certain that she would be left looking red and watery, like a rabbit she had once owned as a child. It could not be helped. She had suffered from the hay fever for years, but it was unfortunate that she had had to experience an attack in public.

She felt her nose run and groped desperately for her handkerchief. One large blow was all the delicate cambric could take. It simply was not up to the task. As Juliana hesitated between the twin shame of wiping her nose on her sleeve or leaving it to drip, a large, white gentleman's kerchief was pressed into her hand. Juliana grabbed it gratefully.

'Thank you, sir,' she said again.

'This way, Lady Juliana,' the gentleman repeated. His grip on her arm increased as he urged her down the church steps. Juliana stumbled a little and felt one of his arms go about her. She drew breath to protest, for this was downright improper, but it was already too late. Through streaming eyes she saw a carriage draw up before them, then the door was thrown open and the gentleman bundled her inside. She did not have time to scream. She barely had time to breathe before the gentleman had leaped in beside her and the coachman gave the horses the office to move off. Tumbled on the seat, out of breath, her skirt rucked up about her knees, her eyes still blinded by tears, Juliana strove to regain her balance and her dignity.

'What in God's name do you think you are doing?'

'Calm yourself, Lady Juliana.' The gentleman sounded amused. 'I am abducting you. Surely that is all par for the course for a lady of your reputation? Or do you prefer to do the kidnapping yourself?'

Juliana sat up straighter. She recognised that voice with its undertone of mockery. Now that her vision was clearing she could see her companion's face. She sat up straighter.

'Mr Davencourt! I did not request your escort anywhere! Kindly instruct your coachman to halt the horses so that I may get down.'

'I regret that I cannot do that,' Martin Davencourt said imperturbably. He had taken the seat across from Juliana and now sat negligently at ease, watching her with casual indifference. Juliana felt her blood fizz with irritation.

'Pray, why not? It seems a simple enough request.'

Martin Davencourt shrugged. 'Did you ever hear of an abduction ending so tamely? I do not think so. I cannot let you go, Lady Juliana.'

Juliana felt as though she was going to explode with annoyance. Her eyes were still streaming, her head ached and this insufferable man was acting as though one of them was mad and she knew which one. She tried to speak calmly.

'Then the least that you can offer me in all courtesy is an explanation. I can scarce believe that you make a habit of abducting ladies like this, Mr Davencourt. You would be in Newgate if you did, and besides, you are far too respectable to do such a thing!'

Martin tilted his head to look at her. 'Is that a challenge?'

'No!' Juliana turned her face away haughtily. 'It is an insult!'

She diverted her gaze to the window, where the London streets were slipping past. She briefly considered jumping from the carriage, but rejected the idea as foolhardy. They were not travelling quickly—London traffic seldom did— but it was still a reckless idea and she would end up looking untidy or, worse, twisting her ankle.

She glanced back at Martin Davencourt. Perhaps he had conceived a hopeless passion for her the previous night and thought to carry her off to press his attentions on her. Juliana had a certain vanity, but she also had common sense and she knew this was unlikely. Only a half-hour earlier, Martin had looked at her with contempt, not appreciation. He was looking at her again now. His gaze moved over her thoughtfully as though he was making an inventory of her features. Juliana raised her chin.

'Well?'

A smile twitched Martin Davencourt's firm mouth. There were sunburned lines about his eyes that suggested that he laughed often. There were also two long grooves down his cheeks that deepened when he smiled. With a jolt of memory, Juliana recalled the curious pull of attraction she had felt for that smile when she was a girl.

It was very appealing. He was very attractive. Juliana was irritated to realise that she found him so.

'Well what?' Martin said.

His coolness set Juliana back a little. She cleared her throat.

'Well…I am still awaiting your explanation, sir. I realise that you have been absent from London for a long time, but it is not customary to behave in such a manner, you know. Even I seldom get abducted these days.'

Martin laughed. 'Hence the need to create a stir in other ways, I suppose. I do feel that disrupting your lover's wedding is particularly bad *ton*, Lady Juliana.'

Juliana frowned. 'Disrupting… Oh, I see! You thought that I intended to make a scene!'

Despite herself, Juliana could not help a smile. So Martin had thought that she was intending to act the discarded mistress, throwing herself before the altar in a last passionate, tearful farewell. She stifled a laugh. Andrew Brookes was scarcely worth such a scene even if she had been inclined to make one. She looked at Martin, her eyes bright with mirth.

'You are mistaken, sir. I had no such intention—'

But Martin had seen her smile and misinterpreted it. His lips set in a hard line.

'Save your breath, Lady Juliana. I thought that your escapade last night was outrageous enough, in all truth, but this is beyond everything. The scarlet dress…' His gaze flicked her again. 'The crocodile tears… You are a consummate actress, are you not?'

Juliana caught her breath. 'Tears? I suffer from the hay fever—'

Martin looked out of the window as though her explanations were of no interest to him. 'You may spare me your denials. We have arrived.'

Juliana peered out of the window. They were in a pretty little square with tall town houses that were much like her own. The carriage rattled through a narrow archway and into a stable yard. Juliana turned to look at Martin.

'Arrived where? The only place at which I wish to arrive is my own doorstep!'

Martin sighed. 'I dare say. I cannot leave you alone, however, so I have brought you to my home. I promised my aunt that I would keep an eye on you and prevent you from ruining the wedding.'

Juliana sat back. 'Your aunt? I collect that you mean Miss Havard's mama?'

'Precisely. She heard that you were Brookes's mistress and was afraid that you would do something outrageous to ruin her daughter's wedding day. It seems that she was quite right.'

'I see.' Juliana took a deep breath. 'I thought that I was inventive, Mr Davencourt, but your imagination far outruns mine. Still, with such madness in the family, who can be surprised? I assure you that you—and Mrs Havard—are quite mistaken.'

'I would like to believe you,' Martin said politely, 'but I fear that I cannot take the risk. If I let you go now, you would surely be in time to ruin the wedding breakfast.'

'Perhaps I could dance on the table,' Juliana said sarcastically, 'unveiling myself as I did so!'

'You did that last night, as I recall.' Martin Davencourt's gaze pinned her to the seat. 'Now do you come inside willingly or must I carry you? It would be undignified for you, I fear.'

Juliana glared at him. 'I never do anything undignified.'

Martin laughed. 'Is that so? What about the time you visited Dr Graham's famous nude mud baths in Piccadilly and insisted on the servants taking the bathtub outside?

That must have provided quite a spectacle for the populace! How decorous was that?'

'The mud-bathing was for the good of my health,' Juliana said haughtily. 'Besides, one would hardly bathe with one's clothes on. Think of the dirtiness.'

'Hmm. Your argument is unconvincing. And what about the occasion on which you dressed as a *demi-mondaine* to trick Lord Berkeley into betraying his wife? Was that dignified? Was it even kind?'

'That was only a jest,' Juliana said sulkily. She was beginning to feel like a naughty child receiving a telling off. 'Besides, Berkeley did not fall for it.'

'Even so, I doubt that Lady Berkeley found the joke prodigiously amusing,' Martin said drily. 'I hear she cried for several days.'

'Well, that is her problem,' Juliana said, her temper catching alight. 'And what a bore you are proving to be, Mr Davencourt! What do *you* do for entertainment? Read the newspaper? Or is that too dangerously exciting for you?'

'Sometimes I read *The Times*,' Martin said, 'or the parliamentary reports—'

'Lud! I might have known!'

Martin ignored her. A footman opened the carriage door and let the steps down. Juliana accepted Martin's hand down on to the cobbles with a certain distaste, removing herself from his grip as quickly as possible. The whole situation seemed absurd, but she could not immediately see what she could do about it. Martin Davencourt was disinclined to listen to her explanations and by now she was so angry with him for his accusations that she was unwilling to elucidate anyway. They were at an impasse.

She looked about her with some curiosity. They were

in a neat brick coach yard at the back of the row of town houses and now Martin guided her towards a door leading into the building. His hand was warm on the small of her back, his touch decisive.

A strange sensation crept through Juliana. Annoyed with herself, she retorted, 'Smuggling me in through the back door, Mr Davencourt? Are you afraid that I will kick up a fuss if you allow anyone to see me?'

'I certainly do not trust you,' Martin said, with the hint of a smile. He held the door open for her. 'This way, Lady Juliana.'

The door closed with a quiet click behind them and the stone-flagged passage was cool after the sunshine outside. As Juliana's eyes adjusted to the dimness she saw that Martin was leading her into a wide hallway floored in pale pink stone and decorated with statues and leafy green plants. Most of the light came from a large cupola set above the stair and the sunlight filtered through the leaves, making dancing shadows on the floor. It was charming and restful.

'Oh, how pretty!' Juliana had spoken before she thought and now she saw that Martin was looking a little surprised at her unfeigned enthusiasm. He also looked pleased.

'Thank you. I was very pleased when the reality matched my plans.'

Juliana looked at him in surprise. 'But surely you did not design it yourself?'

'Why not? I assure you it was not difficult. I saw plenty of Italian palaces to inspire me when I was travelling. My sister Clara helped with the colours and the design. She has a flair for these things.'

Juliana sighed. She, too, had travelled in Italy, but the sights that she had seen had been as far removed from palaces as it was possible to be. Lodging houses with flea-ridden beds and damp running down the walls; stinking canals where rotten vegetables and the decaying corpses of dogs floated together... The heat, the smell, the noise...and the constant, drunken ranting of Clive Massingham, who had run away with her to escape his debts, only to abandon her within two weeks of their wedding.

Juliana shuddered.

Martin opened a door for her and Juliana preceded him into a small drawing room. It was painted in lemon and white and consequently seemed full of light. The rosewood furniture complemented it perfectly. Juliana reflected that Clara Davencourt must indeed have an eye for style.

'May I offer you some refreshment, Lady Juliana?' Martin asked, with scrupulous courtesy.

Juliana gave him a level stare. 'I will take a glass of wine, thank you. Or will my stay be a protracted one? Perhaps I should request an entire dinner?'

Martin smiled. 'I hope that you will not have to stay here too long—'

'Oh, you hope it, too! Well, that is an encouragement!' Juliana gave him a wide smile. 'I shuddered to think that you intended to inflict your company on me for hours!'

Martin sighed. 'Please sit down, Lady Juliana.'

Juliana sat on the rosewood sofa, jumping up a moment later as something sharp pressed into her hip. Investigation proved that it was a small, wooden sailing ship, a child's toy. She placed it carefully on the table.

'My sister Daisy's boat,' Martin said. He passed her a glass of wine. 'I do beg your pardon, Lady Juliana. Daisy leaves her toys all over the house. Ships are a particular favourite with her at the moment for I have been telling her about my travels.'

He broke off abruptly as though he had just remembered that he was not chatting to an acquaintance but that there was another purpose to their engagement. A rather strained silence descended.

After several minutes had passed, the exquisite white gold clock on the mantel struck twelve. They both jumped at the loud chime.

Juliana was starting to feel amused.

'I do believe, Mr Davencourt, that now you have me you are not sure what to do with me! It occurs to me that as we are to be here some little time we might get to know each other better, so why don't we—?'

'No!' Martin did not wait for her to finish. He was scowling. 'I have no wish to take up your offer, Lady Juliana. Besides, my younger brother is returning from Cambridge shortly—'

'Then perhaps I may talk to him, if you do not care to speak with me,' Juliana said neatly. She saw with satisfaction that she had actually put him to the blush. Caught, fair and square.

'Talk! I thought that you meant—' Martin Davencourt stopped abruptly.

'You thought that I meant to proposition you again.' Juliana rearranged her silken skirts demurely about her and took a sip of wine. She watched him over the rim, a smile in her eyes. 'My dear Mr Davencourt, I do assure you that I can take a hint as well as the next person. Besides, you yourself suggested that you were not an appropriate conquest for me and that I should be more particular.'

'I suppose that I deserved that.' A faint, self-deprecating smile touched Martin Davencourt's mouth. He looked rueful. Juliana rather liked him for it. She could not help herself. So many men were so proud that they could not bear to be caught out, but Martin had the confidence to admit when he had been worsted.

'As you do not care to be seduced by me,' she continued sweetly, 'why do we not talk about old times? How long ago was it that we met at Ashby Tallant? Fourteen years? Fifteen?' She put her head on one side and gave him an appraising look. 'I might have guessed that you would turn out like this. A dull boy so often becomes a dull man, although I suppose that you have improved in looks at least.'

Martin did not appear remotely insulted by this backhanded compliment. He laughed. 'You have changed, too, Lady Juliana. I thought you such a sweet child.'

'Either your memory is faulty or your judgement was not sound at the age of fifteen,' Juliana said. 'I am sure that I was exactly as I am now. Though I am surprised that you remember me at all, sir, for you were forever damming the stream or building fortifications or doing whatever it is that boys do.'

Martin smiled. 'I am sure that we both found the other tiresome, Lady Juliana. Adolescent boys and girls seldom have much common ground. You were interested only in balls and dancing and you fell asleep when I tried to explain to you Nelson's battle plan at Trafalgar—'

'And you could not have performed the quadrille to save your life,' Juliana finished. 'I dare say that we had little in common then and nothing in common now.' She smoothed her scarlet skirts and yawned ostentatiously. 'This is going to be an unconscionably long hour or so, is it not?'

Martin sat back in his chair and studied her thoughtfully.

'Indulge my curiosity then, Lady Juliana. Did you truly imagine that Andrew Brookes would leave Eustacia at the altar for you? Or were you merely seeking to cause trouble?'

Juliana sighed. So they were back to that again. She knew that he had not believed her before.

'Mr Davencourt,' she said, with heavy patience, 'you do not strike me as a stupid man so I shall repeat this only once. Your suspicions of me are false. I had no scheme to wreck your cousin's wedding, still less to keep Brookes for myself. Why, I have exhausted all *his* potential! I assure you I would not have him if he were packaged in gold!'

She saw a flicker of a smile in Martin Davencourt's eyes, but it vanished as swiftly as it had come. His blue gaze was keen on her face. 'Yet he was your lover.'

The colour came into Juliana's cheeks. She raised her chin. 'He was *not*. And even had he been, I would not have stooped so low as to spoil your cousin's wedding day.'

Martin looked thoughtful. 'No? Love can prompt one to all kinds of irrational acts.'

'I am aware. But I doubt that you are, Mr Davencourt. I think it unlikely you have ever fallen in love. No doubt you would consider it too dangerous.'

Martin laughed. 'You are mistaken, Lady Juliana. I am sure that all young men fall in love at some point in their salad days.'

'But not when they have reached the age of discretion?' Juliana pulled a face. 'I expect you are too old for that sort of thing now.'

Martin sat back in his chair. '*Touché*, Lady Juliana. I confess that I have not felt any partiality for a lady for many years. And better that way. Matters such as marriage are best conducted with a clear mind. But we were speaking of your past loves, not mine.'

'No, we were not,' Juliana snapped. 'I have no desire to rehearse my past history, nor to debate morality with you, sir. I find that men are tiresomely hypocritical on such matters.'

'Are we? You mean that you dislike the double standard that is so often applied?'

'Of course I do! What right-thinking woman would not dismiss it as unreasonable? A tenet that says a man may behave as a rake without censure, yet if a woman does the same she is branded a whore? It has to be a man who made that rule, do you not agree?'

Martin laughed. 'I concede that it is unjust, but there are plenty of people, women as well as men, who believe in it.'

Juliana turned her shoulder. 'I am aware. Let us change the subject, or I fear I shall become very ill-tempered.'

'Very well. Let us return to the case in point.' Martin sighed. 'If I have made a mistake about your intentions at the wedding, then I apologise, Lady Juliana. It was an honest mistake.'

'Based on a ridiculous assumption,' Juliana said.

'Not quite ridiculous. Not after your behaviour last night.'

'I do wish you would stop raising that!' Juliana said furiously. She felt very frustrated. 'Last night was intended as a jest. As for my tears at the wedding, if you suspect that I am deceiving you about my hay fever—' she invested the words with a heavy sarcasm '—then approach me with that vase of roses from the mantelpiece and I will sneeze for as long as it takes to convince you.'

She put her wineglass down and got to her feet. 'I do believe that we have exhausted this topic, Mr Davencourt. Certainly I am becoming quite dreadfully bored of your company. I assume that I am free to go now?'

Martin made a slight gesture. 'Of course.'

'You are not concerned that I will return to disrupt the wedding breakfast?'

'I think not. You have said that that is not your aim and I believe you.'

Juliana inclined her head frigidly. 'Thank you. Then it would be helpful of you to procure me a hack. I do believe it is the least you can do.'

Martin got to his feet. 'I will send for the carriage for you.'

He came across to her and looked down into her face for a moment. 'Hay fever,' he said slowly. 'When I saw you in the church I was so sure that you were crying…'

He raised a hand and gently brushed away the smudge of a tear on her cheek with one thumb. Juliana felt her pulse skip a beat.

'Andrew Brookes is not worth anyone's tears,' she said abruptly.

Martin's hand fell. He stepped back. Juliana felt relieved. Just for a second he had completely undermined her defences.

'I share your opinion of Brookes, Lady Juliana,' he said, 'but I want Eustacia to be happy. It would be a shame for her to be disillusioned so early in her marriage.'

'It will happen to her sooner or later,' Juliana said, moving towards the door, 'and you would be a simpleton to think otherwise. Andrew Brookes is not capable of fidelity.'

Martin pulled a face. 'I bow to your superior knowledge of the gentleman, Lady Juliana. You sound very cynical. Do you then believe all men faithless?'

Juliana paused, swallowing the confirmation that instinctively rose to her lips. There was something about

Martin Davencourt that always seemed to demand an honest answer. It was disconcerting.

'No,' she said slowly. 'Where a man truly loves I believe he may be faithful. But there are some men who are not capable of love or fidelity, and Brookes is one of those.'

'I hear that it is your preferred type. Brookes, Colling, Massingham…'

Juliana had herself in hand again. 'Lud, I do not choose men for their fidelity, Mr Davencourt. What an odd notion! I choose them for their entertainment value.'

'I see,' Martin said, heavily ironic. 'Then I had better detain you no further. I cannot imagine that you will find what you are seeking in this house.'

Juliana grimaced. 'No. Nor can I.' She paused. 'The wedding service will be over now, I suppose.'

'Indeed.' Martin checked the white gold clock on the mantle. 'Do you have regrets about letting Andrew Brookes go after all, Lady Juliana?'

'No,' Juliana said pleasantly. 'I was merely concerned about your sister Daisy—the little bridesmaid? She will be wondering where you are.'

There was a pause. For a second Juliana saw a quizzical look in Martin's eyes, as though she had surprised him.

'My sister Araminta is taking care of Daisy and the other girls,' he said. 'Besides, she is in such high good spirits to be a bridesmaid that I am sure she will scarcely miss me.'

'I doubt that,' Juliana said, feeling a small pang for Daisy Davencourt. 'I assure you that children notice these things.'

She realised that her tone had been more wistful than she had intended. Martin was still watching her with speculation in his eyes. His perception unnerved her. She gave him a bright smile.

'If you will excuse me, sir, I will leave. So many more marriages to blight, you know! I cannot afford to waste time here. Although...' her voice warmed as a thought struck her '...perhaps it will enhance my bad reputation for it to be known that you whisked me away from the wedding service. Yes, I do believe I shall encourage that rumour. We were overcome with wild passion and could not restrain ourselves.'

'Lady Juliana,' Martin said, a thread of steel in his tone, 'if I hear for one moment that you are putting that story about I shall denounce it—and you—publicly.'

Juliana opened her eyes wide. 'But this is all your fault, Mr Davencourt, with your ridiculous suspicions of me! Most young ladies would take advantage of their abduction to oblige you to marry them!'

Martin's lips twitched. 'Doing it too brown, Lady Juliana. I cannot imagine that you would wish to marry me even for a minute!'

'No, of course not. But the very least you could do is permit me to use it to enhance my poor reputation.'

'Certainly not.'

Juliana pouted. 'Oh, you are so stuffy! But I suppose you are correct in one sense—no one would believe in a hundred years that I could possibly be attracted to *you!*'

They stared at one another for a long moment, but before Martin could respond there was the sound of voices and footsteps on the tiled floor of the hall. The door was flung open and a gentleman burst in.

'Martin, I've—' He stopped abruptly, looked from Martin to Juliana and back again. 'I beg your pardon. I had thought you to be at the wedding, and when Liddington said that you were home I did not realise you had company.'

'I was at the wedding and I do have company,' Martin said. He smiled slightly. 'Lady Juliana, may I make you known to my brother Brandon? Brandon, this is Lady Juliana Myfleet.'

Brandon gave his elder brother a look of lively astonishment, which had been tempered to one of mischievous amusement as he came forward to take Juliana's hand.

'Good gracious,' he said mildly. 'I am delighted to meet you, Lady Juliana.'

Juliana saw Martin frowning, and deliberately gave Brandon a very warm greeting. She guessed that Martin's young half-brother could not be above two and twenty, and he had all the dash and charm that Martin lacked. It would be very difficult to resist Brandon Davencourt and most ladies probably did not try. Where Martin's personality seemed deliberately banked down and controlled, Brandon was at full blaze. Juliana suddenly wondered whether Martin had always been the responsible older brother. She thought that he probably had.

Brandon bowed with an easy grace and fixed her with a frankly admiring glance from his blue eyes.

'I had no notion that you were acquainted with Martin, Lady Juliana.'

Juliana gave Martin a mocking look, which he met with a particularly wooden one of his own. 'We are only very slightly acquainted, Mr Davencourt. We met as children, but have not seen each other these sixteen years past.'

'Dashed good luck for me that you are acquainted,' Brandon said, smiling into her eyes. 'I have been wanting an introduction to you for months, Lady Juliana!'

'You should just have come up and introduced yourself,' Juliana said sweetly. She was watching Martin out of the corner of her eye and saw the disapproving look he had bent on her. 'I love meeting good-looking young men!'

Brandon laughed and Martin cleared his throat pointedly.

'Lady Juliana was just leaving,' he said.

The door opened to admit a liveried butler. 'The Reverend Mr Edward Ashwick is here, Mr Davencourt. He says that he has come to escort Lady Juliana Myfleet home.'

Juliana permitted herself a small, satisfied smile. 'Dear Edward. How chivalrous he is. So useful to have a few beaux to one's string!'

Martin took her hand. 'Good day, Lady Juliana. Once again, I apologise for my mistake.'

'Good day Mr Davencourt,' Juliana said pertly. 'Please try not to abduct me again.'

Chapter Three

'What the deuce was that all about, Juliana?' Edward Ashwick asked, with the familiarity of long acquaintance. 'Must say, you caused quite a stir leaving with Davencourt when the marriage service had barely started. I sometimes wonder if you can do anything without drawing attention to yourself!'

'Probably not.' Juliana sighed. She felt suddenly tired, as though the laudanum of the previous day had caught up with her again and was urging her to sleep. Except that she could not simply go home and go to bed. It was barely afternoon and the house was empty and she would be alone, which was not to be tolerated. She turned impulsively to her escort.

'Can we not go back to the wedding breakfast, Eddie? Please? It would be such fun!'

Edward's ruddy face blushed, as it always did when she called him by his pet name. She could see that he was debating the idea and knew she could twist him around her little finger.

'Please, Eddie…'

'Don't think so, Juliana.' Edward spoke gruffly to hide

his embarrassment. 'You've caused enough of a distraction already. Let it be. I will take you home—'

'No!' Not for anything did Juliana want to admit that she was lonely. It was far easier to pretend to boredom, reinforce the impression that her butterfly mind needed entertainment. 'Can we not visit Joss and Amy, then? Or Adam...'

'They will all be at the party for hours,' Edward said. 'Should have thought of that, Juliana, before you caused such gossip. Besides, everyone's talking about what you got up to last night. Can it really be true that you had yourself served up to Brookes on a silver salver?' Edward looked as though he was about to suffer an apoplexy.

'I fear so,' Juliana said. She sighed. 'It was only a joke, Eddie—'

'Joke! God help us, Juliana! Your idea of humour becomes ever more extraordinary!'

'You are beginning to sound like my father,' Juliana said crossly. 'Or Mr Davencourt. What did I do to deserve to be surrounded by such tedious bores?'

Edward frowned. 'Can you be surprised that we are all appalled? And Joss is furious with you—'

Juliana felt her heart sink. Her brother Joss was the only person whose good opinion truly mattered to her. If she lost him as well it would be dreadful. It had been bad enough when he had married and she had had to share his attention.

'You and Joss and my father are all the same,' she said bitterly. 'I cannot bear to be told what to do by you all! You used not to be such a dull old stick, Eddie.'

She could see Edward fidgeting with his signet ring. His face was very red and he was avoiding looking at her. 'You know I only mention it because I care about you, Juliana. None of us wishes to see you ruin yourself.'

Juliana knew it was true. Edward cared deeply for her. He had been one of her most constant admirers and she knew she took his regard for granted. Dear, steady Edward. He was very kind, but he was not at all exciting.

'You should marry again, Juliana,' Edward said. He looked directly at her now, his dark gaze hopeful. 'You were very happy with Myfleet and might be again.'

Juliana knew what he meant and she could not bear the entreaty in his eyes. He had proposed to her once and she had gently rejected him, and the matter had never been mentioned between them again.

'No one is likely to offer these days, Eddie,' she said lightly. 'My reputation is such it must scare all honest men away!' And with a slight sinking of her heart she knew it to be true.

Edward was looking dogged and devoted. 'Dearest Juliana, you know that that is not entirely true. I would deem it an honour if only you would consider my suit.'

Juliana looked around desperately for an avenue of escape and, finding one, grabbed it with both hands. Walking along the pavement beside the carriage was Emma Wren, with her bosom bow Lady Neasden hanging on her arm. No matter that they had parted in anger the previous night. Hopefully Emma had been so drunk that she would not remember. Juliana rapped on the carriage roof to ask the coachman to stop, and pulled down the window, cutting Edward off in mid-declaration.

'Emma! Mary! Wait for me!'

Juliana saw Edward slump in the corner of the coach. She bent a consoling smile on him. 'Eddie dearest, you know that we would not suit. But thank you so much for rescuing me from Mr Davencourt's clutches. I was quite afraid I would be bored to death! Now I must fly!' She leaned over and gave him a brief kiss on the cheek, then opened the door of the coach and gestured quickly to the groom to put the steps down.

'Are you going shopping, Emma? Wait, I am coming with you!'

'What the devil do you think you're about, Juliana?' Joss Tallant demanded one evening the following week, in almost an echo of Edward Ashwick's question. His tone was considerably milder than it might have been, owing to the excellent dinner that his sister had served for him and the bottle of very fine malt whisky that was standing by his elbow. It was a warm night and they were sitting on Juliana's terrace as the moon rose higher above the trees and the moths buzzed around the candle flame. Occasionally Juliana and Joss would take dinner alone together—Juliana thought of it as time when Amy let Joss off his leash—and she usually enjoyed their tête-à-têtes, but not tonight. Tonight, Joss had joined the long and tiresome list of people quizzing her about her behaviour.

'First there was that outrageous story about you being delivered to Brookes on the silver salver,' her brother continued, 'and then—'

'Pray do not remind me, Joss!' Juliana interrupted sharply. She was heartily sick of being hauled over the coals for her behaviour at Emma Wren's party. 'I keep telling everyone that it was only a jest, but you are all gone odiously censorious on me!'

'Perhaps we do not see the amusing side,' her brother said. He gave her a long look. 'As if that were not enough, then there was the tale about Brookes' wedding! I heard some ridiculous gossip that Martin Davencourt abducted you.'

'Ridiculous is the word,' Juliana said grumpily, pouring

herself another glass of port. 'Martin Davencourt would not know how to abduct someone properly!'

'You mean improperly?'

'Whichever. The man is as stuffed as a piece of taxidermy. I do not know what politics is coming to when we are to have such dull Members of Parliament!'

Joss laughed. 'I presume, then, that seduction was not Davencourt's aim?'

'Of course not! I thought that you knew him? Then you must realise how unlikely that is,' Juliana said sulkily. 'At least, he *did* abduct me, but not for the reason that everyone is thinking. He thought that I was intending to throw myself before the altar and beg Andrew Brookes to come back to me, or some such nonsense. As though I wanted Brookes in the first place!'

'There are plenty who thought that you did,' Joss said.

'Only because I gave them to believe that it was so.' Juliana reached out a lazy hand to steer a wayward moth away from the candle flame. 'You know that I was never Brookes's mistress, Joss.'

'I also know that you do not have the roll call of lovers that everyone believes.' Joss narrowed his eyes against the light. 'Why do you mislead them, Ju?'

Juliana relaxed a little. When her brother called her Juliana in an odiously strict tone she knew that he was genuinely angry, but when he used the diminutive she felt on safer ground. She shrugged lightly.

'I might as well be hung for a sheep as a lamb. Since everyone believes the worst of me, why disabuse them?'

Joss frowned, answering her question with a question. 'Why make it worse for yourself?'

Juliana hesitated, because the honest answer was a mixture of things, all of them reasons she did not wish to admit to. *I play my games because I am bored, because*

I am lonely, because I dare not risk loving once more...
Confessing to such weakness made her feel impossibly
vulnerable.

'I have an obstinate determination to live down to my
bad reputation.' Juliana flashed her brother a smile. They
had had this discussion before, and Joss was always trying
to persuade her to reform.

'Lud, Joss, you know that my reputation was lost when
I ran off with Massingham.' Juliana's voice warmed with
real feeling. 'Nothing that I could say or do now would
make matters any better, so why should I try?'

Joss sighed. 'Juliana, you married Massingham. When
that happens all becomes respectable again. If you were
only to live a little more quietly, people would soon overlook your past indiscretions. Even Papa would forgive
you.'

Juliana flashed him a glance in which there was equal
mockery for herself as well as him.

'Gain Papa's forgiveness? It would take more than that,
Joss! As for the rest of society, how hypocritical can people be? They are prepared to sweep everything under the
carpet as long as I behave myself in future. All my scandals can be overlooked if I reform. After all, I was *married* to Massingham—' she spat the words out '—even
though he deserted me after two weeks! The marriage
lines are all that count.'

Joss shrugged. 'I agree that it is hypocritical, but those
are society's rules.'

'I hate them! They are so dishonest.'

'We are all aware that you dislike conforming. However, the fact remains that you are the widowed daughter
of the Marquis of Tallant, and as such acceptable in society.' Joss flashed her a grin. 'Just.' His tone softened.
'Make it easy on yourself, Ju. Drop those so-called friends

of yours and their foolish pranks. Find something better to do with your life.'

Juliana turned her face away. Home truths always made her uncomfortable. Speaking of Clive Massingham aroused yet more unhappy memories. The pain of his desertion some two years before had faded now, but she still felt angry and betrayed. She had been infatuated and helplessly in love with him, and had been sadly disillusioned. He had killed all her love the day he left, taking her money with him, abandoning her alone in a foreign land. Juliana had been in love twice in her life and both affairs had ended in tears of one sort or another. She had vowed never to make herself so vulnerable again.

She turned back to Joss, her head high, and her eyes bright.

'Lud, Joss, you speak like a Methodist! Now were Massingham still alive, then you would have some scandal to complain about! I shudder to think of all the chaos he would have wreaked by now!'

'Lucky for him that he is dead.' Joss's voice was hard, but he put out a hand to her. 'I am sorry, Ju. I know you cared for him—'

'Once. I cared for him once. Now I detest his memory.'

'Is that why you never took his name?'

Juliana swallowed a warming draught of the port. 'I wished to ignore the humiliation of my marriage.' She shrugged. 'Ironic, since it is that that gives me what little semblance of respectability I possess! It is all dead and buried now, at any rate, but they say that scandal never dies, does it, Joss? So I may as well give the gossips their due and outrage the crusty old dowagers with my exploits.'

Joss sighed. 'And the latest piece of gossip is your abduction by Davencourt. A vastly different type of man from Massingham!'

Juliana laughed. 'Yes, indeed. I warned him that I would ruin his good reputation!'

'So what do you think of him?'

Juliana pulled a face. 'Disappointing. The whole abduction débâcle might have been quite fun, only Martin Davencourt is one of those odiously principled types who take everything so seriously. Did you know that we met as children? His godfather was that eccentric old man over at Ashby Hall.'

Joss raised a brow. 'I do not recall ever meeting him when we were younger.'

'No, you had gone to Oxford when Martin Davencourt came to stay at Ashby. He was a tediously dull youth with pimples and greasy hair—'

'Juliana!'

'Well, I suppose he has improved in looks,' Juliana said fairly, 'but he is still deadly dull. I suppose it is in part the result of taking responsibility of all those siblings, and in part the fact that he was born boring.'

'You seemed to be getting on with him well enough at Lady Everley's dinner the other night,' Joss observed.

Juliana lifted one shoulder in a careless shrug. 'One has to try. We all get lumbered with the tedious dinner guest every so often. I believe Mary Everley put me next to him on purpose.'

'What did you talk about?'

Juliana's brow wrinkled. 'Well, it was the strangest thing… I started off trying to flirt with him but somehow he turned the subject and we ended speaking of Davencourt. It sounds the most prodigiously grand house and it is evident that Mr Davencourt is very fond of it.'

'I am surprised that you sustained the conversation, then,' Joss said, smiling, 'for you hate the country.'

'Very true.' Juliana felt a vague surprise herself.

'I rather like Martin,' Joss said. 'He seems a sound man. I understand that Charles Grey rates him highly. He will definitely be a Member of Parliament come the next election, and I believe Grey thinks he has a bright future.'

'Lud, politics! You have me yawning already, Joss.' Juliana smiled. 'Even so, I am not surprised that you like Martin Davencourt, for he reminds me of you in some ways. Or do you not think it a compliment to be described as principled? Have you met him before then?'

'Yes. Davencourt is a friend of Adam Ashwick's from his army days, so I understand. He was dining at the Ashwicks last week when we were there.' Joss shot Juliana a look. 'You were invited as well, I believe.'

Juliana shrugged again. 'I was invited as a partner for Edward, so I declined. You are all so transparent in your matchmaking plans. As though I would ever be a suitable wife for Edward Ashwick!'

'Why not?' her brother asked mildly. 'He is prodigious fond of you—'

'I dare say. And I love him, too, as a brother.' Juliana smiled. 'Though not a *favourite* brother. Not like you, Joss!'

She saw the shadow of a smile touch Joss's mouth. 'Thank you, Ju. Your regard warms me. So why do you not take Ashwick—and let him redeem your reputation?'

'Ugh!' Juliana grimaced. 'I have no wish for Edward to sacrifice himself to save me, and you know how all the old tabbies would scratch if a clergyman married a fallen woman. A twice-wed widow with a tarnished name! Besides, Joss, I do not wish to reform.' She settled her silk shawl more firmly about her shoulders. 'I shall not marry again, my dear. There are too many reasons why I cannot.'

There was a silence.

'You would still have enjoyed the dinner,' Joss said. 'The Ashwicks have a very fine chef.'

'I dare say he serves more substantial puddings than at Emma Wren's dinners.'

'Considerably.'

They smiled at each other, and then Juliana sighed.

'I suppose I should have accepted. I get very few respectable invitations these days.'

Joss laughed. 'You might even have enjoyed yourself.'

'Perhaps. Though I find wives to be a rather worthy breed, yours included, I fear, dear Joss.'

Joss gave her a faint smile. 'I know. But you might like Amy if you took the trouble.'

Juliana shook her head. Try as she might—and Juliana had to confess that she had not tried very hard—she could not like Amy Tallant. There was something so sweet and wholesome about her that Juliana found difficult to stomach.

'I do not think so, my dear,' she said now. 'Amy's interests and mine are entirely opposite. As for Annis Ashwick—well, I confess she quite terrifies me, she is such a bluestocking!'

'You talk the most arrant nonsense, Ju,' Joss said bracingly. He checked his watch. 'I must go. Amy will have returned from the theatre. She and Annis have been to see *King Lear*.'

'Shakespeare, ugh!' Juliana gave an exaggerated shudder. 'You have proved my point, Joss. I would rather pull my hair out with tweezers than sit through one of Mr Shakespeare's tragedies!'

After Joss had gone, Juliana sat for a little longer

watching the candle burn down and the moths singeing their wings on the small flame. It was getting cooler out in the garden. She stood up and pulled her shawl closer. Her new silver dress, the result of her shopping trip with Emma Wren the previous day, was a sad disappointment for it pinched under the arms. Juliana was prone to buying on impulse, but she never regretted it. She would send the gown back to the shop the following morning and refuse to pay for it. No matter that she had worn it already and there was a spot of port on the silver gauze skirt.

She drifted inside as the clock struck eleven thirty. There were a number of cards on the mantelpiece, but Juliana had been correct in what she told her brother— very few of them were respectable. Fortunately there were enough unrespectable invitations to make up. Juliana picked up a silver-edged card and tapped it thoughtfully. Crowns was a new and most exclusive gaming hell, established by a former Cyprian, Susanna Kellaway. It was the perfect place for a disreputable widow to gamble away her money. Why sit in and be miserable when there was money to be won and lost? Juliana ran upstairs, calling for her maid as she went.

The first person that Juliana saw when she entered Crowns an hour later was her brother Joss who, with Adam Ashwick and Sebastian Fleet, was taking a drink in a quiet corner. Juliana smiled to herself. The hypocrisy of the male never ceased to amaze her. There was Joss, virtuously proclaiming that he intended to return home to Amy, only to be found an hour later in a gaming hell. And Adam, too, who had been married all of a twelve-month. Juliana shook her head, a cynical smile curving her lips. They should both be ashamed of themselves. *She* was ashamed of them. She examined her feelings and realised that a tiny part of her actually *was* disappointed in her brother and his friend. Which was interesting. Perhaps she had not completely lost her faith in human nature after all.

Juliana noted that she was not the only one watching them; a gaggle of high-class Cyprians were even now moving purposefully in the direction of the three men. She did not blame them. Her brother, Adam and Seb were three of the most handsome men in London and a downright temptation to any ambitious courtesan. Juliana cut the girls out neatly, sliding into the booth beside Adam and smiling over her shoulder as she did so.

'I shall be but a moment and then they are all yours, ladies.'

The girls gave her a watchful smile in return and drifted a little distance away. Joss did not look pleased to see her, though both he and Adam stood up politely. Sebastian Fleet moved away, murmuring something about fetching her a drink.

'I did not expect to see you again tonight, Juliana,' Joss said.

'Evidently not,' Juliana said, pointedly looking at the Cyprians. 'What do you think you are about, Joss? I feel very let down by your behaviour.'

Joss looked unamused, but Adam's lips twitched. 'That is rich coming from you, Juliana,' he murmured. 'What are you doing here?'

'I came to play, of course.' Juliana narrowed her eyes on him. 'Do not change the subject, Adam. We were talking of your choice of entertainment, not mine. I suppose that too much sweetness at home becomes cloying after a time and you need a sharp antidote? I cannot blame you. I find virtue absolutely stifling myself.'

'We have all noticed that you and virtue are natural

enemies,' Joss said drily. 'However, you have the matter quite wrong, Ju. We are not here for the play and even less for the courtesans.'

Juliana raised her brows incredulously. 'Indeed?' A smile curved her lips. 'Oh, I see! Yes, of course, how slow of me. When I next meet Annis and Amy I shall remember how very wrong I was in thinking that you were looking for entertainment. I suppose they must deserve to be cuckolded or you would not be here.'

Adam's cool grey eyes held hers. 'Do you know, Juliana,' he said slowly, 'if you had been a man I would have called you out plenty of times before now?'

Juliana smiled at him. 'Except that you would not wish to offend Joss by shooting me!'

Adam's eyes met Joss's. 'Oh, I would not let that stand in my way,' he said easily. 'Just be grateful that I retain a modicum of chivalry where you are concerned. All the same, you are a shrew.'

Juliana threw back her head and laughed. 'You are only saying that because I have caught you out.'

'Not so. You have not caught us out, whatever you may think. Besides, you know you enjoy being so malicious.'

Juliana turned to her brother. 'Joss? Are you going to let that stand?'

Joss shrugged. 'You will not find me disagreeing with Adam's assessment, Ju.'

Juliana laughed again. 'Upon my word, you two are the most ungallant gentlemen that it would be possible to find. I will not take offence, however.'

'I know,' Joss said ruefully. 'It is one of the few aspects of your character that makes you still likeable, Ju. Now run along, for we have business to discuss.'

Juliana opened her eyes wide. 'Oh, business! I see!

What possible business could you two have to talk about in a gaming hell?'

'Political business,' Joss said.

'Of course. This being so much more appropriate a place than White's—'

'Davencourt is here,' Adam said, looking up. He got to his feet. 'Excuse us, Juliana.'

Juliana stood up, too. Martin Davencourt was coming towards their corner seat, cutting a path through the crowds thronging the gaming hell with an easy grace. Suddenly the Cyprians were whispering together like a group of excited schoolgirls as they watched Martin's approach. Juliana could see why. Amongst the effeminate and perfumed crowd he looked tough, uncompromising and devastatingly handsome. She felt a sudden, inexplicable pang of jealousy.

Martin saw her standing there and gave her a quizzical look from his very blue eyes. It made Juliana feel *de trop* in a way that Adam and Joss's impatience had not. She even felt herself blush slightly and hated herself for it. There was no reason why he should make her feel this slightly edgy awareness and yet he did...

'Good evening, Mr Davencourt,' she said. She cast a meaningful look at the hovering Cyprians. 'I will leave you gentlemen to your...business.'

An hour and a half later, having lost a moderate sum of money to Sebastian Fleet at the card tables and drunk several glasses of excellent wine, Juliana was bored with gambling and wandered away from the piquet table. Adam and Joss were just leaving and she stood behind a pillar as she watched them shrug themselves into their coats, shake Martin Davencourt by the hand and turn towards the door. The Cyprians passed close by, but after a succinct word from Adam they veered away, tossing their heads in angry disdain. Juliana felt a flicker of amusement. So it seemed the gentlemen had not been lying after all. Marital fidelity was threatening to become fashionable.

'It is slow tonight, is it not?' Susanna Kellaway said in Juliana's ear. 'What can I do when such eligible gentlemen as your brother and Ashwick prove faithful to their wives? It is most annoying.' She gave Juliana a comprehensive look. 'I heard about your escapade at Emma Wren's dinner. Why do you not spice things up a little for us tonight, my dear?'

Juliana was about to decline and call for her carriage when she saw Martin Davencourt watching her, his dark blue gaze direct and disapproving. She frowned. What with Joss and Adam and now Martin Davencourt regarding her with such censure, it was like having an entire squadron of tiresome older brothers. She was determined to do something to shock him. Since he was so intent on criticising her, the least she could do was to give him just cause. She flashed Susanna a smile, grabbed a glass of wine from a startled footman and downed it in one gulp.

'Why not? Get the string quartet to strike up a jig, Susanna.'

Holding out her hand to the surprised gentlemen on the nearest card table, Juliana scrambled up on to the tabletop and sent the playing cards flying. There was a murmur of surprise followed by a ripple of anticipation. The orchestra struck up.

Juliana took her skirts in one hand, displaying a swathe of petticoats and some very trim ankles. Various gentlemen leant forward eagerly to peer up her skirts.

The music was fast and furious. Juliana swung her hips provocatively, spinning around, her hair falling from its pins about her shoulders. The crowd, getting into the spirit of the occasion, started clapping in time to the music. One of the Cyprians scrambled up on to the next table and joined in, to many cheers and lewd calls. Juliana lost her footing and almost tumbled off the table, but was pushed back up by enthusiastic hands. She danced so hard that one of her breasts fell out of the bodice of her gown and caused the largest cheer of the evening.

At the end she was pink and ruffled, out of breath and eager to accept the glass of wine someone pressed into her hands. Over its rim she caught sight of Martin Davencourt, his expression set and grim. In his hands was Juliana's cloak. Before she could divine his intention, he had taken the glass from her hand, slapped it down on the table, wrapped the cloak around her, and pulled her hard against him with an arm about her waist. His voice was clipped.

'Come along, Lady Juliana. I am taking you home now.'

Juliana gave him a melting look and snuggled up to him. She thought he deserved a bit of embarrassment. This was the man who had thought she would ruin his cousin's wedding. This was the man who believed she had lovers all over London, so she might as well to act as though she did…

'There is no need to be so hasty, Martin darling. I am all yours,' she said sweetly, smiling up at him. 'Take me away!'

'Lucky you, Davencourt,' someone said jocularly.

Martin looked murderous. He practically carried her out of the door, with Juliana clinging artistically to his arm like trailing ivy. She was very conscious of the smiles and comments of the crowd.

'Do slow down, Martin, darling,' she said loudly. 'You are in a great hurry to get me alone!'

'Be quiet!' Martin hissed in an undertone.

Once they were out in the foyer, away from their audience, Juliana let go of him and straightened her rumpled clothes. There was no audience here so she felt no need to pretend.

'Mr Davencourt, your tendency toward abduction will get you into trouble one of these days. I should like to flatter myself that you were anxious for my company, but I know that cannot be the case.'

Martin shot her a furious look. 'I am merely assisting you as a favour to your brother, Lady Juliana. I cannot believe that he would wish you to disport yourself in such a place.'

'Disport myself? How medieval you sound, Mr Davenport! Positively antediluvian!' Juliana laughed. 'And you are fair and far out in your reading of Joss. I assure you that he would have left me to drink myself under the table.'

She saw Martin's mouth turn down disapprovingly at the corners. 'I do not wonder at it.'

'So in future you may leave me to my own devices. Thank you for your help, but there is no need for your knight errantry.'

They had reached the steps at the front of the club. The cold night air hit Juliana like a bucket of water. She had not realised that she had drunk quite so much and now she clutched instinctively at Martin's arm to steady herself. She heard him sigh with exasperation.

'Oh, I do believe that I have had a tiny bit too much to drink.'

'You are foxed,' Martin said. 'Do you wish me to leave you to your own devices now?'

Juliana laughed. 'You may take me home with my blessing, Mr Davencourt, just as long as you realise the damage it is doing to your stalwart reputation.'

Martin made a sound like a snort and bundled her up into her carriage. 'Portman Square, please,' he said.

Martin deposited her ungently on the seat of the coach and climbed in after her. Juliana found that she rather liked being so close to him. There was something about Martin's physical presence that stirred a tingling awareness in her. There was also something about the amount of drink she had taken that made her uninhibited. The combination was too powerful to resist. She wrapped her arms about Martin's neck, refusing to let go even when he tried to disengage himself.

'Unhand me, please, Lady Juliana,' he said coldly, prying her arms away from his and pushing her into a corner.

Juliana was not to be outmanoeuvred. She felt a sudden and surprising pang of alcohol-induced desire, scooted across the seat and climbed into his lap. Martin tried to push her away again.

'Get off!' He sounded as though he was speaking to a recalcitrant dog. 'Leave me alone, please.'

Juliana wriggled on his knee. She felt him tense beneath her. He smelled deliciously of cinnamon cologne and fresh air on the skin. She felt another flash of desire. It seemed ridiculous to be attracted to Martin Davencourt; stuffy, uptight Martin whose idea of enjoying himself was to read the Treasury reports. Nevertheless, there was something very appealing about such stern masculinity. She reminded himself that she found him dull. Immediately her brain flashed back the message that Martin Davencourt was not in the least bit dull; rather he was dangerously, distractingly attractive. When he tipped her gently back on to the seat, Juliana sighed plaintively.

'Don't you want me?'

Her hand crept across his thigh and his own hand closed like an iron vice about her wrist before her fingers could reach their destination.

'Ouch!' Juliana winced as the pain helped to clear her head. 'I must congratulate you on the rigidity of…your moral principles, Mr Davencourt.'

'Please do not touch me!' Martin said sharply, releasing her. 'I have no wish to be the object of your drunken amorous attentions, Lady Juliana.'

'You do yourself an injustice, Mr Davencourt,' Juliana said, straightening up and moving away from him. 'I do not believe a lady would need to be *completely* inebriated to find you attractive.'

Martin turned his shoulder, ignoring her.

Juliana sighed, abandoning her attempts at flirtation. 'I know that you do not like me. You made that plain enough when we met before.'

Martin sighed, too. 'You are drunk, Lady Juliana. You will regret this conversation tomorrow.'

'That is most unlikely. I never regret what I cannot change. It is a waste of time.'

There was another silence.

'Are you not going to talk to me at all?' Juliana asked. Her fingers walked across the velvet squabs of the seat and touched the back of his hand. He felt warm and vital, and she wanted to touch him. She risked slipping her hand into his, and after a moment he sighed with resignation and leaned his head back against the seat, his body relaxing. Juliana drew a little closer, sliding along the seat next to him.

'So you do not mean to speak to me and you do not mean to kiss me…'

Martin turned his head slightly towards her. 'I certainly do not.'

'As I said, you are a very principled man.'

'Hmm.' Martin did not sound flattered.

'Why are you going to all the trouble to take me home if you do not like me?'

Martin looked at her. The light from the carriage lantern skipped across his face, emphasising the slant of his cheek and the hard line of his jaw. Juliana felt an insane urge to put up a hand and touch him, and almost had to sit on her hands to prevent herself doing so.

'I am not sure why I am going to the trouble.' Martin smiled ruefully, a shadowed smile. 'It is not that I do *not* like you, Lady Juliana. I do. God knows why, but somehow I cannot seem to help myself. It is most perplexing.'

Juliana smiled sweetly. 'That is all right. I am such a nice person really...'

Martin laughed. 'That is putting it too strongly, Lady Juliana. Besides, you do not like *me*. You have told me so often enough.'

'Events prove to the contrary, do they not?' Juliana tilted her head to look at him. 'I do not seem able to resist you, Mr Davencourt.'

'Then try harder. You are only interested because I turn you down. I am a novelty to you.'

Juliana put her head on one side. 'That could be the explanation, I suppose, but... No, I do not think that it is. I do believe that there is some strange affinity between us. Perhaps it is that we are both such nice people.'

Martin laughed. 'You said that before. What on earth makes you think that you are a nice person?'

'Under the surface I am. Truly.'

'Then why behave so badly?'

Juliana was aware that she was more than a little cast

away. However this seemed important. She struggled to frame her answer.

'I do not really behave like this. I only pretend.'

'You are turning in a fairly convincing performance,' Martin said drily, 'for someone who is merely pretending.'

Juliana tried again. 'It is only a game. For fun.'

'Fun. I see.' There was a sardonic note in Martin's voice. 'And is it?'

'Is it what?'

'Is it entertaining?'

Juliana shrugged a little petulantly. 'I will concede that it is not much fun at the moment. Talking to you is like trying to complete a crossword when one has had too much brandy.'

'Difficult for you.' Martin's tone was still dry. 'Answer something else for me, then.' He leaned a little closer. 'Is it a game to you to pursue me?'

Juliana thought hard about that one.

'No…yes, I suppose so. It was only a whim. I knew you would not succumb.'

'Would you have been surprised if I had?'

'Vastly. And more than a little taken aback.'

Martin laughed. 'You are honest, I will say that for you, Lady Juliana.'

Juliana shrugged. She cast him a little sideways look. 'I told you before that I do not lie. Anyway, why should it matter if I acted on a whim? I knew that you would not play my games and I was right.'

Martin's blue eyes held hers and there was a disturbing quality in his regard that made Juliana shiver, though not with cold. She leaned towards him a little.

'Mr Davencourt…'

'Lady Juliana?' Martin's voice was slightly husky. His gaze was intent on her. Juliana drew back a little.

'Mr Davencourt, if you do not intend to kiss me, pray stop looking at me like that. I find it most disturbing.'

Martin sat back with a muttered oath. 'I am not looking at you in any particular manner, Lady Juliana.'

'Yes, you are,' Juliana said. She smiled. 'Come, come, Mr Davencourt. I thought you a truthful man. I have been honest with you and now it is your turn. Admit that you find me attractive.'

There was a loaded silence.

'Perhaps we should start with something simpler,' Juliana said, after a pause. 'I believe you once thought me quite pretty.'

'I did.' Martin's tone was unrevealing. 'I was fifteen years old at the time.'

'Ah. And now?'

Again there was a pause, and then Martin spoke reluctantly. 'Now I think you are quite beautiful, Lady Juliana.'

'You are too honest to be a politician, Mr Davencourt. But thank you for the compliment.' Juliana put her head on one side. 'Shall I question you further? You may pretend that you are in the House of Commons if it makes matters easier for you. That will give you a little practice.'

'Thank you,' Martin said, 'but I do not think that that would help. I fear I must decline to answer any further questions.'

Juliana laughed. 'So you do have the makings of a politician after all! Just as I was about to ask you if you were sure you did not want to kiss me, too. You are fortunate, Mr Davencourt, for I do believe that we have reached Portman Square. A lucky escape for you this time.'

Segsbury, Juliana's butler came to open the door, but Martin helped her down from the carriage himself and, to her surprise, carried her up to the front door. Juliana lay quite still in his arms, her cheek pressed against his shoulder, his breath stirring her hair. In the entrance hall he placed her gently on her feet, whilst Segsbury discreetly melted away.

'Sleep it off,' Martin said pleasantly. 'I think you need to.'

His arm was about her waist and Juliana found it incredibly difficult not to rest her head against his broad shoulder. She put one hand on his chest.

'Mr Davencourt—'

'Yes?' Martin bent closer, the slight stubble of his chin brushing her cheek for a moment. Juliana felt quite weak at the knees.

'Thank you for bringing me home, Mr Davencourt. You are such a gentleman. But then, I knew that.'

Martin smiled, a smile that made Juliana feel even dizzier. He put his lips to her ear.

'Not such a gentleman. Your questions put all sorts of ideas into my head, I fear.'

Juliana turned her wide green gaze on his face. Martin was smiling slightly.

'The answer to your question was yes. Yes, I did want to kiss you. But as a gentleman I had to resist taking advantage…'

Juliana smiled very sweetly. 'Oh, confess it, Mr Davencourt! You are making excuses. You resisted because you were afraid that kissing me would be far too dangerous a pastime.' She laughed. 'Never mind. You are excused.'

'A dangerous pastime?' Juliana saw the unholy amusement light Martin's eyes. 'I do believe that I could survive it…'

He still had one arm around her and now he pulled her

towards him, bringing his mouth down on hers with a shocking mixture of power and gentleness. Juliana gave a gasp of astonishment that was smothered by his lips. Up until the very last minute she had not really believed that he would do it. That had been her first mistake. Her second had been to think that kissing Martin Davencourt would be unexciting…

Martin angled his head so that he could kiss her more deeply. His arms were strong about her and it felt so right to be there. The touch of his lips on hers was sweet, fierce and frighteningly seductive. Juliana struggled to regain some semblance of her customary detachment and found herself hopelessly undermined by a desire that held her captive and would not let her go. She trembled helplessly in his arms. What had Martin said to her only a few days before?

If you proposition a gentleman, be sure that you are prepared to deliver on your promise.

Well, she had played the game and he had called in the promise and now…now she had to pay. And Juliana, who had not kissed any gentleman in the whole of the previous three years, found that it was not difficult after all. With a tiny sigh she kissed him back, sliding her arms about his neck, instinctively pressing her body against the whole, hard length of his. For a long, breathless moment they stood locked together until the loud tap of Segsbury's footsteps on the marbled floor heralded his return and Martin let her go. The expression in his eyes was dark and heated and made Juliana catch her breath.

'Dangerous,' Martin said again. He gave her a faint smile that caused the heat inside her to soar again. 'You may be correct after all, Lady Juliana.' He took her hand and pressed a kiss on the back. 'Goodnight.'

Juliana watched Martin leave and stood still in the hall

whilst Segsbury locked the door behind him. She could see her reflection in the long, gilded pier glass on the wall; hair tousled, green eyes still hazy with passion, lips swollen from Martin's kisses. Damnation! She had never intended to go so far. It was too intimate. She felt as though she had given too much of herself away. She did not want anyone so close. That dangerous sense of affinity had betrayed her when her native caution had told her to keep him at arm's length.

Juliana suddenly felt tired and light-headed from the drink, but beneath her tiredness was another sensation, and she had a sinking feeling about it, a strange suspicion that it would be difficult to shift. God forbid that she was forming an attachment to Martin Davencourt. How could such incorruptible morality *ever* appeal to her? It was inconceivable. It was absurd. It was out of the question.

One thing was certain though. There was nothing gentlemanly about the way that Martin kissed and she would never think of him as dull ever again.

Segsbury was looking at her with concern. 'Are you quite well, madam? May I fetch you anything?'

'Yes, thank you, Segsbury,' Juliana said slowly. 'I shall have a glass of port in my bedchamber. Port is a cure for all things, I find. Especially if one drinks a lot of it and nips the problem in the bud early enough.'

Chapter Four

Martin watched Mrs Lane settle Kitty and Clara on two rout chairs prominently arranged beside the dance floor. A slight frown touched his brow. Both of the girls looked glum and he was at a loss to understand why, when they were attending one of the most prestigious fancy dress balls of the season. Kitty, in pale pink satin, was supposed to be Sleeping Beauty but looked more Sleeping Misery. Clara, wearing an ivory gauze gown, looked like a voluptuous fairy. Martin, in a conservative back domino and mask himself, wondered why on earth his sisters looked as though they were having their teeth pulled when by rights they should be the happiest young ladies in the room.

He turned away and made his way through the throng to the refreshment room. He had thought it politic to attend Lady Selwood's ball himself in order to quell any gossip about Kitty and Clara's exploits. His presence would ensure that his sisters behaved themselves and that any further scandal would be squashed before it had started. All the same, it promised to be a dull evening. The majority of the guests were débutantes and their suitors, for Lady Selwood had two daughters to settle and was determined to get at least one of them off her hands that season. Martin knew débutante balls to be slow affairs; he had no desire to dance with any simpering innocents and his acquaintance in London was small after so many years abroad.

When he had first returned, Araminta had offered to host a few dinners for him but Martin had been lukewarm in accepting the suggestion. He preferred small dinners with real friends at which he might relax and discuss all manner of interesting topics. He disliked the empty small talk of the drawing room, though he was perfectly proficient in it. Years of diplomatic missions had ensured that he could talk to anybody about anything. Except his siblings. Martin frowned as he recalled the difficulties of communication between himself and his half-brothers and half-sisters. His role in the Congress of Vienna had been a triumph of simplicity in comparison.

He took a glass of champagne from a footman and scanned the room. Adam Ashwick, his wife Annis, and Joss and Amy Tallant were standing a little distance away, chatting amongst themselves. Adam raised a hand in greeting, and Martin acknowledged him with a grin. He was about to go across and join their group, when he caught sight of Lady Juliana Myfleet.

At least, he assumed that it was she. The lady who flitted across his line of vision was a wraith in silver gauze. She had glorious copper hair caught up in a headdress adorned with the moon and stars. Her eyes were shadowed behind a silver mask and a gossamer cloak swirled about her shoulders. She looked fey and insubstantial, a lovely Cinderella.

Martin's instinct told him that it was Juliana, and that in itself was cause for concern. How he had come to recognise her instinctively after only a handful of meetings was something that he could not explain. It had to be something to do with the fact that he had kissed her. A dangerous pastime, she had called it, and he had thought that amusing at the time. He had had no idea just how dangerous it would turn out to be. Kissing, Martin thought ruefully, was not a static activity, and now that he had kissed Juliana once he seemed possessed of a strong compulsion to repeat the experience.

He almost groaned aloud. Damnation. This was not the rational response of a sensible man, especially not a man who was looking for a sober, respectable woman to be his wife. He would do better to forget about the entire kissing episode in the hallway and concentrate on his search for a spouse.

Despite himself, Martin could not help watching as Juliana darted past without so much as a sideways glance for him. She looked innocent and pretty, and far too young to be the tawdry widow of all the gossip, the woman with the damaged reputation who was alleged to be the veteran of affair after affair. Martin frowned. There was something mysterious about Juliana Myfleet, something that did not quite fit the image. There had been too much diffidence in the way that she had kissed him that night. She had been reserved, almost shy. There was nothing of the courtesan in her kiss.

Martin pondered the mystery. There was a quality of innocence about Juliana that was utterly at odds with her behaviour and reputation. He was reminded of her shocking behaviour at Emma Wren's dinner, when the look in her eyes had completely contradicted the shamelessness of her behaviour. There was something vulnerable about Juliana that called forth his most protective instincts. He grimaced. If he were honest, that was not the *only* emotion that she aroused in him, and he was discovering that protectiveness mixed with strong desire was a heady brew. He had to try to resist her. It was the only way, but he had a strong feeling that he was about to do precisely the opposite.

Martin knew that he could not afford to become entangled in Juliana's games. Not now. Not ever. She was complicated and difficult, and the last thing that he needed at the moment was more complexity in his life. Not when Kitty and Clara were acting as though they were enduring a public execution rather than a fancy dress ball, Brandon was refusing to explain why he had left Cambridge so precipitately, and kept disappearing at odd hours of the day and night, and Daisy was still having nightmares.

Juliana Myfleet had disappeared and Martin turned to find his sister at his elbow. A couple of days before, he had let slip to Araminta that he was looking for a bride, and since then his sister had thrown herself into the project with a zeal Martin found slightly worrying. Araminta had introduced him to so many respectable ladies in the space of three days that Martin was in real danger of confusing their names. He noted with a sinking heart that tonight's candidate was being put forward now. He felt absolutely no enthusiasm at making her acquaintance.

There was a diminutive blonde at Araminta's side, whom his sister was pushing slightly forward. Martin frowned slightly, then caught Araminta's significant stare and rearranged his features into a pleasant smile.

'Martin, may I introduce Mrs Serena Alcott?' Araminta said, in a voice heavy with meaning. 'Serena, this is my brother, Martin Davencourt.'

Martin bowed. Mrs Alcott returned his greeting with a shy one of her own, casting her eyes bashfully down. A faint blush tinged her cheek. She was extremely pretty and dainty as a china figurine. Martin observed this and noted a second later that, curiously, he felt nothing at all. No interest, no anticipation, certainly no nervousness at meeting a potential bride. But perhaps that was to be expected—even welcomed—where choosing a wife was concerned. One should make the decision in cold blood. The selection of his spouse was an entirely rational process, thank God. It was certainly not like the start of a love affair, where one's emotions were engaged at the expense of one's intellect. For a second, the image of Juliana Myfleet imposed itself between Martin and Serena Alcott—Juliana as she had looked when he had left her the other night, with her face pink and flushed and her lips stung by his kisses. He cleared his throat.

'Erm…how do you do, Mrs Alcott?'

Serena Alcott fluttered her eyelashes at him. There was the tiniest smile at the corner of her mouth that suggested that she liked what she saw. In the most modest way imaginable of course. One could not imagine Mrs Alcott ever moved by strong emotion, Martin thought. He remembered the histrionics in his household, and knew that he should be relieved.

Araminta cleared her throat meaningfully and Martin jumped to see her basilisk eye fixed on him again.

'Oh! Yes… Mrs Alcott, would you do me the honour of dancing with me?'

Serena Alcott consulted her dance card. It was impressively full.

'I could squeeze you in for a cotillion later in the evening, Mr Davencourt,' she said, with a pretty smile. 'That would be delightful.'

Martin bowed again, a little stiffly this time. He felt ever so slightly patronised, but was unsure why. He could hardly have expected her to keep her dance card free for him when she had not even met him until this moment.

Araminta and her protégée moved away, and Martin turned to scan the ballroom once more. He could see Kitty, looking lumpen and miserable, sitting alone beside Mrs Lane. Clara was dancing, but with the air of a young lady who finds it almost too much trouble. She was at least five bars behind everyone else, which played havoc with the rest of the couples in the set. Her partner, the young Earl of Ercol, was looking slightly put out at her lack of enthusiasm. Martin sighed. Ercol was an extremely eligible *parti*, but it was obvious that he would not be making Clara an offer when she looked as though she was about to yawn in his face. He wondered where Lady Juliana Myfleet had gone, then he forced himself *not* to wonder about her. Damn the woman for disturbing his peace of mind.

'Well,' Araminta said expectantly, materialising at his side again, 'what do you think of her?'

Martin blinked at her. For a moment he thought that she was referring to Juliana, then he realised that she was talking about Serena Alcott.

'Who? Oh, Mrs Alcott! Yes…I do believe that she would fulfil all my criteria. She seems a calm and sensible woman.'

Araminta looked dissatisfied. 'Gracious, how very dry and pompous you sound, Martin! You might show a little more enthusiasm. Did you not think her pretty?'

'Vastly.'

'Well, you do not sound very pleased about it. I shall not put myself out on your behalf again.'

'I am sure you shall not need to,' Martin said. 'Mrs Alcott seems perfect in every way.'

Far from appearing pleased by this accolade, Araminta was frowning at him. 'I cannot see how you can have made such a judgement in two minutes! Why, she might be quite unacceptable, for all you know. This is not like buying a new horse, Martin!'

'Of course not.' A twinkle came into Martin's eyes. 'I should spend a great deal of time checking over a new purchase for my stables!'

Araminta tutted. 'If you must take an equine approach, then Serena's pedigree is immaculate. She is the niece of the Marquis of Tallant, you know, and first cousin to Joss Tallant and Lady Juliana.'

Martin felt an unpleasant jolt. The thought of paying court to Juliana's cousin was distasteful. It felt like a betrayal. 'One could scarce have a worse recommendation,' he said.

'Stuff!' Araminta was bracing. 'Joss Tallant is the most charming and handsome man, and very sound besides. Good God, he is a friend of yours!'

'Yes, and I doubt that even he would deny that the Tallants are wild to a fault!'

'Oh, Lady Juliana is, perhaps, and Joss was certainly a rake in his younger days, but I doubt those faults are inherited. Serena Alcott's papa was very proper and her mother was sister to the current Marquis and was a very staid and respectable figure. As for Serena herself, she had a placid childhood, made a creditable marriage and has lived a life of quiet retirement in her widowhood.'

Martin grimaced. He was not sure why the thought of Serena Alcott's perfect history should irritate him, but it did. Profoundly.

'You make her sound quite tragically boring, Minta.'

Araminta frowned. 'Gracious, but you are contrary tonight, Martin! What is it that you want—calm good sense or a dash of wilfulness? For you may be sure that you will not find both in the one package!'

She stalked off in a huff and Martin sighed, reflecting

that he was not at all sure what he *did* want. Certainly
Serena Alcott had all the attributes of a conformable wife.
It was his own fault if he suddenly found that insuffi-
cient...

Lady Juliana Myfleet was dancing now. Martin caught
sight of her in the cotillion, partnered by a man in a garish
harlequin suit. He leaned against a pillar and studied them.
Juliana Myfleet and that blackguard Jasper Colling. He
was surprised that Lady Selwood had stooped so low as
to invite Colling to such an affair. Still, the man had both
title and money and Martin knew how far some matchmaking mamas would go to catch a husband for their
daughters.

If it came to that, he was attracting some débutante
attention himself. Martin looked round to see that a small
knot of young ladies had formed up close by, like a flotilla
of ships blockading him into a corner. They were peeking
at him from behind their fans and giggling amongst themselves. He just managed to prevent a grimace of distaste
from showing on his face. With a general bow in their
direction, Martin slid adroitly past the group and went in
search of a drink.

'How famous to see you again, Lady Juliana!' Brandon
Davencourt, smiling broadly, approached Juliana as she
came out of the card room. 'May I procure you a glass
of wine, ma'am? Or would you care to dance?'

Juliana smiled. 'I should be delighted, Mr Davencourt.'

She seldom danced, but now, seeing that Martin Davencourt was watching them darkly from across the ballroom, she smiled charmingly at Brandon and took his
arm, positively daring Martin to express his disapproval.
She had not seen him since the night he had escorted her
home from Crowns a week before, and Juliana thought

drily that that showed more clearly than anything his attitude towards her. The kiss in the hallway, sweet as it had been at the time, was an aberration and one which both of them were intent on forgetting. It was just a pity that she seemed to be spending so much time reminding herself to forget it.

'Capital of you to agree, Lady Juliana,' Brandon said, steering her on to the dance floor. 'I thought you would refuse me.' He flashed her a grin that was a more boyish version of his brother's. 'They said you wouldn't dance—that you never do.'

'They?'

'All the other fellows. They will be sick with envy.'

Juliana laughed. Such uncomplicated flattery was difficult to resist and balm to her feelings. 'Well, Mr Davencourt…I like to be unpredictable.'

'Dashed good luck for me.' Brandon gave her his heartbreaking smile. 'Just plain Brandon will do, Lady Juliana.' He swept her into the waltz. 'As you are so well acquainted with the family…'

Juliana grimaced. 'Scarcely that. I do believe that your brother disapproves of me, Brandon.'

'Lord, Martin disapproves of everything these days.' A frown creased Brandon's brow. 'He gave me the most fearful dressing down today, you know. All about how my studies should come first and that I was throwing away my education by leaving Cambridge in my final year. I do believe that he is very disappointed with me.'

Juliana looked up at him. There was a frown still lingering in his eyes, but when he saw her scrutiny Brandon seemed to shake himself and gave her his quick smile.

'I beg your pardon, ma'am. This is melancholy talk for a ball.'

'It does not matter,' Juliana said. Talking to attractive

young men was, after all, no hardship. She narrowed her eyes slightly. 'I had not realised that you had completed your studies, Brandon.'

Brandon nodded. 'Prematurely, I am afraid, ma'am. I am not cut out to be a scholar.' He pulled a face. 'I believe that is one of the reasons that Martin is disappointed in me. He was quite prodigiously academic in his own time.'

Juliana smiled to hear Martin Davencourt discussed thus. It made him sound like a greybeard, which he most certainly was not. She looked across at him. He was leaning against a pillar and had his arms crossed in slightly forbidding fashion. Juliana flashed him a dazzling smile then quickly turned away.

'I remember your brother being fearfully studious when I first met him,' she said. 'He must have been about fifteen, I suppose, and he was forever devising new mathematical equations or reading poetry or philosophy. I am afraid his learned activities quite sent me to sleep!'

Brandon twirled her around boisterously. 'Philosophy, eh? I shall remember that if I suffer an attack of insomnia! I expect the library is stuffed full of Martin's books.'

'I dare say Mr Davencourt has little time for the philosophers now that he has the responsibility for seven siblings,' Juliana said drily. 'Or six, perhaps, since you should be able to look after yourself, Brandon. He must count himself fortunate if he even has the time to read a newspaper, let alone a learned book.'

The frown returned to Brandon's brow. 'I suppose we are rather a trial to him,' he said. His frown deepened. 'I have scarce helped the situation with my precipitate return, but—' He broke off.

'Financial difficulties, was it?' Juliana asked sympathetically. She knew only too well that there were usually two basic reasons for young men to abandon their studies.

Brandon shot her a quick look and a rueful smile. 'No, not money problems. The other sort.'

'Ah. A romantic entanglement.' Juliana smiled. She could see how *that* had happened. Most right-thinking women would be susceptible to Brandon's charm. One need only look around the room to see the truth of that. The débutantes were all glaring at her as though she had stolen the most eligible gentleman at the ball from under their noses.

'Yes. I have got myself into a fearful mess,' Brandon said frankly. He sounded so despondent that Juliana smiled.

'Oh, dear. Does your brother know about this?'

Brandon looked shifty. 'Not yet. The right moment to tell him has not presented itself.'

'The right moment never will,' Juliana said, with a sigh. 'Take my word for it, Brandon. I know a little about difficult confessions. Best to get it over with, particularly if your problem is of an embarrassing or potentially expensive nature.'

'It is not like that!' Brandon said, flushing. 'The truth is, Lady Juliana, that there is a young lady whom I... I esteem her greatly, but her parents do not approve of the match and nor, I am persuaded, would Martin...'

They executed another turn, enabling Juliana to get another quick look at Martin Davencourt. He was still watching them, his blue gaze steady and thoughtful. It sent a tickle of feeling down Juliana's spine.

'I see,' she said. 'Yet your affections are sincere, Brandon?'

Brandon blushed boyishly. 'Well, yes, they are. I suppose,' he added with spirit, 'that you will say I am too young to think of marriage?'

'No,' Juliana said. 'I was younger than you when I first

married and my husband was only a few years older. We were both very happy and I truly believe that if Myfleet was still alive, I would be the luckiest woman on earth.' She gave him a bright smile. 'What is important is for you to be certain that you have made the right choice.'

The music was swirling to a finale. They executed a final flourish and Brandon released her, grinning exuberantly.

'I say, that was splendid!' He sobered. 'Thank you, Lady Juliana. And thank you for the advice. I have enjoyed talking to you. It was not at all like talking to a female.' Juliana thought that he sounded vaguely surprised. 'In fact, it was rather like talking to another chap, only different of course, since we do not speak about our feelings.'

Juliana burst out laughing. 'Of course not! But to be likened to a man is quite a new experience for me, Brandon. Should I be flattered?'

Brandon flushed. 'I beg your pardon. I intended it to be a compliment, but perhaps it did not turn out quite right.'

'I am happy to accept it as such,' Juliana said, smiling. She took his arm for the customary turn about the room, but almost immediately they walked straight into the Martin Davencourt. He had evidently been waiting to intercept them. And he did not look pleased.

Juliana felt herself blush. All over. It was as though she was being slowly toasted over an open fire. Such acute physical awareness had never affected her before, not even in the long-ago days when she had been a débutante. She felt as though all her town bronze had worn off in one go.

Martin was surveying his half-brother's cheerful demeanour with a slightly sardonic smile, a smile that deepened as his thoughtful gaze rested on Juliana's face. Juliana felt hot and flustered, but she drew on all her self-control and gave him back a very straight look. She had been taught decorum as a girl and had never rated it highly before, but now she thought that the lessons might at least have been a little useful if they enabled her to withstand her curious attraction to this arrogant man.

'Brandon, I am persuaded that Lady Juliana would like a glass of wine after her recent exertions,' Martin said. 'Would you be so good as to fetch one from the refreshment room? And a glass for me as well, if you please.'

Brandon gave Juliana an apologetic look. She knew that he was not going to argue. One did not argue with the Martin Davencourt, particularly if one had the misfortune to be his younger brother.

'Excuse me, ma'am,' Brandon said. 'I shall be back shortly.'

'Do not hurry,' Martin said. He offered Juliana his arm. 'Lady Juliana and I have plenty to speak about.'

Juliana reluctantly rested her hand on Martin's arm. Brandon was charming and uncomplicated, easy to manage. Martin was quite a different matter. She felt very on edge. What had started as a game for her own amusement was threatening to turn into something quite different and she had a lowering feeling that she was not entirely equal to the situation.

'I am flattered that you should think we have much to discuss, sir,' she said lightly. 'I should have thought that we have nothing to say to each other at all.'

Martin smiled. 'Why do you say that?'

'Well, we have managed to keep apart for this week past, have we not?' Juliana said. 'That scarcely argues a burning need to seek out each other's company.'

Martin nodded slowly. 'I thought it best to stay away, Lady Juliana.'

Their eyes met and the tension seemed to stretch between them like a string of beads about to snap.

'How very measured of you.' Juliana looked away. 'I would have expected nothing less. I hope that you did not shock yourself when we last met, Mr Davencourt. I should hate to be responsible for that.'

The smile was still in Martin's eyes. It reminded Juliana forcibly of their encounter in the candlelit hall.

'I assure you that I did not shock myself,' he said gently, 'though I may have surprised you.'

'Oh, you did.' Juliana had no intention of allowing him to see quite how much he had disturbed her. 'You have hidden depths, Mr Davencourt. And there was I, thinking that it was quite safe to play in the shallows!'

'But then I am good at confounding your expectations.' There was a wry twist to Martin's lips. 'It would not do to become too sure of me.'

Their eyes met again and this time Juliana found it even more difficult to drag her gaze away. She was trembling slightly. And she was not in the least bit sure of him. She felt rather as though she had put a match to a powder keg and was waiting for the explosion. His gaze moved over her with unsettling thoroughness, just as it had done in Emma Wren's hall. Hair, eyes, mouth… It lingered on the curve of her lips and a light came into his eyes, dark and dangerous. Juliana took a shaky breath.

'Mr Davencourt, we are in a crowded ballroom—'

'Then step outside.'

His sheer effrontery took her breath away. She was supposed to be the one with the experience here, the one with the bad reputation. It seemed absurd. She was really struggling.

Someone bumped against Juliana's arm and apologised. She had no idea who it was, but it broke the spell. She drew away a little.

'Perhaps you are right, Mr Davencourt,' she said, as lightly as she was able. 'You are full of surprises, are you not? For example, I did not expect to see you here tonight. Do you intend to keep an eye on your siblings?'

Martin accepted the turn of the conversation with an expressive lift of his brows. It suggested that he was prepared to allow her to dictate the pace—for now. Juliana did not feel reassured.

He gave her a rueful smile. 'You make it sound like a children's ball, Lady Juliana.'

'Why and so it is—for you.' Juliana cast him a mocking sideways look. She felt safer now, away from the edge of that dark attraction. 'The days of your youth are over now, sir. How could it be otherwise with a brood of children to oversee?'

Martin pulled a face. 'Must you be so crushing, Lady Juliana? I am scarce in my dotage.'

'No, but you might as well be, for you will have no time to yourself now. I have heard that the rigours of child rearing are quite exhausting. One imagines that you will not have any time for your future parliamentary work, riveting as it will be.'

Martin laughed. 'Then I suppose I must marry and set up as a family man.'

Juliana's heart unaccountably sank even whilst she kept a smile pinned on her face.

'And I note that you are already making great strides in that direction,' she observed. 'My cousin, Mrs Alcott, will make you the most perfect bride.'

Martin looked startled. 'You are precipitate, Lady Juliana. I have only met Mrs Alcott this evening.'

'Why waste time?' Juliana said. 'I am persuaded that she is the ideal woman for you.'

Martin raised his brows. 'Is your cousin at all like you?'

'Not in the least. She is the exact opposite, which is why I am sure that you will have so much in common. Besides…' Juliana smiled sweetly '…you offer a woman a tempting situation, sir. A ready-made family of seven! Serena need not bother to produce any children of her own. What could be better?'

Martin looked taken aback. 'I would still hope for a family of my own,' he said.

'Oh, well, you will need your strength then.' Juliana took a small hip flask from the silver reticule on her arm. 'May I offer you a sip, sir?'

Martin laughed. 'What is it—brandy?'

'No, port. A very good one. I find it a necessity when I am attending a débutante ball.'

'Thank you for the offer, but I prefer a good brandy myself.' Martin smiled. 'One must wonder why you have bothered to come here tonight, Lady Juliana. If you thought it surprising that I should be here I would say it is even odder in you. I should not have thought this to your taste at all.'

'You are correct of course. It is very slow.' Juliana took an ostentatious swig of port. The heat of it hit her stomach and made her feel slightly less shaky. Several matrons in their vicinity were staring, their mouths forming tightly pursed circles of disapproval. 'I did it on a whim,' Juliana said, screwing the top back of the flask and slipping it back in the bag. 'Another of my wayward whims, I am afraid. I once heard Lady Selwood refer to me as that dreadful Myfleet creature and say that I should never be invited to one of her events. So I thought to prove her wrong and come and grace her ball as a punishment.'

Juliana gave Martin a dazzling smile. 'As it was a fancy dress occasion, the poor lady did not recognise me at once and welcomed me most warmly. I especially invited Jasper Colling to escort me, as Lady Selwood thinks him a disgusting lecher.'

'So he is.'

'I know. But do you not see the piquancy? Her ladyship cannot throw us out now, for it would create even more of a scandal. Yet she knows who we are and so do all her guests. I have made her a laughing stock. Why, even now Jasper is dancing with Miss Selwood!'

She saw that Martin was watching her, an indefinable expression in his blue eyes. The sensual awareness had gone, to be replaced by something very different but no less disturbing. He looked sorry for her. Sorry and disappointed. Juliana recognised the expression with a twist of the heart and she felt the anger flower inside her. How dare he pity her? She gave him back a defiant look of her own.

'I see that your idea of amusement and my own do not accord, Mr Davencourt. That being the case, you need not torture yourself by spending any further time in my company. Unless there was something particular you wished to say to me?'

'There was one thing,' Martin said slowly. He was not looking at her; his gaze was resting on Brandon, who had been ambushed in conversation by a particularly pretty débutante.

Juliana narrowed her eyes suspiciously. 'It is something to do with your brother, perhaps?'

Martin's blue gaze came back to focus on her with disconcerting intentness. 'You are correct.' He looked amused. 'Am I then so transparent?'

'As glass, Mr Davencourt.' Juliana gave him a look. 'You would like me to discourage the acquaintance.'

'Of course I would. Brandon is young and susceptible—'

'I did not find him either of those things. He seems extremely mature for a boy of his age.'

'His age,' Martin said, an edge coming into his voice, 'is two and twenty, Lady Juliana. He is a mere stripling, and quite out of his depth with you.'

Juliana laughed. It seemed absurd that Brandon should be confiding in her his love for another lady whilst Martin had cast her in the role of seducer of innocents. 'Young men in their salad days will always be looking to fall in love, Mr Davencourt,' she said. 'You said so yourself, as I recall. But perhaps you have forgotten your youth. Certainly you are acting as though you are thirty going on ninety-five.'

She heard Martin take an exaggeratedly deep breath. 'I should appreciate it if you did not encourage Brandon, Lady Juliana,' he said, with commendable calm. 'That is all I ask.'

'I see,' Juliana said. She flashed him a smile. 'How very predictable you are, sir. You disappoint me. That is exactly what I would have expected you to say.'

Martin made a slight gesture. 'Surely you cannot be surprised?'

'No, of course not.' Juliana was not surprised but she was conscious of a sharp disappointment. 'Hypocrisy never surprises me. So it is one rule for you and another for Brandon? But then I suppose that no one could describe you as young and susceptible, Mr Davencourt, not even your dearest and most deluded relatives.'

'Of course not.' Martin's gaze narrowed on her. 'And

neither are you, Lady Juliana, so we understand each other.'

Juliana turned away. She felt hurt, as though she had expected Martin to have a better opinion of her than this and was disappointed that he did not. At the same time, she was annoyed with herself. After all, she had been the one to give Martin the impression that she pursued men for entertainment. She could hardly blame him for believing her. And she had to cure herself of this inexplicable attraction to him.

'You must excuse me,' she said. 'I see Sir Jasper Colling across the room and he is undoubtedly looking to engage me in the cotillion. Good evening.'

Martin caught her arm. 'A moment. You have not agreed to discourage Brandon.'

Juliana looked disdainful. 'No, nor shall I. Your brother is quite delightful and excellent company. It is a shame that you did not inherit the same good qualities. Furthermore, being of age, Brandon can surely make his own decisions. Excuse me, Mr Davencourt.'

Juliana saw the flash of vivid anger in Martin's eyes before he let go of her arm. She walked away, and the relief she felt was intense. Uppermost in her mind was the thought that she had taken on more than she could handle with Martin Davencourt. As lover or as adversary—and she was not entirely sure which he would be—he was formidable.

Halfway across the room she met Brandon, who was carrying two glasses of wine and breathing heavily, as though he had been hurrying despite what his brother had said. Knowing that Martin was watching, Juliana deliberately paused and put out a hand.

'Thank you for the dance, Brandon.' She bent closer so that their heads were almost touching. She was sure that

Martin would view it as an unacceptable piece of intimacy. She lowered her voice.

'I do urge you to confide the truth in your brother. Whatever you have done, I am sure he will be able to help you.'

Brandon gave her a pale imitation of his dazzling smile. He looked tired. 'I swear I shall try to find the right moment, Lady Juliana and...' he touched her wrist lightly '...thank you so very much...'

Juliana watched as Brandon rejoined Martin and handed over one of the glasses of wine. Martin took the glass with a word of thanks, but his cool blue gaze did not move from Juliana's face and, though his expression was quite unreadable, she knew he was still angry. The thought raised a little shiver along Juliana's skin. She went slowly across to join Sir Jasper Colling, but she knew that Martin was watching her all the way, even though she did not turn around. She could feel his gaze like a physical touch and it disturbed her.

Colling distracted her attention by pulling on her silken sleeve, his moist breath in her ear.

'Juliana, my dear, I have a little proposition for you. You will find it most entertaining...'

With one final backward glance at Martin, Juliana allowed herself to be led away. She smiled beguilingly into Colling's face.

'Entertain me, then, Jasper,' she said.

Chapter Five

It felt very cold in Hyde Park at ten o'clock at night. Standing in the shelter of a group of knotted beech trees as the moon poured down, Juliana was thinking that perhaps this was the most foolish action of all her life. She shuddered to think what her father, or Joss, or even Martin Davencourt might say if it all came out. They would shake their heads over her latest misdeed but somehow that disapproval, which had always spurred her on in the past, seemed all too justifiable now. For the first time in her life she was having second thoughts.

It had all seemed such a marvellous joke in prospect. She and Jasper Colling and Emma Wren had planned it all the previous week, in the card room at Lady Selwood's ball—how she and Colling would waylay Andrew Brookes's carriage in the Park and pretend to hold it up. Juliana had always wanted to play the highwayman and it sounded like fun. But now she had changed her mind, only it was too late to renege. Though her teeth chattered and her toes were frozen within her riding boots, she could not simply give up and go home. That would entail too much of a loss of face in front of her friends.

'This hat is so damnably ugly,' she said, shifting her

weight in the saddle and hoping that Colling could not
detect the quiver of nerves in her voice, 'and the breeches
are disgusting. Could you not have found something more
becoming for me to wear, Jasper? I declare that if we are
caught, the worst they will be able to charge me with is
not highway robbery but crimes against fashion!'

Jasper Colling laughed. 'Juliana, my love, we shall not
be caught so you need have no fear of being exposed as
a frump. Besides, 'tis only a jest. We shall give Brookes
and his bride a welcome they will not forget!'

Juliana shivered. The moon was full and it was a chilly,
white night. She had chosen a long black masquerade
cloak and had tied her auburn hair back and thrust it out
of sight. Colling had provided her with an old tricorne hat
that belonged to his coachman and had also given her a
little silver pistol that she had no idea how to use. Only
a quarter of an hour before it had all seemed such fun.
Now, suddenly, the escapade suddenly held all the allure
of a stay in the Fleet. Which was where she was likely to
end up if they were caught.

Colling touched her arm. She could sense his excitement and it lit an uneasy mix of exhilaration and nervousness inside her. 'There they are!'

There was a coach lurching towards them along the
road, squat and dark in the moonlight. Juliana caught her
breath.

'I do not think—' she began, but Colling was already
urging his horse forward. The skittish bay half-reared and
almost unseated him, and then he was galloping into the
path of the coach. After a second's hesitation, Juliana followed.

It took her about a minute to realise that this was not
the right coach and by then it was too late. Colling had
put a shot across the box, causing the coachman almost

to tumble from his perch. He cowered there, his face bent to the horses' necks, his voice trembling.

'Who are you? What do you want?'

Juliana saw that Colling was almost choking with laughter.

'Your money or your life!'

He threw open the carriage door at the same moment that Juliana caught hold of his arm.

'What are you doing? This isn't Brookes's coach.'

'What the devil is the difference?' Colling said recklessly. ''Tis only in jest.'

There was a little old lady shrinking against the squabs in the corner of the carriage. Her eyes were terrified and there was a pitiful tremor at the corner of her mouth. Her shaking hands had already gone to the diamond necklace at her throat, but she could not unfasten it for trembling. Juliana bit her lip. An unaccustomed emotion swept over her, causing her to pull back and catch Colling's arm again, harder this time.

'No! Leave her be.'

'One hundred guineas or your honour!' Colling said, trying not to laugh.

The old lady, seventy if she was a day, by Juliana's reckoning, looked fit to swoon at the thought of this young blood throwing her down in a ditch.

'Take my purse, but spare me! I am so old and so tired—' Her voice broke on the words.

'For pity's sake!' Juliana felt sick. She broke away from Colling and wheeled her horse about. 'Leave her! This is too dangerous. I am going back—'

There was a crack of a bullet passing close by her ear. Colling swore. He was not laughing now. Without another word he whipped up his horse and galloped off the way that they had come, leaving Juliana in the carriage doorway where the old lady's purse was in danger of being trampled by her horse's hooves.

Juliana looked round. Another coach was coming along the road now and both the coachman and the passenger were firing on them. She swung herself quickly to the ground and scooped up the purse, leaning into the carriage and thrusting it into the old lady's hand.

'Take it. I am sorry! It was only a jest…'

She scrambled up into the saddle and kicked her horse for home. Colling came out of the shelter of the beech trees and drew alongside her, but he could hardly match her hell-for-leather pace and was reduced to bringing up the rear, interspersing pleas for her to slow down with irritable questions about what the devil was the matter with her. Juliana did not answer. A couple of times she dashed the tears fiercely from her cheeks, but she was careful that Colling did not see her do so, and when they reached the lighted city streets she slowed to a decorous trot and thanked him for the adventure.

Colling was still abuzz with excitement. 'They shot at us! Upon my word, what a splendid escape! Did you see who it was, Juliana? Davencourt, of all people! Davencourt fired on us!'

Juliana felt a sharp apprehension mix with her feeling of nausea. 'Martin Davencourt? Are you sure? He did not see you, did he, Jasper?'

'I doubt it,' Colling said cheerfully. 'Can't prove a thing, at any rate. We stole nothing and did no harm…'

But Juliana was thinking about the terror in the old lady's pansy blue eyes. There was more than one sort of harm.

Colling put his hand over hers on the reins. 'The night is still young. Why do we not change our clothes and go to Lady Babbacombe's soirée? Or perhaps…' his voice dropped suggestively '...we could celebrate our career of crime together...just the two of us...'

Juliana pulled her hands out from under his. She felt repulsed. 'I think not, Sir Jasper. The evening has been entertaining, but here it ends.'

'Except that we share our little secret, eh?' Colling leered. 'I will have you yet, Lady Juliana! See if I don't.'

Juliana did not like the sound of that. It smacked of blackmail and she did not like to think of herself in Colling's power. Then there was Emma Wren, who had also been privy to the plan to stop Andrew Brookes's coach. Emma had thought it a great joke, but as soon as she heard what had happened in the Park that night she would put two and two together and realise what had happened... Juliana's heart sank. The whole matter was becoming intolerably complicated.

She parted from Colling in Portman Square and went into the house alone. There were a dozen candles burning in the hall for no particular reason other than that Juliana preferred it so. It made the place seem less empty. However, she could do nothing about the silence. It was the silence that needed to be filled. She could not possibly sit in at home alone.

The door from the servants' quarters opened and Juliana's maid Hattie emerged. Seeing her mistress in breeches, she gave a small shriek.

'Lord lawks, my lady, whatever do you look like? Surely you have not been riding around London dressed in boy's clothes?'

Juliana immediately felt more cheerful. 'I fear so, Hattie. Now, I need your help. I must transform from tomboy to lady in the space of a half-hour. And pray ask Jeffers to have the carriage brought around. I am for Lady Babbacombe's soirée.'

It was only when she had stripped off the breeches and the linen shirt that Juliana discovered that her silver necklace, the one with the half-moon that had been a gift from her husband, was missing. She searched frantically to see if it had snagged on the material of the shirt, but it was in vain. It was not on the floor and it was not amongst the folds of the cloak. She had lost it.

'Have you not heard?' Emma Wren dealt the cards, then sat back in her seat to appraise her hand and to pass on the gossip. 'The Countess of Lyon's carriage was held up in Hyde Park not two hours ago! Highwaymen, Ju! In Hyde Park! I thought that such savagery went out of fashion years ago.'

Juliana kept her hand steady as she discarded one playing card and picked another up. They were playing whist in a group of four, and she was partnered by old Lady Bestable, who was erratic at the best of times. Now, with the knowledge that she might be stopped and robbed on the way home, the old lady was shaking so much that she could barely see what was in her hand. Juliana knew they were bound to lose.

Her own concentration was not wholly on the game either. Alongside the concern that Emma might suspect her was the memory of the Countess of Lyon's face, old, lined, terrified...

Take my purse but spare me! I am so old and so tired—

Juliana repressed a shudder. She had tried to forget the incident and with it the vivid impression of the Countess's terror. She had tried to tell herself that she did not care. She knew she was lying and she felt sick. For the first time, the effects of her own actions had been brought home to her, and she was appalled.

She sensed Emma's gaze on her, bright and malicious, and forced her mouth into a smile.

'Was anyone injured?' she enquired lightly.

'Apparently not.' It was Lady Neasden, who was making up the group, who answered, her eyes snapping with the excitement of it all. 'The fiends were driven off by the arrival of another coach.'

'How fortunate,' Juliana said politely. She kept her eyes on her cards.

'There is a rumour that it was no common highwaymen but some young bucks out on the rampage,' Lady Bestable commented. She shuddered. 'If it had not been for Mr Davencourt's prompt arrival, no doubt poor Lady Lyon would have been robbed and left in a ditch. All to amuse some young rake with too much money and time on his hands, and no moral principles!'

Juliana felt her smile stretching to breaking point. 'You are harsh, ma'am. Perhaps it was only intended as a jest—'

'Jest!' Lady Bestable looked as though she were about to succumb to the apoplexy. 'That is precisely my point, Lady Juliana. Anyone who thinks that it is a joking matter to frighten an old woman practically into her grave is fit for Bedlam!'

They played on in silence for a couple of minutes. Juliana won, and felt a savage satisfaction at having worsted Lady Bestable. Yet her excitement felt hollow and underneath was a sickness that was all too real. She wondered how soon she might go home. Just for once, the thought of her quiet house was most appealing.

'Mr Davencourt is quite the hero of the hour,' Lady Neasden murmured, nodding towards the open door leading into the ballroom. 'I do believe that I shall go and congratulate him.'

She drifted off, taking Lady Bestable with her.

Emma Wren leaned forward. 'I had thought that *you* were planning to be in the vicinity of Hyde Park this evening, Juliana dear. You remember—that escapade we planned involving Jasper Colling—'

Juliana met her gaze very straight. She did not want Emma asking any awkward questions and there was one explanation that was sure to distract her.

'Jasper Colling and I have indeed been enjoying each other's company this evening, albeit not in the way that we had originally intended,' she said, hitting just the right, suggestive note. 'Alas, we were far too preoccupied to venture as far as Hyde Park!'

Emma Wren tittered, her eyes opening wide. 'Indeed! I thought that Jasper was looking a little fatigued when I saw him earlier. You are to be congratulated, my dear.' She leaned forward, inviting confidence. 'I hear that he is very talented.'

Juliana shrugged, evading her eyes. 'I have known worse.'

Emma wriggled with excitement. 'Oh, do tell! I know Massingham was dreadful when he was in his cups. Why, I heard that he fell asleep on top of Harriet Templeton once, but as he was paying her she did not care and merely charged him extra!'

Juliana let Emma's chatter wash over her. Once, when she had been younger and more thin-skinned, such talk had disgusted her. Now she was almost inured to it. She had, after all, encouraged the likes of Emma Wren and Mary Neasden to include her in their easy-going sisterhood. She had even cultivated a reputation for wildness. She could hardly turn prudish now and complain that Emma's conversation was fit only for a bordello.

Out of the corner of her eye she saw Martin Davencourt, surrounded by admiring ladies. For some reason she felt on edge. She had resolved to avoid him anyway, but now it seemed essential. If he had approached the carriage and spoken to Lady Lyon, he would know that one of her assailants had been a female. Even though Juliana knew that Martin had no reason to connect her with the event, the thought made her turn quite cold with horror.

Martin looked up and for a second his unfathomable blue gaze met hers. Juliana's hand strayed to her throat, where the silver chain usually rested. She had put on a different necklace that evening, but as her fingers caressed the heavy emeralds she felt another sharp stab of alarm. She saw Martin's gaze go from her eyes to her throat and linger there, watching the way her hand plucked nervously at the necklace.

Juliana turned hastily away.

'Another game?' she said.

Martin Davencourt finally managed to shake off all the toadies who were bent on congratulating him and prowled into the refreshment room in search of a strong drink. His half-sisters had been quite impressed by his prowess in fighting off several desperate highwaymen and had been dining out on the story all evening. Martin, however, had found the attention irksome. Particularly in view of what he knew of the identity of one of the lawbreakers…

Martin had been in a filthy mood all day. He had arrived back in town from Davencourt only that afternoon, following an unpleasant incident involving a light-fingered maid and the family silver. As soon as Martin had dismissed the girl he had received a message from Araminta telling him that Kitty had lost several hundred guineas at faro and that the house was in uproar. Martin had arrived home into a nightmare of chaos and recriminations, with Mrs Lane accusing Kitty and Clara of bare-faced wickedness whilst Kitty remained defiant and Clara cried her eyes out. Her tears soon set off her younger sisters, who had wailed like banshees until Martin had thought that his head would split. In the end he had banished Kitty and Clara to their bedrooms, the rest of the children to the nursery, and Mrs Lane to the employment agency. The chaperon had been outraged to be dismissed and Martin darkly suspected that, even now, she was spreading the most vengeful rumours about his sisters' lack of moral fibre.

In the early evening he had sat in his study and reflected that something had to be done about Kitty. And about Brandon and Clara and Maria and Daisy and Bertram. Sometimes it felt as though his life was running completely out of control. It was not sufficient to employ a competent governess or chaperon or nursemaid and to rely on additional help from Araminta. She had a young family of her own. He definitely needed a wife. A practical, managing female who would take on the running of the household and guide his children with a firm hand. For a moment he had allowed himself a beautiful dream of an ordered household in which there was no stewed apple in the beds or mice released to run rampant in the ballroom. Then he had returned abruptly to reality.

He had escorted Kitty and Clara to Lady Babbacombe's soirée himself, in an effort to preserve appearances and refute any rumours in the *ton* that his household was in uproar. He knew that Serena Alcott would be there, for Araminta had told him so. She had impressed upon him what a wifely paragon Mrs Alcott would be. A steady widow who could be a good influence…

His eye fell on Lady Juliana Myfleet. He could see her through the doorway to the card room. The candlelight glinted on the tiny emeralds in her auburn hair and the matching necklace about her slender throat. She looked distant and haughty. Martin smiled grimly. Of all the *un-*suitable widows… Yet he could not deny that there had been a strong pull of attraction between them. He realised that it had started as a game; Juliana had made a play for him and he had turned the tables, responding with the male's fundamental need to pursue and possess. Yet almost immediately it had seemed more complicated than that. He enjoyed her company. He liked her. Or rather, he had liked her until tonight in Hyde Park…

He felt an appalled disgust at what Juliana had done. When they had come up to the Countess of Lyon's carriage, the poor lady was still sitting huddled in a corner, clutching her purse and repeating, 'Pray do not hurt me…' over and over again. It had taken Martin at least ten minutes to reassure her that she was safe. The coachman was little better. He was almost as ancient as his mistress and had been quite unmanned by the whole experience. When Lady Lyon had murmured, 'I thought that she would kill me…' Martin had thought that he had misheard. It was only as he was stepping down from the carriage that the lamplight had glinted on a thread of silver in the grass. He had bent down and found that it was a filigree chain with a silver crescent moon dangling from its delicate links. He had remembered at once where he had seen it before. He could even visualise it around Lady Juliana Myfleet's neck, the crescent moon resting in the hollow at the base of her throat…

The silver chain was in his pocket now. Glancing back at Juliana's serenely composed countenance, Martin felt a sudden hot and irrational anger. If she had been to blame for the outrage in Hyde Park then it was the most appalling, irresponsible piece of delinquency he could imagine.

And all in the name of entertainment, no doubt. He himself had witnessed the tricks that Lady Juliana got up to in order to alleviate her boredom, but after the misunderstanding at the wedding he had wondered if some of the stories was not entirely true. She had assured him that her wildness was merely a pretence and he realised now that he had hoped she was in earnest. He had hoped that she was a far better person than she pretended to be. Now he knew she was not. She was worse.

He found himself clenching his hands in his pockets. He had liked Juliana as well as desired her. It had been irrational, utterly inexplicable. But now he was angry with her—and with himself for being taken in.

Juliana had risen from the whist table and was walking slowly towards the ballroom now, acknowledging the greetings of her acquaintance with a slight, feline smile. Most of these acquaintances appeared to be men, and they seemed to be rather familiar towards her. Unaccountably, Martin felt another rush of anger. So Lady Juliana Myfleet was amoral, with a penchant for cruel tricks and an obsession with gambling. That should not matter to him. It should not matter one iota. But it did.

He reached Juliana's side in three strides.

'Would you care to dance, my lady?'

He thought that she looked a little startled at his sudden approach—startled and something else. For a moment her green eyes were wide with something like fear before she masked it and smiled politely.

'Thank you, Mr Davencourt, but I seldom dance. It is too fatiguing.'

'Surely not as fatiguing as a brisk ride,' Martin said grimly, falling into step beside her. 'Do you ride, Lady Juliana?'

'Indifferently, sir.' Juliana's smile seemed fixed. 'I regret that almost all exercise is repugnant to me.'

She started to walk a little more quickly. Martin kept up.

'So you do not keep a hack when you are in London?'

Juliana gave him a malicious little smile. 'If you are anxious to find a livery stable, sir, I shall ask one of my friends to recommend one.'

'I was concerned about your activities rather than my own,' Martin said. 'Do you ever frequent Hyde Park, Lady Juliana?'

This time he felt her jump and felt a sharp satisfaction that he had pierced her façade. When she spoke, however, she sounded quite calm.

'Occasionally I drive there. Why do you ask, sir?'

'I am curious about how you pass your time. This evening, for example.'

She gave him another smile, narrowing those glorious green eyes thoughtfully. Her lashes were very dark against the pale cream of her skin. She was laughing at him now, determined to discompose.

'You will have to apply to Sir Jasper Colling if you wish to know about my activities this evening, sir. However, I hope that he is too much of a gentleman to tell, or that you are too much of one to ask further...'

Martin's lips twisted in a parody of a smile. He was forced to admit that she was a cool customer. Yet even now she unconsciously betrayed herself, for her hand strayed nervously to her throat, where the emerald necklace lay above the neckline of her copper silk gown.

'I do believe you have lost your silver chain,' he said, very gently.

'A chain?' She sounded indifferent and he was almost

convinced. Almost but not quite. He allowed a note of contempt to creep into his voice.

'Surely you remember? The little silver moon that you were wearing when they served you up to Brookes on that tray? And again at the wedding? A trinket from one of your lovers, perhaps.'

Her lips tightened and she raised her chin as she met his steady regard. 'It was a present from my late husband, Mr Davencourt. And it is not lost.'

'No, indeed it is not. I have it here. I knew it was yours as soon as I found it. Distinctive, is it not?'

Martin took the necklace from his pocket. He saw Juliana whiten and shoot a quick look about the ballroom to see if anyone was watching. Her breath came quickly.

'I must have dropped it here tonight.'

'A fair attempt, but I am afraid I do not believe you. You see, Lady Juliana, I found this in the grass by the Countess of Lyon's carriage. You must have heard the tale by now?' He raised a brow ironically. 'How the Countess was stopped by highwaymen in Hyde Park tonight…'

Juliana made a little fluttering gesture with her hands. 'I have heard it! In fact, I have heard of nothing else. If you wish me to add my congratulations on your heroism to all the other plaudits you have received tonight, sir, you will be sadly disappointed. I believe you are just showing off.'

Martin laughed. 'Perhaps if I had put a bullet through you in the Park you would take me more seriously now?'

Her eyes jerked up to meet his, furious now. 'You were not a good enough shot, were you? I will take my necklace and leave you to find someone who actually enjoys your stories—'

'Oh, no!' Martin whipped the silver chain away as she

put out a hand to grasp it. With his other hand he caught her wrist, drawing her behind an arrangement of potted palms in a secluded corner. It was like trying to hold a wild cat. She was as tense as a loaded spring and braced to resist him, and once they were out of sight of the milling crowd she struggled with a will. Martin grasped both of her arms above the elbow and held her still.

'Let me go! I shall scream and create a scandal.'

She spoke quite calmly and Martin believed her. Creating a scandal in a crowded ballroom would be nothing to Lady Juliana Myfleet. It would be child's play compared to her other tricks.

'By all means,' he said pleasantly. 'If you wish to create a scandal, carry on. I shall create a greater one when I denounce you to the Constable!'

He saw the flicker of doubt in her eyes. 'You have been away too long, Mr Davencourt. No one behaves with such bad *ton* as to betray one of their own.'

'Oh no? Then perhaps your brother or your father would like to hear of your latest escapade? Or maybe you do not respect their opinion either? Maybe you would not have sunk so low if you did. For how much lower can you go, Lady Juliana?'

Martin gave her a brutal little shake. His anger was white hot now, stoked by her casual insouciance. One of the emerald pins in her hair came lose and fell on the tiles with a soft tinkling sound. Neither of them looked down. Their attention was locked on each other and even if the entire ballroom had been standing watching, they would not have noticed. Martin let her go and stood back, repudiation in every line of his body.

'Taking your clothes off and playing the whore is nothing in comparison to tonight's behaviour! Do you understand what you did to that old lady? Do you understand her fear and her pain? Do you even care, or did you lose that ability long ago?' He thrust the silver chain at her with a gesture of disgust. 'Take it! But if I ever hear of you doing the like again...'

She had gone. As the mist of anger cleared from his head, Martin saw her threading her way through the crowds on the far edge of the ballroom, walking quickly away from him, head down. She had not taken the necklace; it was still in his hand.

A wave of feeling swept him, for there was something so vulnerable about that downbent head and slumped shoulders. He felt ashamed of himself, and angry that he should feel so when he knew he was in the right. He felt a pity for what Juliana Myfleet had become.

As though sensing his regard, Juliana squared her shoulders and he watched her pause to speak to a knot of gentleman, her smile roguish, and her stance defiant. She threw him one look over her shoulder, and then she slipped her hand through the arm of the nearest of her admirers and swept from the room. Martin was torn between admiration of her aplomb and a sinking feeling that his words had made no impression on her whatsoever.

Juliana was not certain how she had managed to walk from the ballroom on legs that felt so shaky she was afraid they would buckle under her. She had no recollection of the faces of the people she passed and Edward Ashwick had to address her three times before she even noticed that he was there. No one seemed to realise that she was upset, however. Edward cheerfully gave her his arm out of the ballroom when she said that she wished to be escorted to her coach, only expressing disappointment that she was not to stay longer. He chatted inconsequentially of this and that as they walked, and seemed to expect no reply, which was fortunate, as all Juliana seemed capable of hearing was Martin Davencourt's furious tones: *Do you understand what you did to that old lady? Do you understand her fear and her pain? Do you even care, or did you lose that ability long ago?*

And like an echo, the voice of the Countess of Lyon: *Spare me. I am so old and so tired—*

'Are you quite well, Juliana?' Edward said suddenly. 'You are looking dreadfully pale.'

Juliana grasped the excuse gratefully. 'I feel a little weary. Please excuse me, Eddie. I...I need to rest for a moment. I will go to the Ladies' withdrawing room.'

'Of course,' Edward said at once. 'If you are sure you will be all right on your own—'

'I am quite sure, I thank you.'

'Then I shall call tomorrow to see how you are.'

'Please do.'

The lights were making Juliana's head ache. The marble corridor was cool and, for a moment, deserted. She leaned against the nearest doorway and put a hand to her forehead. She felt so tired. And she felt dreadfully miserable.

A tear slipped from the corner of each eye and Juliana brushed them away. She tried to pretend to herself that she was not crying, but in fact she was. She cast a furtive look down the corridor, but no one was there, so she allowed herself one sob. Its intensity surprised her and it was very difficult to keep the next one inside.

Perhaps your brother or your father would like to hear of your latest escapade? Or maybe you do not respect their opinion either?

She had once thought Martin Davencourt dull and boring, yet there had been so much anger and passion in his eyes that she had at once recognised her error. What would it be like to arouse love in a man like that—instead of fury and derision? Only a week ago he had held her in his arms, and she had wanted all that love and passion then. Now she would never know it.

Juliana gave a little hiccupping snuffle and then another full-blown sob, which escaped despite her attempts to keep it in. She covered her face with her hands, struggling for self-control. This was so embarrassing. And quite inexplicable. She never cried. But then, she had never felt so miserable before.

Someone put a gentle hand on her arm. 'Lady Juliana?'

For a second, confused and longing, she thought that Joss, her brother, had found her. She was eight years old again and she knew he would give her a rough, boyish hug. He would be embarrassed and gruff, but she would feel better.

Then she recognised the voice. *His* voice. Martin Davencourt. She backed away from him as though she had been stung, miserably aware that her face was streaked with tears and there was no concealing it.

For a long moment they stared at one another. Martin's face was dark and severe, but there was a kindness in his eyes that made her want to fling herself into his arms and beg to be loved and protected forever. It reminded her of the kindness he had shown her at Ashby Tallant that summer. Even at fifteen, Martin Davencourt had shown her the true meaning of honour and integrity. Now she wanted it desperately.

She was horrified by her feelings.

'I am sorry if—' Martin started to say, but she met his gaze defiantly and spoke over the top of him.

'If you think for one moment that I am upset because

of anything that *you* said, Mr Davencourt, then you are most definitely mistaken.'

She walked away down the corridor with her spine ramrod straight and she did not turn to look at him again. But she knew that he was watching her.

Chapter Six

'May we speak, please, Juliana?'

Joss Tallant's incisive tones cut through the card-room babble and brought his sister reluctantly to her feet. She excused herself from her companions at the faro table and allowed her brother to take her arm and steer her to a quiet corner. Juliana suspected that she knew what it was that Joss wanted to discuss. In the past five days she had been playing very deep indeed and the stories of her losses had made her the talk of the town. She had known that Joss would eventually catch up with her and demand to know what was going on. She did not want to try to explain her current misery when she barely understood it herself. She had seen Martin Davencourt a couple of times and had been frigidly polite to him, but that had only been a part of her wretchedness. The rest had been compounded of miserable dreams in which the Countess of Lyon's face had haunted her, and an unhappy feeling that everything was going wrong and yet she had no way of putting it right.

And now Joss had come to find her, and judging by his expression, she was in for a dreadful lecture.

'You are looking well, Joss,' she said lightly as her

brother passed her a glass of wine from the tray proffered by the footman. 'Married life seems to suit you so well, my dear. I hope that Amy continues to flourish?'

She saw Joss smile as he recognised her diversionary tactics. 'It is a good try, Juliana, but it won't wash. You do not care about Amy's health and I am here to talk about your debts, not to make small talk.'

Juliana grimaced. This was going to be quite as bad as she had imagined, if not worse. 'You might at least make some concessions to courtesy first, Joss,' she said plaintively. 'And it is harsh to say that I do not care about Amy. Of course I do.'

Her brother sighed. 'Amy is very well,' he said. 'We are planning to go to stay at Ashby Tallant in a month or so. Why do you not join us, Juliana? You might find it just the thing you need.'

Juliana shuddered. The thought of being immured in the country with Joss playing the doting husband to curds-and-whey Amy was enough to turn her stomach. Taken together with no company, no gambling and no shopping, it was out of the question. If she was miserable now, she would run quite mad then.

'I have no wish to play the unwelcome third to the two of you,' she said airily. 'You are still so dotingly in love that it makes the rest of us feel inadequate. Besides, you know I hate the country, Joss. I have no need to rusticate and my entertainments are all in town.'

'So I hear,' Joss said, a little grimly. He fixed his sister with a particularly penetrating look, one under which she winced. For a horrid second Juliana wondered if he had heard about the Hyde Park escapade, but then she realised that it was only her gambling that concerned him. Thank God for that. It was bad enough, but not as bad as it might be.

'How much is it this time, Ju?'

Juliana sipped her wine and debated whether to tell him the truth. On the one hand it would be useful to borrow some money from Joss, but on the other he would be disappointed in her. She had done this so many times before.

'A mere fifteen thousand, my dear,' she said, neatly halving the figure.

Joss raised his brows disbelievingly. 'And the rest?'

Juliana shrugged a pettish shoulder. 'Well, maybe a little more.' She gave him a winning smile. 'If you could see your way to lending me a few thousand, Joss…'

Joss put his glass down sharply. 'I am afraid not, Juliana. Not this time.'

At first Juliana thought that she had misheard him. She frowned a little. 'Why not? Have you been playing and losing yourself? Oh, Joss! Amy will be so displeased—'

'No,' her brother said sharply. 'I have not been playing at all. It is simply that I cannot continue funding you as you ruin yourself, Ju. Time and time again you have touched me for money. Or our father.'

Juliana's face puckered. She felt confused and panicky. 'But you *must* fund me! Or Papa must. For the family honour.'

Joss's expression was cynical. 'How much do you care for that, Ju?'

'But I…' Juliana swallowed the rest of her wine, feeling stronger as she felt the warmth of it hit her stomach. It gave her courage. 'I suppose that Amy has put you up to this! Little disapproving Amy!'

'Amy has nothing to do with this,' Joss said calmly. A muscle twitched in his cheek. 'It is for your own good, Juliana. You must master this.'

'Well, you are a fine one to talk!' Juliana almost

smashed the glass on the marble floor in her frustration. 'Upon my word, when you were the most inveterate gambler of them all! I suppose you will say that you were saved by the love of a good woman? How odiously mawkish you are these days!'

'If you like,' Joss said. A flicker of a smile touched his lips. 'You were very happily married once, Juliana. Would you not recommend it?'

Juliana's throat closed. 'Lud, no,' she forced out. 'I dare say it suited me when I was young and dreamy, but now I need entertainment, not some tedious routine. You would not catch me marrying again!'

'A pity,' Joss said. 'It might just be what you need. And nor will we tempt you to the country? Well…' he shrugged and turned away '…you must just hope to start winning, my dear, and soon. Otherwise we shall all be visiting you in the Fleet.' He paused. 'Papa has been ill,' he added abruptly. 'I do beg you not to trouble him with your latest exploits. He is too weak at present to deal with any of your melodramas and Mr Ivinghoe is referring all financial matters to me.'

Juliana's fear pressed down, a crushing weight on her chest. 'Joss, wait! If Papa is too ill and you refuse to help me—'

'Yes?' her brother said. Juliana could see his determination and she could see how much it was costing him. She and Joss had always been close, drawn together in mutual support during a lonely childhood. She wanted to rail at him, to denounce him for deserting her. But another part of her whispered that Joss was trying to help her and that the cost to him was high as well. She wanted to blame him, but found she could not. All the fight went out of her in a long sigh.

'I cannot believe that you are doing this to me,' she said.

Joss pulled a face. 'Juliana—'

'I know.' Juliana put out a hand and touched his arm. 'I *know* you want the best for me. I even know that you love me.' She sighed again, sharply. 'But if I have no money, how am I to entertain myself?' She could hear the pleading note slip into her voice and despised herself for it. 'I need to go shopping, and to have money for play, and… Oh!' Her voice broke in exasperation. 'How am I to manage, Joss? I cannot attend all the balls and parties in the same outfits every day!'

'I am sure that you will think of something,' her brother said smoothly. 'I will see that your household bills are paid, of course, and if you agree to come to Ashby Tallant I will pay off your gaming debts.'

For a moment Juliana was sorely tempted. To have all her debts paid, to start again with a blank sheet, was extremely appealing. Then she imagined how it would be to be trapped in the country; to have no play and no visitors and no entertainment. To watch Joss doting on his wife when she felt sick with envy because no one ever looked at her with an ounce of that devotion; to suffer her father's indifference and cold contempt. She knew that she had been difficult with Joss that evening, but it was only because she was so afraid…

'I thank you, but no,' she said, trying to salvage her pride for she knew that Joss could enforce her rustication if he chose. 'I am persuaded that I shall fend for myself quite well.'

Joss was shaking his head. 'You know where to find me if you need me.'

'There is no point in finding you,' Juliana said crossly, 'since you will not fund me.'

For a moment they stared at one another, then Juliana made a muffled noise and threw herself into Joss's arms, regardless of the curious stares of the card players. For a long moment she held him tightly, her face pressed to his chest.

'Oh, Joss…'

Her brother hugged her back. 'Please, Ju…please try. For all our sakes.'

Juliana released him. She nodded. 'I will. Now go, before I get really cross with you.' She gave him a watery smile. 'As you said, I know where to find you. And I know you will not let me moulder in the Fleet.'

'Well, not for long,' Joss said. He gave her a kiss on the cheek. 'Goodnight, Ju.'

Back at the card table, Juliana found that Emma Wren and Mary Neasden had been joined by a pale girl of about twenty. She was dressed in a dull but expensive gown and she was clutching her cards desperately in her hand. Her darting dark gaze seemed intensely nervous.

'Juliana dear, this is Kitty Davenport,' Emma said comfortably. She was using her most reassuring tone, the one she used to draw unsuspecting innocents into her trap. 'Kitty is new to town and I know she will be pleased to make new friends. Kitty, my love, this is Lady Juliana Myfleet.'

Juliana jumped. For a moment she thought that she had misheard and that Emma had said Davencourt, but then she realised that she knew the Davenports, a fabulously wealthy but deadly dull family. No doubt this poor little girl was a young matron or wayward daughter, looking for a little excitement.

'How do you do, ma'am?' the girl said submissively.

'How do you do?' Juliana said politely. She caught Emma's eye and Emma gave her the ghost of a wink. It suggested that here was a young lady about to be parted from her allowance.

Juliana shrugged inwardly. She was still burning with a mixture of annoyance and misery over Joss's refusal to fund her, but there seemed a certain justice in the fact that fate had just offered up a means for her to win some money. She flicked Kitty a glance, and then set about fleecing the girl.

It was all over very quickly. Within a half hour, Kitty had lost to the tune of twelve thousand guineas and she was looking very pale. Emma Wren shuffled the cards and yawned.

'Heigh ho! Your luck is in tonight, Ju, and no mistake! With the ten thousand I owe you, plus little Kitty's twelve, you will soon be riding high again.'

Kitty had been very quiet as the game had worn on. Now she said, stuttering a little, 'I beg your pardon, ma'am, but may I offer you an IOU? I cannot meet the debt until…' her voice wavered '…until I receive my next allowance.'

Juliana looked at her. It seemed very unlikely to her that any young lady would receive a quarterly allowance of twelve thousand guineas. Emma Wren was trying not to laugh.

'You are certain that you will not renege?' she asked cruelly. 'You should not play above your capabilities, my dear…'

Poor Kitty looked about to faint. 'I assure you that I shall pay!' She threw Juliana a pleading look. 'If I might write you a promissory note, ma'am?'

Juliana sighed. 'If you wish,' she said indifferently. Now it could be months until she got her money. If it arrived at all. It was a shame, for she had planned to use it to win more.

Emma got up from the table and beckoned to a footman to bring pen and ink. Kitty started to scribble.

'Excuse me.' Emma gave Juliana a broad smile. 'I will see you in a little while, my dear.'

Juliana sat drumming her fingers on the card table as Kitty wrote. After a few minutes she looked at the girl's bent head and hectically flushed cheeks. Really, it was as though she was writing an entire novel. What on earth could be taking so long?

Then she saw that a big fat tear had plopped down onto the paper beside Kitty's right hand. Juliana stared whilst the girl tried to rub it away and only succeeded in smearing the entire document. She gave a smothered sob.

'Good gracious!' Juliana said blankly.

Kitty gave a start and shot Juliana a guilty look. 'I beg your pardon, ma'am. If I might have another piece of paper?'

Juliana took a deep breath. The candlelight was reflecting off the tears on Kitty's cheeks. The girl looked guilty and desperate and about twelve years old. Juliana found herself reaching out and taking the promissory note and tearing it in two.

'Do not trouble to write another one,' she said. 'The debt is cancelled.'

Kitty caught her breath. 'My lady—'

'You do not have the means to pay it, do you?' Juliana said.

Kitty looked away. 'No, but I was going to tell my brother—'

'Do not.' Juliana's heart clenched. At the back of her mind was an old, old memory—another young girl, not twenty years old, who had lost eighty thousand pounds and had almost brought her family down. Joss had saved her then. If she could do a little for Kitty now… She leaned forward.

'Do not tell him, Kitty. There is no need. Only—' she reached across and touched Kitty's hand '—do not gamble if you cannot afford the stake. No, ignore that advice. Do not gamble at all. The game is not worth the candle.'

The unlooked-for kindness of her words opened the floodgates. Kitty burst into tears, sniffed, snorted and generally made Juliana wish she had said nothing at all. After several minutes, when Kitty's torrent of crying had barely slowed and they were attracting a great deal of curious attention, Juliana got up and took her by the arm.

'Miss Davenport—Kitty—let me take you somewhere else…'

She steered the girl out into the corridor and down to a discreet sitting room where she poured Kitty a half-inch of brandy and pressed it into her hand. 'Here, take this.'

'I hate brandy,' Kitty said, with the first flash of spirit she had shown.

'I dare say,' Juliana said calmly. 'It will help you to recover, however. Do you have a handkerchief?'

Kitty did not. With a sigh, Juliana took her own out of her reticule and handed it to the girl to mop her face. After a moment, Kitty sat back, took a sip of brandy, gulped, coughed and drew a deep breath.

'That's better,' Juliana said. 'So tell me, Kitty—why *do* you gamble?' She laughed at the irony of her question. 'Lord knows, it is rich coming from me, but it is not at all the done thing for young ladies, you know.'

Kitty sipped her brandy and looked embarrassed. 'I know it is quite dreadful, Lady Juliana.' She drew a deep breath. 'The truth is that I was hoping to lose and lose, until matters got so bad that my brother sent me home. It was the only way I could think of to get into such disgrace that I might be allowed to live quietly in the country!'

Juliana stared in disbelief. Of all the explanations she was expecting, this was the last. 'You wanted to be sent home in disgrace?' she repeated incredulously. 'That was not such a good plan, Kitty.'

'I know.' Kitty hung her head. 'It was all I could think of, you see. For how else may a young lady disgrace herself?'

'Well, you could have run off with some ineligible man—' Juliana began, then stopped. 'No, perhaps not. Pray forget that I said that. So tonight you set out to run up a huge debt...'

'Yes,' Kitty's gaze was tragic. 'I have lost a considerable sum over the past few weeks, Lady Juliana, so I am in complete disgrace. I knew that to gamble now would be the last straw. But when I had done it I felt sick with fear and could not believe how much I had lost.' Kitty hung her head. 'I suddenly realised what a particularly stupid thing it was to do.'

'It was,' Juliana said thoughtfully. 'But why did you wish to be sent home in the first place, Kitty?'

Kitty's lip quivered. 'I want to go home because I *hate* London! I hate the noise and the people and the dirty streets. I thought that I might find someone sympathetic to marry, but all I meet is bores and rakes and gentlemen who wish to talk about themselves! If I could find someone who liked the country it might be different...'

Juliana tried to find a crumb of comfort. 'There are plenty of men who enjoy hunting and fishing—'

Kitty made a desperate gesture. 'Yes, but I would wish to marry a man who conserves nature rather than trying to destroy it!'

'That is a rather unusual point of view, and I am not

surprised that you have yet to meet this paragon.' Juliana looked thoughtfully at Kitty. 'I will have to see if I can think of anyone who might suit you, Kitty. And, if not, we must come up with a different plan—something a little more likely of success than trying to get yourself banished to the country in disgrace.' She checked the clock on the mantelpiece. 'Now you had better hurry back to your chaperon before you are missed. I am surprised that she has not raised a hue and cry for you.'

'I do not have a chaperon at the moment,' Kitty said, 'and Lady Harpenden, who was supposed to be keeping an eye on us, does not like chaperoning us because my sister Clara is prettier than her daughter.'

'Yes, I see,' Juliana said. 'Even so, you had better run along.'

Kitty's eyes, dark as pansies in the rain, filled with grateful tears.

'Thank you for your kindness, Lady Juliana!'

'Pray do not cry again, Kitty,' Juliana said hastily.

'No, no! Nor shall I ever gamble again,' Kitty said stalwartly. 'You are so kind and good, Lady Juliana! Thank you so much!'

After Kitty had gone, Juliana poured herself a good inch of brandy and drank it all down. She felt that she needed it to recover from the shock of being described as kind and good. She could not quite believe what she had done. Cancelling a debt, offering advice to a débutante, acting as confidante… She must be mad. Juliana sighed, and poured herself some more brandy. It had been the memories that had undermined her. Kitty's plight had reminded her of her own unutterable folly when, at seventeen, she had played and lost, played and lost, until she had run up the huge debt that almost ruined her family.

Juliana shook her head to dispel the memory. Well, she

had done her bit to save Kitty. And though she had promised her help, there really was no need to see the girl
again. Kitty's family would never allow it anyway. Which
was all to the good. She did not wish to get drawn in any
further.

Martin Davencourt arrived on Lady Juliana Myfleet's
doorstep the following morning as though all the hounds
of hell were on his heels. The information that Lady Juliana was still abed was imparted by the butler and
brought him up a little short, but he decided that he would
wait. After a half-hour he wondered suddenly if Juliana
was not alone and if the early morning was possibly the
worst time to call. He had no wish to meet one of Juliana's
lovers, or worse, find himself obliged to share breakfast
with the two of them. By the time a full hour was up,
Martin was practically chewing the carpet with tension
and unaccustomed indecision, and he was about to leave
when Juliana herself walked into the library.

'Mr Davencourt.'

Martin got to his feet. 'Good morning, Lady Juliana.
Thank you for seeing me. I beg your pardon for arriving
at such an unfashionably early hour.'

Juliana gave him a dazzling smile. Martin felt his heart
contract. 'There is no need,' she said politely. 'I was not
occupied with anything else. I am only surprised that you
sought me out at all, Mr Davencourt. Or is it to ring another peal over me? I assure you that the last one was
effective enough. There is no need for a repeat performance.'

Martin shook his head. He realised that despite the long
wait, he had not prepared what he was going to say. It
was unusual for him to be so impetuous. He plunged
straight in.

'I came…I wanted… That is, there is something that I wished to speak with you about.'

Juliana raised an eyebrow at his tangled sentences. 'I see. Will you take coffee? I have not partaken of breakfast yet.'

'Of course.' Martin forced himself to relax and match her coolness. 'And yes, I should be delighted to have coffee with you.'

Juliana nodded. Martin repressed a grin. Lady Juliana's defences were very firmly in place that morning. The façade of the society sophisticate was almost impenetrable. If he had not seen her cry at Lady Babbacombe's ball he would have sworn that she had no softer feelings. If he did not know Kitty to have been telling the truth about the previous night, he would have thought that generosity was beyond her. And yet he knew there was more to her than that…

Martin watched Juliana whilst the footman brought a silver tray with a coffee pot and two cups. He knew that she was conscious of his regard, but that she was making strenuous efforts to appear calm. She did not look at him, but he knew she was as achingly aware of him as he was of her.

The coffee smelled delicious. Martin was suddenly aware that he had not stopped for breakfast that morning and that he was hungry. Juliana poured, precisely and efficiently. She passed him a cup and raised her brows enquiringly.

'So—what did you wish to speak about, Mr Davencourt?'

'It is to do with Kitty,' Martin said. 'My sister, Kitty Davencourt. She tells me that she lost twelve thousand guineas to you at play last night.'

Juliana turned her head sharply. She looked very slightly put out. She put her coffee cup down gently.

'I was not aware that she was your sister. I thought… That is, she was introduced to me as Kitty Davenport.'

Martin raised his brows. 'Would it have made a difference to you if you had known the truth?'

He saw a glint of amusement in Juliana's eyes. 'Perhaps I would have thought twice about letting her off the debt.'

Martin wondered if she was teasing him. He cleared his throat. 'Yes. Well…she told me that you had cancelled her debt to you. I wondered why you had done so.'

Juliana gave him a stare as protracted and considering as that of a predatory cat. '*I* wonder what Miss Davencourt was doing there in the first place.'

Martin immediately felt defensive, which he knew was exactly what Juliana had intended. He gave her back a look as straight as her own.

'I asked you first,' he said evenly. 'Why did you let Kitty off the debt?'

He sensed that Juliana was irritated by his persistence, although nothing of her feelings showed on her face. She waved a dismissive hand.

'I cancelled the debt because I wanted to do so. I was feeling generous last night.'

Martin stared at her. 'You threw away twelve thousand guineas on a *whim?*'

Now she looked very irritated. 'It was not a whim precisely. But yes, I decided to let her off because I felt like it.'

Martin sat forward. He knew she was hiding something, knew that there was more to this, but he doubted that she would tell him the truth.

'It was not because you felt sorry for her? Not because

she is young and you knew she was out of her depth and you took pity on her?'

Juliana smiled faintly. 'Certainly not. There is no place for pity in the card room, Mr Davencourt. Play or pay.'

Martin repressed a prickle of anger at the thought of all the young sprigs of fashion and impressionable young ladies who fell under the spell of the card tables. 'A philosophy that you follow yourself, I suppose,' he said softly, 'although I hear that you owe rather a lot at present and cannot actually pay.'

Juliana gave him a hard stare. 'That is none of your business.'

'I suppose not. But my younger sister is my business and I do not wish her falling under the influence of hardened gamesters.'

Juliana looked disdainful. 'Then you should keep her away from the card tables, Mr Davencourt. You did not answer my question. What was she doing there in the first place?'

Martin sighed. He did not feel that he owed Lady Juliana Myfleet an explanation, but he found himself offering one anyway. 'My sisters have recently lost their chaperon. Last night Kitty was supposed to be under the care of Lady Harpenden. It seems that her ladyship became distracted and did not notice when Kitty slipped away to the card room. Lady Harpenden was quite distraught when she found out, which was why Kitty was obliged to confess the whole to me.' He paused. 'She told me that you had advised her not to tell, Lady Juliana.'

Juliana shrugged. 'What was the point when I had let her off the debt?' She sighed. 'Unfortunately, young ladies seem to suffer from an overwhelming urge to confess their sins.'

Martin's held her gaze. 'And older ones?'

'Experience teaches one never to divulge secrets,' Juliana said lightly. She frowned. 'There is something troubling your sister, Mr Davencourt. She confided in me last night and I do believe that you should talk to her.'

'I will do,' Martin said shortly. Once again he felt profoundly irritated. Why did Kitty appear to have found it easier to talk to Juliana Myfleet than to her own brother? First Brandon, now his sister…

'There is no need for you to trouble yourself further on Kitty's behalf, Lady Juliana,' he said austerely. 'I will deal with the matter.'

'I see.' Juliana looked at him thoughtfully. 'More coffee, Mr Davencourt?'

Martin stood up. 'No thank you. I must thank you for your kindness towards Kitty, I suppose. Or should I call it your generous impulse?'

Juliana stood up, too. She was tall; she did not have to tilt her head up far to meet his eyes.

'You may call it whatever you wish, Mr Davencourt.'

'If you should come across her in the card room in future—'

'Have no fear. I shall fleece her mercilessly.' Juliana gave him a measuring look. 'Keep Kitty away from the cards, Mr Davencourt. I am persuaded that you would not wish her to develop a passion for them.'

Martin sighed heavily. He felt depressed. 'It may be too late for that.'

'Not at all. She is not playing because she wants to do so—she is playing as a means to an end. She promised me that she would not gamble again, but you really need to speak to her. But we have already discussed this and you do not appreciate my interference.'

Juliana whisked across to the mantel and reached out to pull the bell. Martin put his hand over hers. He knew that there was something here that was deeper than a careless caprice on Juliana's part. Once again she had surprised him and he was no closer to solving the enigma.

'A moment, Lady Juliana. Would you know how to break a dependence on the cards?'

Juliana paused. Martin thought he saw a flicker of temper in her eyes. She raised her chin, her gaze cold.

'Is this a question about my own gambling rather than Kitty's, Mr Davencourt?'

Martin gave her a searching look. 'If you like. Would you give it up?'

Juliana laughed shortly. 'Certainly not. Cards entertain me.'

'Along with a penchant for reckless tricks.' Martin felt in his pocket. 'I still have your necklace.'

'Thank you,' Juliana said. She held out a hand and Martin put the silver chain into it.

'I am sorry about what I said that night,' he said slowly.

There was not the slightest hint of warmth in Juliana's expression. 'Why should you be sorry, Mr Davencourt? You spoke the truth as you saw it.'

'I was too harsh.'

Juliana turned a shoulder. 'I can deal with that, Mr Davencourt. You are not speaking to some shrinking débutante now. I have heard plenty of harsh words spoken. Besides, you were correct. It was the most appalling error of judgement on my part.'

Martin felt a pang of surprise at her honesty. He looked at her. Her composure was flawless, yet in his mind was another image; her face tearstained and white as she sought to hide her misery at Lady Babbacombe's ball. The memory was like a wrench to his heart.

'I hear that someone sent Lady Lyon a huge basket of flowers and an apology,' he said.

Juliana's expression did not soften. 'I believe that someone was most sincerely sorry for what happened. I also believe that you have overstayed your welcome, Mr Davencourt. The door is over there. Pray give my regards to your sister.'

Martin hesitated. 'I must ask you to stay away from Kitty,' he said carefully. 'She has some inappropriate idea about seeking you out again. I am sure you understand. She is young and impressionable and I would not wish her to fall under any undesirable influence.'

'You are offensive, Mr Davencourt,' Juliana said coldly. 'So I am good enough for you to kiss me if the whim takes you, but not suitable to speak to your sister. I think that tells me all I need to know of your opinion of me! As for Kitty, she does not wish to speak to you, does she? I may be unacceptable, but you are inadequate. In so many ways.'

Martin's eyes narrowed. He caught her arm. 'I do not believe that you found me inadequate the night we returned from Crowns.'

Juliana laughed. Her bright gaze mocked him. 'How like a man! I was not referring to your amatory capabilities, Mr Davencourt, as I am sure you know. I suppose that in that respect you were passable.'

Martin knew perfectly well that he should not pursue this, but found he could not help himself. Juliana angered him, as she was wont to do. She was like a prickly burr under the saddle of a horse. No matter how he tried, he could not prevent the irritation. And yet she puzzled him. He wanted to find out what was beneath the façade.

'In comparison to your long list of admirers, I suppose,' he said softly.

He saw a flicker of some expression in Juliana's eyes before she shrugged his comment away. 'Your words, not mine, Mr Davencourt. I told you once before that I had no wish to discuss my conquests with you.'

Martin's temper caught alight. 'The hell you don't. Well I do! I want to know—'

'Want to know what, precisely, Mr Davencourt?' Juliana was ice cool. 'The names and details of all my lovers? Why do you wish to know? Can it be that you are jealous?'

There was a fraught pause.

'Yes,' Martin said. 'Yes, I am. I am damnably jealous.'

He saw beneath Juliana's façade then; saw the colour leave her face, saw her eyes widen in disbelief. She looked suddenly vulnerable. 'Devil take it,' she said, a little unsteadily. 'Somehow I expected you to lie.'

Martin closed the gap between them. Time paused for a heartbeat as he lowered his head to hers. The touch of his lips was soft, but it lit something in both of them. Within a second, he had crushed Juliana closer to him and kissed her again, no longer gentle. Juliana leaned into him, her lips parting under the irresistible pressure of his. Now there was no pretence and no performance, just a sweetness and an urgency that poleaxed Martin, knocking the breath from his body and igniting a ferocious desire. His tongue tangled with hers in a hungry, dizzying kiss, but then Juliana was stepping back, holding him off. Martin could feel the effort it cost her and though a part of him wanted to override her scruples and draw her back into his arms, he let his hands fall to his side.

Juliana was biting her lip. 'No,' she said. She looked up and met his gaze very straight. 'You are confused, Mr Davencourt. And now you are confusing me. Remember that you have no very good opinion of me. I think that you should go.'

Martin put out a hand. 'Juliana—'

'And,' Juliana added, very clearly, 'I do not respond well to the offer of *carte blanche*.'

Carte blanche. Martin felt the shock go through him. He had not even thought of offering it.

Juliana tugged the bell pull sharply. Segsbury appeared as though he had been waiting on the other side of the door and Martin found himself out on the steps of the house in short order. He walked away from 7 Portman Square so blindly that he could have been run over by a hackney cab for all the attention he was paying.

He had been wanting to kiss Juliana for a long time. Since the last time, in fact. And now that it had happened, he wanted to do it again. Soon. Often. He groaned. His timing was appalling. He was paying court to another lady, a respectable widow he had identified as the ideal wife. It was hardly the moment to be kissing a different widow, a disreputable one.

As for *carte blanche*, Martin knew he could not offer Juliana that even if he had been the sort of man to set up a wife and a mistress at one and the same time. He could not offer Juliana *carte blanche* because it felt like an insult.

It was not good enough for her.

Martin absorbed the thought.

Why was it not good enough for her? She was a lady with a shady reputation who had apparently had liaisons with any number of gentlemen. She was considered practically unmarriageable now, her reputation in tatters. If she had had a fortune it might perhaps have been different. But she did not. She had a huge pile of gambling debts. She was practically ruined and it was only her widowed status and her position as the daughter of the Marquis of Tallant that gave her a scant protection in the *ton*.

Oddly enough, this reminder of Juliana's situation did not make Martin feel any better. It made him angry.

You are confused, Mr Davencourt. And now you are confusing me.

She was right, Martin thought ruefully. He was damnably confused and damnably jealous. When he held her in his arms it felt as though she belonged there. It reminded him uncomfortably of the contentment he had felt that summer at Ashby Tallant.

But he could not allow such thoughts to cloud his judgement. Juliana was unpredictable and dangerous, and her influence on Kitty could be dreadfully damaging. He frowned, thinking of Juliana's generosity in letting Kitty off the debt. It was not the act of a woman intent on ruining his sister by leading her deeper into a web of gambling.

He felt torn. He wanted Juliana Myfleet, but he knew he could not have her and just at the moment he could see no way out at all.

Chapter Seven

'There is a young lady here to see you, madam.' Segsbury said, when Juliana returned from a shopping trip the following afternoon. He sounded quite impassive, despite the fact that young ladies never called at 7 Portman Square. 'Two young ladies, to be exact. Miss Davencourt and Miss Clara Davencourt, madam. I showed them into the blue drawing-room, thinking perhaps—'

'Thinking that the nude sculptures in the Library might shock their delicate sensibilities,' Juliana finished for him. 'Thank you, Segsbury. I am indebted to you.'

She passed her hat and coat to the butler, ran a satisfied eye over the huge pile of purchases that the footman was unloading from the carriage, and went across to the Library door. What Kitty and Clara Davencourt might want was anybody's guess, but Juliana was fairly certain that their brother could not know they were there. She resolved to get rid of the girls as quickly as possible. Chatting to débutantes was not an occupation that held any interest for her and she did not wish to encourage Kitty into thinking of her as a friend. Besides, if Martin found out she would no doubt be subject to another homily on how she was not good enough to associate with his sisters. And the worst of it was that he was right. Visiting Portman Square could damage the Davencourt girls irreparably.

Juliana paused before the mirror, straightened her hair and smoothed down her dress. The worst possible outcome was that Kitty and Clara's visit might bring Martin to her door again. She did not wish to see him, because whenever she did, she wanted him. She did not simply want to be in his arms. She wanted *him*. She wanted his honour and integrity and protectiveness. She ached for him to love her and it was infuriating. She had sworn never to fall in love again and she despaired of herself, particularly for choosing a man whose opinion of her was insultingly low. Particularly because she had no intention of marrying ever again.

Juliana pulled a face at herself in the mirror. She also hated maudlin self-pity. So she would stay away from Martin Davencourt. And from his simpering little sisters.

Both the Davencourt girls got to their feet when Juliana entered the room. Today Kitty looked pretty in pale pink, but Clara eclipsed her completely, for she was a glowing creature, bursting with health and vitality. Clara had inherited the fair good looks of the Davencourt family. She had long blonde hair that curled winsomely about her face, a delicious creamy complexion and huge, dark blue eyes. She looked as luscious as a bowl of strawberries and cream.

'Lady Juliana!' Clara said. She was staring quite frankly and Juliana found herself trying not to laugh. What gossip had this girl heard about her? Did respectable matrons and chaperons use her as a bogeyman to scare young ladies?

Misbehave yourself and you will turn into Lady Juliana Myfleet!

'We came...' Clara pulled herself together with an ef-

fort although she did not stop staring. 'That is, we wanted
to ask you...'

'Yes?' Juliana said. 'Why did you come, Miss Clara?'

Clara looked nonplussed for a moment, then she smiled.
It was glorious, like the sun coming up. Juliana reflected
that she must be fighting her suitors off with sticks.

'We came because we wanted to see you, of course,'
she said artlessly. 'Kitty has told me so much about you.'

Juliana looked at Kitty, who blushed.

'I can imagine,' Juliana said drily. 'I am not a sideshow
attraction, however. Besides, I am tolerably certain that
your brother cannot know you are here. You should be
gone before he finds out.'

Kitty tugged on Clara's arm. She was evidently far
more sensitive to atmosphere than her sister. 'Lady Juliana
is correct, Clara. We should not have troubled her...'

A slight pang of compassion undermined Juliana. Kitty
looked so downcast and disappointed. She remembered
that she had promised the girl her help in finding a husband. She must have been mad.

Surprisingly for someone with such a sweet exterior,
Clara proved to be made of sterner stuff than her sister.
She turned to Kitty with a mulish expression. 'But I
wanted to ask Lady Juliana for her help! She said that she
would help you.'

'I am not a fairy godmother,' Juliana said, but she could
not help a slight softening of tone.

Clara, sensing weakness, gave her unwilling hostess a
winning smile.

'Oh, please, Lady Juliana! We need your advice, and
Kitty said that you were so kind before...'

Juliana hesitated. She had not foreseen that Kitty would
paint her in the light of some sort of ministering angel. It
had seemed so unlikely. She looked at Clara. Clara looked

back at her, a steely light in her limpid blue eyes. Juliana smiled. She had always thought that Martin must be the Davencourt with the most stubborn nature. But that was before she had met Clara.

She sighed.

'Very well, Miss Clara. I am sure that I can spare a little time. Why do we not all sit down and have a cup of tea, and you can tell me all about it?'

Half an hour later, Juliana's head was spinning. Between mouthfuls of muffin and copious cups of tea, Clara had poured out the whole sorry tale of her own and her sister's problems. Kitty had sat quietly, very much in her younger sister's shadow, but occasionally she had nodded, or added a word here and there.

'It is not that we do not wish to marry, Lady Juliana,' Clara said, opening her eyes very wide, 'only all the gentlemen we meet are so unsuitable. Kitty wishes to find a man who loves the country and I…well, I have not been able to find anyone worth staying awake for.' She popped another muffin into her mouth. 'I have a dreadful habit of falling asleep, you see. I find the Season so very fatiguing, and all this hot weather makes me doze off. I am afraid that I fall asleep in the most embarrassing places. Ballrooms, the theatre—'

'Oh, everyone goes to sleep at the theatre,' Juliana said. 'That is, if they stop talking for long enough to do so. But I hope you do not fall asleep when the gentlemen are trying to talk to you, Clara.'

'She does,' Kitty said.

A guilty blush stained Clara's cheek. 'I may do so.' She fluttered her hands languidly. 'All my suitors are so dull, Lady Juliana! I fear they can do nothing to keep me awake!'

Juliana just managed to quell the riposte that sprang to her lips. 'No? Well, men can be tiresomely dull, but there are still a few who are worth your interest. And surely you are not short of admirers, Clara? You are a very pretty girl.'

Clara shrugged lightly. 'Oh, I have plenty of suitors. Kitty and I have a large fortune as well, so we are quite sought after. That just makes matters more difficult, for I have to stay awake for so many people! And I do try. The Earl of Ercol made me an offer yesterday morning, but I fear I fell asleep whilst he was talking to me. Martin was frightfully angry with me, and Ercol cut us dead at the opera last night.'

'One cannot blame him.' Kitty munched her way through a biscuit. 'You were dreadfully rude, Clara.'

'Unfortunately your sister is right,' Juliana said drily. 'Most gentlemen like to think that they are the most fascinating speakers on earth, particularly when they are talking about themselves. Yet,' she added gently, 'if you met a gentleman you liked, Clara, you might find that you wanted to stay awake long enough to enjoy his company.'

Clara's guilty blush deepened. 'I know. Oh, it is so very difficult!'

Juliana raised her brows. 'Is it that you wish to live on your own in the country like Kitty?'

Kitty smothered a laugh and Clara shuddered. 'Certainly not, Lady Juliana! The country is quite exhausting. All that walking and riding and playing of croquet... No, it is simply that I worry because I imagine that the running of my own establishment would be sooooo tiring. I dread to think of it.'

Juliana frowned. 'So Kitty requires a country-loving suitor and you need a gentleman who engages your interest *and* employs plenty of servants to see to the running of your home. That is a tall order. I shall have to think about this, Clara, and see who might fit the bill.'

'Please could you think quickly?' Clara said hopefully. 'Mrs Alcott has intimated that it would be a good match for me to marry her brother and she is such a *managing* female I am sure I shall give in through sheer exhaustion!'

'Oh, you cannot marry Charlie Walton,' Juliana said quickly. 'He is the most dreadful bore. Just like his sister!'

Clara giggled and looked more cheerful. 'She is shockingly dull, is she not? And she is always picking on Kitty and on me. I am too fat, too lazy, too poorly dressed...'

'You are too pretty and too rich,' Juliana said. 'I'll wager she is jealous of you, Clara.'

Clara opened her eyes wide. 'Oh, do you think so? Yes, perhaps you are right! She is gushingly sweet to Martin, but quite horrible to me!'

Juliana thought it unlikely that even Serena Alcott would manage to marry Clara off. Although Clara was indolent, there was something very determined about her laziness.

'It makes me quite cross,' the quiet Kitty said staunchly. 'Martin cannot see through Mrs Alcott at all. I dread that he might marry her. Why are men so hopeless, Lady Juliana?'

'Alas, they cannot help it,' Juliana said. 'They seldom see what is beneath their noses. Could you not talk to Mr Davencourt about your concerns? Confide in him?'

Both girls looked horrified. 'Oh, no!' Kitty said. 'We could never talk to Martin. He is fearfully busy and has no time for us.'

'He is a splendid brother,' Clara put in, 'and we love him dearly, but we are just a tiny bit afraid of him, dear Lady Juliana!'

Juliana's lips twitched. 'Afraid of him? I am sure that you have no need to be.'

'No…' Kitty looked dubious. 'It is simply that he always seems so…'

'Disapproving,' Clara said. 'I fear we are a sad disappointment to him. Brandon, too. There is something troubling Brandon, but he will not tell Martin about it.'

'I know,' Juliana said. She sighed. 'I am sure that you all malign Mr Davencourt. I know he seems daunting, but he does care about you all, you know.' She laughed. 'I have an elder brother, you see, so I know how you feel.'

Kitty's eyes sparkled. 'Are you afraid of him, Lady Juliana?'

'Prodigiously!' Juliana said. 'No, only a little, Kitty—but I do long for his good opinion.' And she realised it was true.

'Your brother is Joss Tallant, isn't he?' Clara said dreamily. 'He is *such* a handsome man. And he has a friend whom I might be persuaded to stay awake for, if only I could scrape an acquaintance!'

Juliana's heart sank. The thought of Clara falling for one of Joss's rakish acquaintances would be any parent's nightmare. Goodness only knew what Martin would say if he found out.

'A friend of my brother's,' she said carefully. 'Which friend would that be, Clara?'

Clara blushed. 'The Duke of Fleet. He is very good-looking, is he not, Lady Juliana?'

'Very,' Juliana said. She frowned. 'Sebastian Fleet is a shocking gambler, Clara, as well as a rake. He is completely unsuitable for you. Your brother would never countenance the match.'

The steely light was back in Clara's eyes. 'But I hear that Fleet is very rich and so he could support me in the indolence to which I have become accustomed. Will you introduce me to him, Lady Juliana?'

'No,' Juliana said. 'Anyone else and I would do it. Well, almost anyone else,' she amended, thinking of Jasper Colling. 'But Seb Fleet is out of the question.'

Clara looked downcast, then perked up slightly. 'Then what about Lady Tallant's brother, Richard Bainbridge? Now he is terribly charming.'

'Richard is feckless and a wastrel,' Juliana said. 'Besides, he has no money. Clara, your taste in men is almost as bad as mine!'

Clara giggled. 'It is strange that these gentlemen are all acquaintances of yours.'

'It is not strange at all,' Juliana said. 'I am the last person to try and make a match for either you or Kitty. All the gentlemen I know are quite unacceptable.'

'There is Martin,' Kitty pointed out. 'You know him and he is very eligible and terribly proper.'

'Your brother is the exception that proves the rule,' Juliana said. 'He is the only respectable gentleman I know.'

And even then, she thought privately, he is not as proper as everyone thinks him. Certainly there was nothing proper in the way he kissed.

Kitty sighed. 'I do so hope that Martin will not marry Serena. It would be far more fun were he to marry you! He has definitely got the wrong cousin.'

Juliana felt a pang and smothered it quickly. 'Thank you, Kitty. Alas, your brother and I would not suit. Never in a thousand years.'

Clara was watching her with a very shrewd look in her eye. There was nothing sleepy about her expression at all. Juliana suddenly thought that the days of Sebastian Fleet's bachelorhood might well be numbered. If there was something that Clara wanted she would go right out and get it…

The bell pealed. Juliana's heart sank. She hoped that it was not Emma Wren, or even worse, Jasper Colling. She felt quite chilled to think what Jasper might say if he found Clara and Kitty in her drawing room.

The girls were both gazing at her in trepidation.

'Do you think—?' Kitty began. She bit her lip. 'I wonder if Martin has guessed.'

'Oh, no!' Clara wailed.

The door opened.

'Mr Davencourt,' Segsbury said, very stately. 'Shall I send in a fresh pot of tea, madam?'

Juliana took in Clara's expression of guilty apprehension, Kitty's pallor and Martin Davencourt's heavy frown.

'Please do, Segsbury,' she said politely. 'I am sure that a fresh pot of tea is just what we all need.'

Martin felt a huge relief when he saw Clara and Kitty sitting innocently on Juliana Myfleet's sofa. It was not that he had believed that Juliana would have corrupted his sisters, more that he could not credit their naïve folly in seeking out the most notorious widow in the *ton*. He suspected that Clara was the instigator. For all her idleness, Clara was not stupid, and Martin knew that when she wanted something she had a pig-headed determination that would overcome most obstacles. And what she had wanted was to talk to Lady Juliana Myfleet. Not to him. None of them wanted to talk to him. Brandon would not talk to him and Kitty and Clara preferred Juliana. It was unaccountable—and annoying.

Martin looked at his sisters. They were looking both guilty and apprehensive, wilting in their seats. Martin felt his anger drain away. He did not want his siblings to be afraid of him. That made him feel quite hollow with horror.

He was aware that Juliana had stood up and was drifting towards him with a social smile pinned on her face. She held out a hand. Martin gritted his teeth and bowed to her. There was a look on her face that said she was well aware of how he was feeling—and also that she was aware that he would not make a scene in front of his sisters. Her perfume enfolded him. It was the light, sweet scent of lilies. It made him think of soft skin and tumbled auburn hair and it sent his senses into a spin. He tried to concentrate. This was not the time to become distracted by Lady Juliana Myfleet's undeniable physical attractions, nor his somewhat contrary feelings for her.

'Good afternoon, Mr Davencourt,' Juliana said. 'Will you take a cup of tea with us?'

Martin almost refused, but then he saw Clara's look of anguish and wiped the black frown from his face.

'That would be pleasant,' he said, in a tone of voice that suggested the contrary. He took a seat opposite the sofa and his sisters wilted further under his scrutiny.

'Martin…' Kitty said, almost in a whisper. 'We came…'

'Kitty and Clara were kind enough to come to call on me,' Juliana said smoothly, pouring Martin a cup. 'Milk, Mr Davencourt? Sugar?'

'No sugar. Thank you,' Martin said automatically. 'There was no need to call on Lady Juliana, girls. I had already visited to convey my sense of obligation for her kindness.'

He saw the faint, cynical smile touch Juliana's lips and felt annoyed all over again.

Clara blushed. 'I thought that Lady Juliana might—' she began, then broke off as Kitty kicked her ankle.

'Might what?' Martin asked.

'Might have picked up the reticule that Kitty dropped at Lady Badbury's rout,' Juliana said. 'Alas, I had not.'

Martin looked at her. He knew she was lying. He knew that she knew he knew. He also knew she did not care. There was a definite challenge in the tilt of her chin, as though she was daring him to question her.

'I understand that Kitty and Clara are without a chaperon at the moment, Mr Davencourt,' Juliana continued. 'Will you be escorting them yourself in future? A male chaperon could become all the rage!'

Clara smothered a giggle.

The conversation languished. Neither the girls nor Juliana seemed inclined to contribute anything and Martin was sure Juliana was being deliberately silent in order to discomfit him. He wondered what on earth they could have been discussing when he arrived. Just for a moment, when the door had opened, Clara had looked excited and Kitty more animated than he remembered ever seeing her. Then he had come in and spoiled it all. He drained his teacup.

'Well…come along, Kitty, come along, Clara,' he said lamely.

In the carriage on the short journey back to Laverstock Gardens he determined to impress on his sisters the imprudence of calling upon fast widows. The conversation did not go at all well.

'Why did you feel the necessity to call on Lady Juliana, girls?' he asked mildly.

Kitty pressed her lips together and Clara evaded his gaze. 'We wished to thank her for her kindness to Kitty, Martin. Oh, and to ask about the reticule, of course.'

Martin ignored the repetition of the lie. 'But I had told

you that I would call to convey our appreciation for her generosity. There was no need for you to do the same. Indeed, it was quite inappropriate.'

Clara's plump shoulders lifted in a little shrug. Martin tried again.

'I would prefer that you did not call on Lady Juliana again. Both of you.'

There was a silence. Kitty nodded dispiritedly but Martin could tell that Clara was working up to something like a volcano about to blow her top. He pressed the point.

'Is that agreed, Clara?'

Clara bounced. 'Why, Martin? Why can we not call on Lady Juliana?'

'Lady Juliana is not the sort of lady you should associate with, Clara,' Martin said severely.

'Why not?'

Martin was reminded of the days when he had been a youth and his little sisters would follow him around and ask him questions all the time. They were the sort of questions that often had very difficult answers. Some things had not changed. He sighed.

'Because she is not a lady of good reputation.'

'Why not?'

Martin glared. 'Clara, I am sure you have reached an age where you understand about good and bad reputation. Lady Juliana has a bad reputation. She is a gambler and—'

'And?'

'And an undesirable influence!' Martin finished.

'Do you think that Kitty and I could be easily led, Martin?' Clara's gaze was guileless but Martin was not fooled. He repressed the desire to snap.

'I would hope not. But it can do you no good—'

'Particularly if we were to meet some *wicked* gentlemen

whilst we were visiting Lady Juliana,' Clara said, with a pleasurable shiver. 'Araminta says that Lady Juliana knows some very wicked gentlemen.'

Martin could feel the situation slipping from his grasp. 'Clara—'

Clara looked at him. 'I *like* Lady Juliana.' She gave Martin a searching look from her big blue eyes. 'Kitty likes her, too. So does Brandon. *You* like Lady Juliana, too, do you not, Martin? I have watched you watching her.'

Martin ran a hand through his fair hair.

'Clara, please. That is neither here nor there. Brandon and I may keep the sort of company that it is not suitable for you to do.'

'How unfair!'

Martin gritted his teeth. He knew she was running rings around him. He knew that in all logical senses, she were right. 'Neither you, nor Kitty, will see Lady Juliana again.'

There was a pause.

'Why not?' Clara asked.

Martin frowned. 'Because I say so.'

Clara's blue eyes stared at him accusingly. Even Kitty looked reproachful. Martin remembered that he had always disliked it when his parents had given him that particular answer to a question. It had not been a good enough reason when they were children and Martin knew it was not good enough now.

'You are ten minutes late, Mr Davencourt.' Juliana greeted Martin coolly on his return to Portman Square.

'I beg your pardon?' Martin raised his brows. He was girded for battle and this apparent *non sequitur* threw him slightly.

Juliana glanced at the clock ostentatiously. She itemised the timings on her fingers. 'Ten minutes to deliver your sisters back to Laverstock Gardens, five minutes to turn around and ten minutes to drive back here. Five and twenty minutes. You are ten minutes late.'

Martin walked across to the fireplace. 'How did you know that I would come back?'

Juliana threw him a mocking glance. 'Come, come, Mr Davencourt! I knew that you would have to come back in order to say all those things that you were too polite to discuss whilst your sisters were here.'

Martin allowed himself a small grin. He had to admire her coolness. She looked completely composed, but for the pulse that beat in the hollow of her throat, just above the silver half moon. He found himself riveted at the sight of it and pulled his gaze away with difficulty.

'Would you like to tell me what it is we have to discuss?' he invited softly.

Juliana gave an elegant little shrug. 'If it saves you the trouble. What was the phrase you used before?' She squared her shoulders. 'You would like me to stay away from your sisters. They are young and impressionable and you do not wish them to be subject to my bad influence.'

Martin gave her a measured look. 'Thank you. I believe you have it almost word perfect.'

'I believe I do. Did you tell Kitty and Clara to stay away from *me*, Mr Davencourt? They were the ones who sought me out, after all, not vice versa.'

'I am aware. They will not be doing it again.'

Juliana turned away. Her voice held biting sarcasm. 'You must have been relieved to find Clara and Kitty blamelessly drinking tea, Mr Davencourt, and not indulging in any of the vices that this house can offer.'

'I was relieved, certainly, but not surprised.' Martin

matched her sangfroid with his own. 'I scarce imagined the girls to have stepped into a den of iniquity, Lady Juliana. That is putting it too strongly. But I confess I wish that they had had the sense to see that it is not appropriate for them to call here.'

Juliana pulled a face. 'Inappropriate. What a damning word. I found both your sisters delightful company, Mr Davencourt. Unlike you, they do not suffer from an excess of disapproval.'

Martin felt profoundly irritated. 'Lady Juliana, do I have your word that you will not approach either Kitty or Clara in future?'

'My word?' Juliana's sparkling green eyes mocked him. She walked across to him and tilted her head to study his face. Martin found her scrutiny slightly unnerving. 'How much credence do you attach to my word, Mr Davencourt?'

Martin shifted. 'I would like to believe that you would honour it—'

'But?'

'But after the episode in Hyde Park I do not know how far I may trust you. I know you said that you regretted it, but…'

'But?'

'There is always the possibility that you might do something like that again. You are unpredictable, Lady Juliana.'

'To the point of folly, you imply.' Juliana grimaced. Martin had the sudden, startling impression that he had hurt her, though her expression did not betray the fact. She moved away.

'One cannot fault you on your plain-speaking, Mr Davencourt. You, too, are honest—to the point of cruelty. Well, let there be no misunderstandings. I will not approach your sisters, but if they speak to me then I shall certainly not send them away. I like Kitty and Clara, Mr Davencourt, and I believe that they need…someone to talk to.'

Martin narrowed his eyes. He felt a hot frustration at the manner in which matters were turning out—and a sinking dread that she was right. He had made precious little progress when he spoke to Kitty and Clara. It had been like wading through treacle and he had had the persistent feeling that he was missing something.

'I do not wish for that person to be you, Lady Juliana.'

'No?' Juliana arched a brow. 'Your new wife might be more suitable?'

'Indeed.'

Juliana spun around to face him in a welter of copper silk. 'Why is that, Mr Davencourt? Spit the words out. Do not boggle at them.'

Martin stared at her. 'I thought that it was understood. My new wife will be a guiding influence. You are—'

'Yes?'

Martin sighed. 'It is not that I believe you would deliberately act as a bad influence, Lady Juliana.' He swallowed. 'I believe you have more integrity than to lead my sisters astray on purpose…'

'Thank you.' Juliana's jewel-bright gaze was fixed on him, pinning him to the spot. 'And yet you will not take that risk and trust them to my company.'

Martin made a slight gesture. 'You must see how others would perceive it! It is not my opinion of you that counts here, but the judgement of society. If Kitty and Clara are seen to spend time with you, it cannot but damage their reputations.'

Juliana turned away from him in a rustle of silks. Martin took a deep breath. He felt the same regret as when he had found her crying the corridor at Lady Babba-combe's ball. An extraordinary part of him wanted to take her in his arms and comfort her, and yet he could not. They both knew that what he was saying was true.

'I merely wish to protect Kitty and Clara,' Martin said quietly.

Juliana nodded. 'Yes, I understand that.' She looked up again and her eyes were quite dry. 'You had best find your bride quickly, Mr Davencourt. Your sisters need someone to advise them.'

'And they thought to ask you?' The words were out before Martin could help himself. He thought he saw Juliana wince, but he was not sure.

'Well, they did not ask you,' she said coolly. 'And very wise of them, too. What do you know of female fashion, Mr Davencourt? Do you know which gloves go with a walking dress and which suit an evening gown? What would you tell a young lady who thought she did not wish to marry? Or one who thought that she did but had chosen an ineligible gentleman?'

Martin felt a chill. 'Are you saying that my sisters are in *love?*'

Juliana smiled serenely. 'Not at all, Mr Davencourt. But if they were, would you know how to advise them?' She met his gaze. 'They do not wish to speak to you, but they choose to speak to me. That should tell you something. Good day, Mr Davencourt.'

Juliana felt cold after Martin had gone. The house, which had echoed with laughter for the duration of Kitty and Clara's visit, now seemed very silent. It felt lonely.

Juliana sent for a maid to light the fire, then sat down beside it and tried to get warm. She told herself that it did not matter that she would not see Kitty and Clara in future, that she did not care about the Davencourt family, but suddenly the words seemed rather hóllow. She was horrified to find that in a short space of time she had become drawn in. She actually cared.

Juliana shivered. It had been very silly of her to start to believe that she could be a permanent fixture in the lives of Martin's siblings. She had not realised that her thoughts were tending that way until Martin had taken it all away from her. And now she felt utterly bereft. It was foolish, but it was true.

Juliana jumped up and started riffling through the invitations on the mantelpiece. She had neglected her old friends a little bit recently. Still, they were always there to fall back on. Emma Wren was hosting a dinner party that night and it might be fun…

Juliana sat down again, the invitations scattering from her hand. She did not want to sit playing cards in Emma's overheated rooms, listening to the malicious gossip, fending off suggestive remarks from Jasper Colling and others. She wanted to be in Lady Eaton's ballroom, trying to find a beau for Kitty, watching Clara engineer an introduction to the Duke of Fleet, as she surely would, and guessing for whom Brandon had a secret passion. She wanted to be *involved*. But she was not a part of it. Not really. She never had been and Martin had recalled her to that fact.

She stood up and rang the bell for Hattie. If Emma's dinner party was all the entertainment on offer, then that would have to do.

Chapter Eight

Martin Davencourt sat listening to an exquisite Italian aria and wondering why he felt so damnably blue-devilled. Beside him sat Clara, her face rapt, looking most elegant in rose-pink gauze. Beyond Clara was Kitty, slender in primrose yellow and at the end of the row, Brandon was fidgeting with his cuffs and making no attempt to appear interested in the music. Behind Martin, out of sight but most forcibly in mind, sat Lady Juliana Myfleet. Although she was three rows back and to his right, Martin was sharply aware of her physical presence.

It was a week since he had last seen her and Martin had thought about her for every one of those seven days. He had wondered if he should call on her to apologise for their last meeting, when he knew he had been utterly pompous and offensive. He had almost gone to see her—until he had gone to a ball and seen Juliana hanging on Edward Ashwick's arm. The sight had made him out of proportion angry and the fact that Ashwick was her escort tonight seemed like another good reason to keep his distance.

Across the aisle, Serena Alcott leaned forward and caught Martin's eye. She smiled and nodded and Martin smiled in return, masking his irritability. When the aria came to an end and the interval was announced, Serena made a little beckoning gesture to summon him to her side. Martin's heart sank, but his good manners prompted him to go across to her.

Serena welcomed him by patting the empty seat next to her. Martin sat, dredging up some social conversation.

'Are you enjoying the music, Mrs Alcott?'

'Oh, yes, indeed.' Serena fluttered her lashes at him. 'It is very fine.'

'Did you not think the high notes a trifle—?'

'Sharp? No, indeed. *La Perla* is outstandingly good.'

'I thought her singing very—'

'Good? Yes, she is marvellously versatile, is she not?'

'This is a perfect room for a—'

'Recital? Indeed, it is. Perfect.'

Martin frowned slightly. He was aware that Serena was watching him very closely, a tiny frown on her brow, as though she was trying to anticipate what he might say next. It was rather disconcerting, as though she had already adopted the habit some married couples had of reading each other's minds—and finishing their sentences for them. Martin tried again.

'Mrs Duston always hosts an—'

'Elegant event? Yes, she does.'

It was uncanny. Martin could not believe that he had not noticed it before. He wondered if he would ever be permitted to finish a sentence again in his life. He got to his feet.

'Would you like me to fetch you some—?'

'Lemonade? Oh, yes, thank you.'

'I will just go to the—'

'Refreshment room. Do bring yourself some wine as well.'

Martin gave her a hard stare. 'Thank you. I will.'

He beat a hasty retreat, wincing when he looked over his shoulder and Serena gave him a coy smile and a little wave. His humour was not improved at the sight of Brandon chatting easily with Juliana Myfleet. She looked animated and supremely elegant in a gown of old gold, a matching circlet of gold nestling in her hair. Martin noticed that she had despatched Edward Ashwick to procure Kitty a glass of lemonade. Kitty was looking pink and happy and was watching Edward as he made his way across the room. Martin felt a prickle of speculation. Kitty could do a great deal worse than Edward Ashwick, but had Juliana deliberately thrown them into each other's company? Ashwick was her most constant beau, after all, and the only respectable one at that. ·

He took a glass of wine for himself and was about to pick up another of lemonade when he saw a flash of rose pink. Clara was standing just outside the door of the card room, engaged in a spirited conversation with a gentleman whom Martin identified as the Duke of Fleet. For a moment Martin was so riveted to see Clara chatting animatedly to any gentleman that he overlooked the fact that the Duke of Fleet was a rake and a gambler, and as such the most ineligible suitor imaginable for his sister. Then he frowned fiercely. By rights Clara should never even have met Fleet, let alone be talking to him with such enthusiasm.

He was about to step forward and intervene when he saw something that made him stop dead. Juliana detached herself politely from Brandon and caught Clara's eye. Clara, apparently obedient to Juliana's smallest gesture, excused herself prettily from the Duke of Fleet and went across to her. Martin saw Juliana say something quietly to Clara and shake her head, saw Clara look obstinate and Juliana shake her head again. He could not hear a word but he understood the byplay. Juliana was warning Clara away from Fleet and his stubborn little sister was actually listening. Martin let his breath go in a sigh of mingled astonishment and admiration.

As though aware of his scrutiny, Juliana looked up and their eyes met. He saw her falter in whatever she was saying to Clara and he felt a fierce pleasure at having so undeniable an effect upon her. For a moment he held her gaze trapped in his own. He saw a faint blush come into her cheeks, saw her glance flicker away and return to him as though drawn irresistibly back, and he was shot through with a desire so strong it made him rock back on his heels.

'Martin?'

Martin took a pull on himself. Brandon was looking at him quizzically.

'Were you having a somewhat laborious encounter with Mrs Alcott, Martin? You looked as though you had swallowed a prune.'

Martin took a mouthful of wine. 'Was it that obvious?'

Brandon laughed. 'Painfully.'

Martin sighed. 'I wonder if it is too late to—'

'Withdraw your suit?'

Martin gave his brother a darkling stare. 'Pray do not start doing the same thing yourself! Does she speak to everyone like that?'

'I fear so.'

'Why did I not notice before?'

Brandon smothered another grin. 'She is very pretty. Perhaps you were besotted?'

Martin stared. It seemed irrelevant to be told that Serena Alcott was pretty when the only woman he seemed capable of thinking about was Juliana. 'Do not be an arrant fool, Brandon!'

'I?' Brandon took his wine and sauntered towards the

door, still smiling. 'I suggest that it is you who has been the fool here, Martin. You are paying court to the wrong woman and getting yourself in a shocking muddle. Lady Juliana Myfleet is charming and kind and generous-spirited. All the things that Mrs Alcott is not. But I doubt that Lady Juliana would have you. She is too good for you.'

They looked at each other for a moment, and then Martin started to laugh.

'Devil take it, Brandon, are you offering me advice on my matrimonial plans?'

Brandon shrugged. He did not smile. 'What is it, Martin? You can give advice, but you cannot take it?'

Martin winced. 'Perhaps you are right,' he said slowly. 'I do not like taking risks.'

A hint of a smile came into Brandon's eyes. 'I am no gambler,' he said, 'but I understand that it is sometimes worth risking all to gain all.'

He raised his glass in a half-mocking salute and went out, and Martin took his drink out on to the terrace for a little fresh air, completely forgetting Serena Alcott's lemonade.

He recalled Juliana's words: *Remember that you have no very good opinion of me,* and like an echo, there was Brandon: *She is too good for you.*

And perhaps his brother was correct, Martin thought. He had been shallow and disapproving. He had ignored the arguments of his own heart in favour of the harsh judgements of other people. He had ignored his instincts out of respect for convention, and there was nothing brave or admirable about that. He had not really given Juliana Myfleet a chance.

A second later, he saw her. She was standing in the shadows at the far end of the balustrade, where the honeysuckle twined over the old stones of the terrace and filled the air with its wistful scent. There was something wistful about Juliana's stance as well. She was leaning on the stone rail and looking out into the dark and there was a very slight slump to her shoulders that spoke of vulnerability and loneliness. Martin felt it like a kick to the stomach.

He must have made some small movement, for Juliana turned and looked at him, her eyes wide and dark.

'Good evening, Mr Davencourt.'

Martin bowed. Every one of his senses seemed to be on the edge. He wanted to speak to her. The subject did not matter. He wanted to touch her, to feel that silky auburn hair beneath his fingers. He wanted to kiss her until they were both trembling. He took a step towards her, then another.

Juliana did not move. She looked very slight in the dark shadows. For a brief moment, Martin battled against the strong protective urge that she always roused in him, along with the equally powerful and devastating desire. If this was all an act on her part, if it were only a game, then he was about to make the biggest mistake of his life. Schooled to rational decision-making, his mind shied away from risk and danger. And yet, she was worth it...

He took the last step to her side. They were too close now to do anything other than kiss. He could smell the wistful scent of the honeysuckle and beneath it, a faint echo, the sweetness of Juliana's lily perfume. He could feel her warmth and hear her breathing. He put out a hand.

And she stepped back from him. He heard her breath catch in her throat, and then she had broken away from him and was gone, in a whirl of gold, and Martin felt colder than he had ever felt before in his life.

The faint strains of the orchestra drifted through the

open windows. There was a step; Serena Alcott was hunting him along the terrace. Her shadow drew nearer, her breathy whispers calling his name.

'Martin? Where are you, my dear?'

Martin's impatience swelled to almost tidal proportions. Without pausing to think, he slipped away from her, through the terrace doors and back into the recital room.

'I suppose that Joss sent you,' Juliana said crossly. Her hand shook a little and she slopped the tea into the saucer as she handed her sister-in-law her cup. 'There was no need for you to call, you know. I am perfectly well!'

'Certainly you sound much the same as normal,' Amy Tallant said calmly. 'I called because I was passing and I remembered that you had looked quite poorly at Lady Stockley's rout two days ago, and I wondered—'

'If I was drunk? If I had finally lost all my money?' Juliana picked crossly at the cake crumbs on her skirt. There was something so irritating about Amy. She was always so *good*. And it did not help that she was right. Juliana had been feeling very miserable indeed for the last few weeks and she was still feeling wretched now.

She had seen the Davencourt girls a few times in the past fortnight, though not by design. They had met in Bond Street, where Clara had fallen on her with cries of delight and Kitty had asked a little more quietly for advice on a scarf to complement her gown. They had exchanged a few words at various balls and at the theatre, and they had chatted at the musicale. Brandon had confessed that he had still not told Martin about his romantic entanglement. Clara was still stubbornly pursuing the Duke of Fleet, but at least Kitty had gained a respectable suitor. As for Martin, there was nothing there for her, despite the peculiar affinity that seemed to bind them together. It had taken all her willpower to leave him on the terrace at the musicale, but she knew it had been the only thing to do.

She turned back to Amy. 'I thought that you and Joss were supposed to be going to the country,' she said irritably. 'Why are you still here?'

'Joss was delayed by business.' There was a flicker of annoyance in Amy's eyes. 'If you want to tell me what is the matter, Juliana—'

'No, thank you!'

Amy got to her feet. 'I sometimes wonder why I bother to call at all. I am clearly wasting my time.'

There was a great big lump in Juliana's throat. 'Yes, you are. Please do not put yourself to the trouble again.'

Amy gave Juliana a very straight look. She put her cup down untouched and got to her feet. 'Very well, I won't. Goodbye.'

Juliana then surprised both herself and her sister-in-law by bursting into tears. She was annoyed and discomposed.

'Damnation! That is the second time I have done that in a month. I cannot think what has got into me.' She looked up to see Amy staring. 'What on earth is the matter with you?'

'I did not know that you could cry.'

Juliana glared. 'Well, of course I can! Everybody can do it!'

Amy smiled. 'Yes, but I thought that you might have some physical impairment that prevented you. You always seem so collected.'

Ridiculously, Juliana felt the flicker of an answering smile starting. It stopped the tears at once. She sniffed.

'I do not suppose you have a handkerchief, Amy? I never carry one because I do not usually need it.'

Amy passed a handkerchief over without comment. Juliana felt herself warming to her. Cloying sympathy or prosy comments would have been the worse thing to come out with. Amy kept silent.

Juliana mopped her eyes, looked at the handkerchief and handed it back. Amy pulled an expressive face and tucked it away in her reticule.

'I will be going, then,' she said.

'No,' Juliana said suddenly. She felt a strange, shaky feeling. She looked at Amy and tried not to look too pleading. 'Please stay and have some tea with me, Amy.'

'Very well,' Amy said. She sat down again. There was a little silence whilst they looked at each other.

'So,' Amy said slowly, 'what is all this about?'

Juliana hesitated. 'I fear that I have fallen in love,' she said. And if, she thought savagely, you so much as say you are sorry, Amy, I shall regret this whole episode and throw the teapot at you.

'I see,' Amy said.

'I suppose,' Juliana said sharply, 'you thought that I might be physically incapable of doing that as well?'

'Not at all.' Amy sipped her tea delicately. 'With whom have you fallen in love?'

'Well…' Juliana avoided her gaze. 'With the entire Davencourt family, I think.'

Amy choked. Delicately. She put her cup down and fixed Juliana with her steady brown eyes. 'Good lord, Juliana! The whole family? How did that happen?'

Juliana took a deep breath. She told Amy everything; all about Kitty's gambling and her unhappiness in town, and Clara's sleepiness and her penchant for unsuitable men, and Brandon's secret romance… Amy nodded and asked a question or two, but mainly she listened.

'And then Martin Davencourt pointed out to me that I was an inappropriate person for the girls to know,' Juliana finished. She met Amy's gaze. 'I felt such a fool, Amy!

I realised that I had secretly hoped I might be permitted to see them, and suddenly Mr Davencourt was pulling the carpet from under my feet.' She shook her head. 'I cannot think how I let it happen, and so quickly.'

'You fell in love with the idea of a family,' Amy said. 'Just as you said. Such things do not happen to order.'

'And now I feel sick—really *ill*—at the prospect of never seeing them again. I cannot believe that I am being so feeble-minded!' Juliana leaped to her feet and paced across the room. 'I never behave like this!'

Amy sat back. 'I expect it is a shock for you.'

'It is! I do not like it. What do you think is the cure?'

Amy shook her head. 'I cannot tell you that, Juliana. I am not even sure that I know the answer.'

'Is it time? Or another interest?' Juliana flung out an arm. Now that she had started confiding she did not want to stop. She had never had a female confidant before, for she had never felt comfortable enough to talk sincerely to Emma Wren, but now she felt surprisingly good. Amy was very easy to talk to.

'I had thought that perhaps I could take up needlework,' she said, a little sadly.

Amy smothered a laugh. 'Do you truly believe that you would feel the same passion for embroidery as you do for the Davencourts?'

Juliana sighed. She knew Amy was right. She had hated needlework even as a child.

'Then perhaps I could buy a dog? They are supposed to be very loving and faithful.'

'It is a thought.' Amy bent a searching glance on her sister-in-law. 'What about Emma Wren and Jasper Colling and all your old friends? Could they not console you?'

'I do not wish them to do so,' Juliana said. She sighed.

'It sounds very ungrateful in me—disloyal, even—but I am not sure I wish to seek out their company again.'

'Why ever not?'

There was a silence. 'They are not the sort of people I admire,' Juliana said slowly. 'Oh, there was a time not so long ago when I thought their company amusing. In a way I still do. But it was as though we were all diverting ourselves because we had nothing better to do with our time. Now…I do not know… Somehow that is not enough.'

Amy nodded. 'You need a cause and you thought that you had found it with the Davencourts.'

'I suppose so.' Juliana gave her a watery smile. 'It is rather melancholy of me, is it not?'

'Not really. I expect you could find some other purpose to fill the space. Climbing boys, or orphanages, or the rural poor.'

Juliana grimaced. It was not an appealing thought. 'Gracious, I am sure that I could never be so good! That is quite beyond me.'

'Well, perhaps we may come up with a cause more appropriate to you. I will give it some thought.' Amy passed her cup over for a refill and helped herself to a piece of cake.

'You have mentioned the Davencourt family,' she said slowly, 'but what about Mr Davencourt himself, Juliana?'

Juliana turned away and made a pretence of checking to see how much tea was left in the pot. Now that she had confided so much in Amy she was starting to regret it. Her sister-in-law was surprisingly acute.

'What of him?'

'Do you like him, too?'

Juliana frowned. 'Certainly not. Mr Davencourt is rude and judgemental. Besides, he is to marry that henwit, our cousin Serena Alcott.'

Amy nodded. 'I had heard as much. How dull for him. Serena is such a bore.'

'They deserve each other.' Juliana pressed her hands together. The thought of Martin marrying Serena was a painful one. 'Truth to tell, Amy, I am a little smitten by Mr Davencourt. For all his problems with his brothers and sisters he does care about them deeply and I want…'

'Yes?'

'I suppose I want someone to care about me like that. I want someone to love me the way Joss loves you.' Juliana tossed her head defiantly. 'How mawkish is that?'

'Not very mawkish. In fact, I should say that it is quite reasonable.'

'At any rate, I am persuaded that I shall be over it quite soon. I suppose it is a bit like the admiration I had for Mr Taupin, my dancing master. I thought him most dashing and was smitten with his charms.'

Amy raised her brows. 'Except that you can only have been about fourteen at the time.'

Juliana sighed. 'The principle is the same. I thought that I admired him, but really it was just a type of schoolgirl infatuation.'

'And that is what you think you feel for Martin Davencourt? A schoolgirl infatuation?'

'Well…'

'Has he kissed you?'

Juliana felt shocked. Her sister-in-law was nowhere near as prim as she looked. 'Amy! What sort of question is that?'

'Well, has he? Surely you must know how you feel if he has.'

Juliana bit her lip. 'He has. Of course, he should not have done, if he is to marry Serena. It was quite ungentlemanly of him. Men are such a grave disappointment, are they not?'

'Frequently, but not always. Do not change the subject, Juliana.' Amy was stern. 'Was it disappointing kissing Martin Davencourt?'

Juliana frowned and smiled at the same time. 'Not exactly.'

'What was it like?'

Juliana hesitated. Her smile grew. 'Oh…warm and sweet and exciting and very, very passionate.' She caught Amy's eye. 'Why are you looking like that?'

Amy laughed. 'You are in love with him, you know.'

Juliana jumped up again, agitated. Hearing someone else put her own thoughts into words made it somehow more true—and more terrifying.

'No, I cannot be. It is quite out of the question.'

There was a twinkle in Amy's eye. 'Love often is.' She sighed. 'There is something powerfully attractive about a man of integrity, is there not?'

Juliana sighed too. 'There can be no future in it. I shall not marry again. I cannot. And Martin cannot marry me! It would be quite unsuitable.'

Amy burst out laughing. 'You know, Juliana, I do believe that you are the one making the difficulties here. Stop protesting and let it happen!' She checked the clock. 'I am sorry, but I am promised to Annis Ashwick for luncheon.' She hesitated. 'Perhaps I could call again.'

'Of course,' Juliana said. 'Thank you, Amy.'

She was surprised how disappointed she felt to lose Amy's company. Part of her even wanted to be invited to join the luncheon party. The thought of sitting staring at her own four walls all afternoon was intolerable.

The doorbell rang and Segsbury ushered in Emma

Wren. Emma looked a little startled to see Amy and gave her a cool nod of greeting, ignoring her immediately.

'Juliana, my love!' she said, in her affected drawl. 'I am for Bond Street, where I intend to spend vast amounts of money and entertain myself in the process. Do you come with me?'

Juliana saw Amy watching her. She looked from her sister-in-law to her erstwhile friend. She had no burning desire to spend the day in Emma's company, but there was loneliness…and then there was Bond Street and Emma's familiar chatter. She nodded.

'I shall be with you directly, Emma. Excuse me, Amy.'

Amy's expression did not change, but Juliana felt guilty and gave her sister-in-law a little, defiant smile.

'One must be entertained, Amy. After all, what else is there when one is disappointed in love?'

'I do not know what it is that Juliana wants,' Joss Tallant said to his wife later that day, in the privacy of their own bedroom. 'It seems to me that she does not know either.'

Amy had related the whole of her encounter with Juliana, and now she put her hairbrush down slowly on the dressing table and turned towards her husband.

'She wants two things, I believe—Martin Davencourt and…a sense of purpose.'

Joss raised a brow. 'Are the two not one and the same thing?'

Amy gave him a hard stare. 'How arrogant you are! A woman's purpose need not be *entirely* dependent on a man, you know!'

Joss laughed. 'I beg your pardon! I merely meant that if Juliana were to wed, that would give her life a purpose.'

'But it is not enough on its own.' Amy crinkled her

brow. 'Juliana is quite a managing kind of woman, curious as that may seem. She is nowhere near the indolent pleasure-seeker we all imagine. Look at the way in which she has tried to help Martin's brothers and sisters. She needs a cause.'

'A political wife,' Joss said slowly.

'Why not? Juliana is charming and clever and well organised. She could be formidable.'

'She is not interested in politics.'

Amy shrugged. 'That does not really matter, Joss. She is intelligent enough to learn.'

'True. But would she be interested? Ju has a mind like a butterfly when she is bored. And can you see her as surrogate mother to seven children?'

'Surrogate sister. It is not as bad as you make it sound. They all love her already. Have you not observed how they seek her company? Besides, Brandon Davencourt is old enough to go his own way and I believe that Kitty will marry soon.'

Joss looked at his wife in the liveliest astonishment. 'Will she? But I thought she had no admirers?'

'Oh, Juliana has already found Kitty a country-loving suitor,' Amy smiled mischievously. 'Did you not observe that Edward Ashwick was paying Miss Davencourt a great deal of attention at the musicale last night?'

'Edward Ashwick? Good lord!'

'You never see what is under your nose,' Amy said contentedly.

'It seems not. I thought that Edward was Ju's staunchest admirer!'

'So he was. Almost to the point of habit, do you not think? I thought it remarkably clever of Juliana to throw Kitty in his path last night.'

Joss stared. 'I had no notion.'

'Of course not.' Amy smiled. 'I shall be interested to see whom she chooses for Miss Clara. Once she has persuaded her against Seb Fleet, of course.'

'There is always Jasper Colling,' her husband commented, with heavy irony.

Amy shuddered. 'Even Fleet is preferable to Colling!'

'And is Martin Davencourt suitable for Juliana?' Joss enquired, with only slightly less sarcasm.

'He certainly has her measure. She wishes to live up to his good opinion.'

'Good God!' Joss looked thunderstruck. 'Juliana is far more accustomed to living down to her reputation!' He frowned. 'I have not seen any sign of partiality for Juliana in Martin Davencourt, all the same.'

'Oh, pooh!' Amy gave him a scornful look. 'When he watches her all the time? I have said that you cannot see what is under your nose.'

'Probably not. Can Davencourt see it, though? I doubt it, since he is as good as betrothed to our cousin Serena.'

'Yes.' Amy tilted her head to study Joss's reflection in the mirror. 'That is unfortunate, but he has made her no formal offer.'

Joss smiled a little. 'Do you require an ally? If so, I may have the very person for you. I had a letter from Papa yesterday, saying that he had heard from Aunt Beatrix and that she was on her way to town.'

Amy's eyes lit up. 'Aunt Trix! The very person! She detests Serena, does she not?'

Joss frowned. 'Yes… She calls her the milksop maid.'

'Capital,' Amy said happily. She caught sight of Joss's puzzled expression and burst out laughing. 'Between us I am sure that Aunt Trix and I may bring Martin and Juliana together. And deal with Serena if need be!'

Chapter Nine

Juliana roused herself slowly from her laudanum-induced stupor. Her bedroom was dark and dim, and she had only a vague memory of the previous day and night, which had begun with the shopping spree to Bond Street and ended with a drunken dinner at Emma Wren's, at which Jasper Colling had climbed the drawing-room walls using the candle sconces as footholds, and had swung from the crystal chandelier. Everyone had screamed with laughter until Colling had lost his grip and had fallen on to the dinner table, landing in the middle of the haunch of venison. After that they had drunk some more, played some piquet and she had lost to Emma and to Colling as well.

Juliana rolled over and groaned. The evening had been an utter bore and she could not pretend otherwise. She had sat like the spectre at the feast, wishing that she were elsewhere. Her old friends and old haunts had finally lost all their appeal, and since she had nothing with which to replace them, she felt herself to be in a very strange no man's land indeed.

Juliana had no clear recollection of tumbling into bed and now it seemed far too early to wake up. From downstairs came the sound of crashing furniture and voices raised in bullying confrontation. Throwing a peignoir over her nightdress, Juliana hurried to the top of the stairs, intent on scolding the clumsy servants who were evidently incapable of moving the furniture quietly.

The scene that met her eyes was shocking. Segsbury was standing in the middle of the hall, hands on hips, a picture of impotent misery as two muscular men in shiny black suits marched in and out through the front door with pieces of the drawing-room furniture. They chipped the corner of the escritoire on the way out, causing Juliana to wince. She flew down the stairs.

'What the devil is going on here?'

Both men stopped dead, dropping the chair on the floor with a crunching jolt. Juliana winced. They appraised her thoroughly and one, with a cheeky face and rubicund cheeks, pursed his mouth into an appreciative whistle.

'Cor! How about arranging a different method of payment, darlin'?'

Juliana felt sick. The memory of Joss talking about her debts flashed through her mind. She had forgotten all about it. Or chosen to ignore it, more accurately. How much had she spent yesterday? How much had she lost last night? She glared at the men.

'I asked what the devil you were doing with my furniture?'

'Takin' it as payment, darlin',' the bailiff said. They picked up the chair again and crashed cheerfully through the front door. 'Forty thousand pounds' worth should just about clear the house out.'

'For pity's sake!' Juliana clutched her brow. She could see the ranks of people lining up on the street outside, peering in, discussing what was happening. So many people gawking at her in her peignoir. She turned furiously to the older bailiff.

'What is the meaning of this? You could at least have had the courtesy to call me before you start to empty my house!'

The man scratched his head. 'Mr Needham's bought up all your debts, ma'am. Told us to collect on them. No time for courtesy, ma'am, not when there's work to be done.'

'I do apologise, my lady.' Segsbury was looking shattered. 'There was no time to wake you before these gentlemen started to denude the house—'

'I would have woken soon enough if these loobies had started carting off my bedroom furniture with me still in there,' Juliana said furiously. She swung round on the bailiffs, who were whistling cheerfully as they returned for a fourth load. 'For pity's sake, bring those items back into the drawing room and put them precisely where you found them. I have a diamond set that will be sufficient and more to settle Mr Needham's demands.'

The older bailiff looked dubious. The younger one licked his lips. 'Diamonds… Might be worth a look, Mr Maggs.'

'Aye, I suppose,' the older man said grudgingly. 'We can always come back.'

'Over my dead body,' Juliana said furiously. She followed them out into the hall and slammed the front door in the face of the crowd. 'I will fetch the jewellery and you will return the furniture from the back of your cart. Understood? And shut the damned door after you!'

She shot back up the stairs and into the bedroom, where she rummaged beneath her underwear to find the velvet case with the diamond necklace, earrings and bracelet. Joss was always telling her that she should keep her jewellery in the bank. Now she was glad that she did not. She had always hated the diamond set anyway. It had been a wedding present from her father and was far too heavy and old-fashioned to wear. She had never had the money to have it reset, nor the inclination to do so. She grimaced to think what the Marquis would say when he heard what she had done. No matter, it was too late now. If only she had not thrown away all those bills without reading them. But she had not needed the bills to know that there were so many debts. Gambling debts, bills for gowns from Bond Street's most fashionable couturiers, tradesmen's demands... She would be a laughing stock when this got around and it was all Joss's fault for being so obstinate about helping her...

Juliana sat down heavily on the edge of the bed, the diamonds still clasped in her hand. She knew that Joss was not really to blame. He had warned her that he would not fund her any longer and she had chosen to ignore him. This humiliation was all her own. Impatient, she threw the diamonds back in the case and hurried back down the stairs. Her bare feet were cold now. The front door was open again and a strong draught blew through. She could hear voices in the drawing room, the grumbles of the bailiffs as they lumped the furniture back into place. She was filled with fury.

'I thought I told you to close that damned door!' Juliana shrieked like a fishwife as she shot into the room. 'And if I find any of the furniture is damaged I shall sue Mr Needham for every penny he possesses!'

She stopped dead. An elderly lady was standing in the centre of the carpet, watching with lively interest as the bailiffs squeaked and creaked the furniture into place, swearing under their breath as they went. She was tall, thin, and very upright in grey silk and immaculate pearls. She turned as Juliana entered the room and her amber eyes lit with unholy amusement.

'Juliana, dear. I thought that I recognised your voice!'

'Aunt Beatrix!'

Juliana stared in horror. Then her gaze switched to the figure at Lady Beatrix Tallant's side. Martin Davencourt gave her back a very straight look in which the merest hint of a speculative gleam betrayed his amusement. Juliana suddenly became acutely conscious of the transparent nature of the peignoir, her bare feet, the tumble of her hair about her shoulders.

'What the devil are you doing here?' she demanded ungraciously. 'I thought that I had seen the back of you!'

Lady Beatrix raised her brows. 'Do you address me— or Mr Davencourt, Juliana dear?'

'Whichever! If the cap fits…'

'Hmm. Well, I am here because I am returned from my travels and need somewhere to stay.' Beatrix turned to Martin. 'Mr Davencourt is here because he most kindly offered to escort me from your brother's house. Which reminds me…' She frowned slightly. 'You are in a state of *dishabille*, my love, which is most inappropriate in front of a gentleman and quite unacceptable in front of tradesmen. Best to go and dress yourself. Hurry along now.'

Juliana saw Martin unsuccessfully try to repress a smile at Lady Beatrix's tone. She glared at him.

'Pray order yourself some tea whilst I am dressing, Aunt. Mr Davencourt, thank you for escorting Aunt Beatrix here. I am sure you will be gone when I come down…'

In this she was wrong, however. Some three-quarters of an hour later, Juliana went out into the conservatory to find Beatrix and Martin seated together on the sofa, partaking of tea and cake and looking extremely comfortable together. Juliana felt her irritation rise.

Lady Beatrix looked up as she came in, and beamed at her.

'It is so very kind of you to offer me a roof over my head, Juliana.'

'I was not aware that I had,' Juliana said crossly. She picked up the teapot and poured herself a cup. Lady Beatrix's air of old-lady distraction did not fool her. She knew her aunt had a mind as sharp as a needle and an astringent tongue to match.

Lady Beatrix poured a fresh cup for herself and Martin. She ignored Juliana's comment.

'I shall only be in London a short while, but whilst I am here it will be pleasant to have the company.'

'There are many good hotels these days,' Juliana said. 'Bertram's, or The Grand—'

'The Grand is very disappointing,' Martin said blandly. 'Though at least you would not be in danger of losing your bed whilst you slept, Lady Beatrix!'

Juliana shot him a poisonous look and ostentatiously turned away from him. She leaned across to Beatrix and rested her elbows on the table.

'Why could you not stay with Joss and Amy, Aunt Beatrix?'

Lady Beatrix smiled. 'Oh, they did press me to stay, but I knew that you needed me more, Juliana.' She shook her head sadly. 'I heard some dreadful tale when I was in Bath last week that you were intending to marry that man who disrupted Lady Bilton's dinner by snuffing the candles with his pistols.'

'Sir Jasper Colling,' Martin said.

'That is correct. Dreadful, common family.' Lady Beatrix shuddered. 'As for the pistol trick—so passé! Why,

Lord Dauntsey did that for the first time when I was a girl.'

'I have no intention of marrying Sir Jasper, so you may be easy on that score, ma'am,' Juliana snapped. 'Not that it is any business of anyone else.' She glared at Martin. 'Especially not you, sir.'

Martin smiled. 'Why *especially* not me?'

There was a warmth in his blue eyes that made Juliana feel suddenly overheated. She waved one of the footmen over. 'It is very hot in here, Milton. Pray open the top windows.'

Lady Beatrix smiled at her. 'I am so relieved to hear that you are not to marry Colling, my dear. These louche fellows can be most *fatally* attractive!' She gave Martin an approving smile. 'Now, if you were to choose a gentleman like Mr Davencourt…'

'I doubt that there are any other gentlemen like Mr Davencourt,' Juliana said. 'He is a complete original.'

Martin's smile grew. So did Juliana's impression that the conservatory was fast becoming the stuffiest place in London.

'I fear that Mr Davencourt is already spoken for, Aunt Trix,' she added. 'Your other niece, Serena, is the lucky lady to whose hand he aspires.'

Beatrix looked from one to the other. 'Serena Alcott. Dear me, Mr Davencourt. Dear me.'

'You should wish him happy,' Juliana pointed out.

'It would not make any difference if I did,' Lady Beatrix said sadly. 'No difference at all. May I pass you another piece of cake, Martin?'

'No, thank you. I must be leaving.' Martin got to his feet in leisurely fashion. 'I hope that it will be acceptable to call on you and see how you go on, Lady Beatrix?'

'Only if you do not bring that gooseish girl Serena with

you,' Lady Beatrix said, tucking into another piece of the walnut cake. 'But do call, Mr Davencourt, do call! I shall be settled here for several weeks!'

'Oh, no, you will not,' Juliana said under her breath, as she ushered Martin out of the conservatory.

'You are mightily bad-tempered this morning, Lady Juliana,' Martin observed, as they crossed the hall. 'I suppose it is the effect of being woken before eleven o'clock? Very difficult for you.'

Juliana glared at him. 'Thank you for bringing Lady Beatrix to plague me, sir.'

'You are very welcome. In many ways you are quite alike, you know.'

Juliana raised her brows. 'Indeed?'

'Both of you prefer plain speaking and neither of you suffer fools gladly.'

'That is true.' Juliana smiled a little, thinking of Serena Alcott.

'So I am persuaded that you will get on famously,' Martin said. He smiled at her. It was warm, intimate and it made her feel a little dizzy. It made Juliana forget that she was standing with him in her hallway and made her think of the strength of Martin's arms about her and the intimacy of his kiss. He took her hand.

'Lady Juliana, I am glad that I called this morning, for I need to talk to you.'

'I doubt it, sir,' Juliana said starchily, withdrawing her hand.

'On the contrary. I have been wanting to apologise—'

Juliana backed away. 'Handsome of you, Mr Davencourt, but I assure you it is not required.'

Martin followed her, trapping her between a pillar and a large potted palm. He moved closer to her until his body brushed against hers. Juliana could feel herself getting hotter and hotter. Out of the corner of her eye she could see the footman at the main door averting his gaze and staring fixedly at the floor. She lowered her voice to a whisper.

'For shame, Mr Davencourt, behaving thus in front of my servants.'

'I apologise,' Martin said easily. He leaned forward until his breath stirred the tendrils of hair by her ear. 'But you have been running away from me since the night of the musicale, so what else can I do?'

'Stop it!' Juliana hissed. 'Stand further off.'

'I only wish to talk to you. I told you, I need to apologise, to discuss certain matters with you.'

'Well, you should not!' Juliana extricated herself from her corner and stood smoothing her dress down with fingers that trembled slightly. 'My cousin, Mrs Alcott, is the one to whom you should be addressing yourself.'

Martin sighed. 'If we could just leave her aside for a moment—'

'Certainly not! How like a man.' Juliana glared at him. 'You are as good as betrothed to her and you think to leave her aside before the knot is even tied!'

'That was not what I meant. I am *not* betrothed to Mrs Alcott and I shall be even less betrothed to her shortly.'

Juliana raised her brows. She crushed down the flare of excitement and nervousness that his words kindled in her.

'I fail to see what that has to do with me.'

Martin caught her wrist and pulled her close to him. Her hands came up against his chest, but she could not break free for his arms were around her tightly. 'I will tell you what it has to do with you. It is not Serena that I want, but you. I am sorry, Juliana. I have been judgemental and wilfully rude—'

Juliana put her hands over her ears. It was a mistake,

since it merely brought her into closer proximity with his body. Her breasts were pressed against his chest in a most disconcerting manner and in order to speak to him she had to tilt her face up until it was almost touching his.

'I hope,' she said loudly, 'that you are not intent on switching your affections from one cousin to the other, Mr Davencourt. It shows a sad instability of character. Leaving aside the fact that I am totally unsuitable, of course.'

The footman blushed bright red. Martin merely smiled and kissed her. His mouth on hers was hot, sweet and hard. Juliana's head spun with surprise and pleasure.

'We will see,' he said, when he released her. 'I will be back later, when I hope to speak with you properly. Good day, Lady Juliana.'

He strode out and Juliana found herself staring blindly at the potted palm, her mind in a whirl, her body still echoing with its response to his touch. After a moment she took a deep steadying breath and marched back to the conservatory.

Lady Beatrix eyed her very sharply as she came in.

'You look quite charmingly ruffled, child. Can it be anything to do with Mr Davencourt? He is most delightful, is he not?'

'He is insufferable,' Juliana said, through shut teeth. 'Arrogant, domineering… I detest him!'

Lady Beatrix beamed. 'That's a good sign. His father was another such man. Very potent, as well. The most fecund man in London.'

Juliana, who had taken a mouthful of tea to calm her shattered nerves, almost choked. 'Aunt Beatrix! How can you possibly know that?'

'Stands to reason,' her aunt said. 'Nine children in all—

and there would have been more if that pea goose Honoria had not locked her door against him towards the end.'

Juliana sat down. 'Where *do* you get your information from, Aunt Beatrix?' she asked. 'You are just like Papa. He always seems to know everything.'

Beatrix beamed. 'I speculate to accumulate, my dear, if you know what I mean. Now, where do we go after luncheon? I have a particular desire to see Mrs Salmon's waxworks in Fleet Street. Very lifelike, I am told.'

'I am afraid you will have to find another escort if you wish to go there,' Juliana warned. 'Society is full of wax dummies as it is, without seeking out more!'

Beatrix did not seem offended. 'Then we shall go to the Royal Academy,' she said. 'You will come with me, Juliana. It is about time you acquired a little culture.'

'It is far too late for that,' Juliana said. 'My tastes were formed a good twelve years ago!'

'It is never too late,' Beatrix corrected. 'And tonight there is a performance of *Romeo and Juliet* at the Coburg. You will like that, Juliana.'

Juliana smiled. 'You are determined to reduce me to tears of one sort or another, are you not, Aunt Trix!'

She remembered that Martin had said that he would call later and she seized on the trip with a kind of relief as an escape. The game she had started so carelessly with Martin had become real. He was pursuing her now, and the thought made her feel quite faint with nervousness. Worse, she had fallen in love, which she had sworn never to do again. She had no idea what she was going to do.

It was eleven thirty and they had only been back from the theatre for ten minutes when the doorbell rang once, urgently, then again almost immediately. Juliana and Beatrix, who had been taking a late cup of chocolate together before retiring, exchanged glances.

'Someone is impatient to see you,' Beatrix observed. 'Whatever can be the matter?'

There was a hullabaloo in the hallway. A man's voice was raised imperatively and over the top of it rose the wails of a baby. A very hungry-sounding baby. Juliana and Beatrix shot out into the hall.

Brandon Davencourt was standing just inside the door, his arm protectively about a young woman. She looked pale and frightened. In her arms she held a bundle that was emitting some very loud screams. Segsbury was hovering nearby, looking as close to panic as a butler of his extensive training could be. Both he and Brandon turned towards Juliana with identical expressions of relief.

'Lady Juliana!' Brandon said. 'Thank goodness you are back. I need your help!'

Chapter Ten

'Your wife!' Juliana said. 'Oh, Brandon!'

Emily Davencourt and her son had been installed in Juliana's second-best guest room, Beatrix had retired for the night and Juliana had borne Brandon downstairs for a glass of brandy and some long overdue explanations.

Brandon ran a hand through his tumbled fair hair. 'Yes, my wife. I know I have made a mull of things—'

'That is putting it mildly.'

'Yes, but now you can see how difficult everything was! I could not tell Martin that I was married, not when he was still in a miff over me leaving Cambridge! Then the longer I put it off, the worse the matter became! In the end it was only because I could not leave Emily and Henry in those damp lodgings any longer that I was obliged to ask your help!'

Juliana sighed. 'I think that you underestimate your brother,' she said. 'I am certain that he would have supported you, no matter what you had done.' She poured Brandon a glass of brandy and he took it with a word of thanks and went to sit on the sofa. Seldom had a man looked so dejected. There were lines about his eyes that made him look far older than his two and twenty years, his shoulders were slumped and his whole demeanour weary and defeated. Juliana sat down beside him.

'Pull yourself together, Brandon,' she said cheerfully. 'At least you *are* married and Emily and Henry are both fit and well.'

Brandon looked up. 'You never asked,' he said, surprisingly. 'When I brought Em in and you arranged for her to be taken up to a room…you never asked a single question.'

'Why should I? A fine thing it would have been if your Emily was exhausted and hungry and I insisted on seeing the marriage lines before I let you across the threshold! You brought her to me, and that is all that matters.'

Brandon gave her hand a brief, convulsive squeeze. Juliana was surprised to feel a lump in her throat.

'Why do you not tell me the entire story?' she said hastily, before she burst into tears for a third time in a month.

Brandon swallowed and straightened up. 'Where to begin?'

'The beginning is customary.'

Brandon smiled faintly. 'Very well. I suppose the beginning was last year, when I was out with some chaps in Cambridge one evening. We were all rather the worse for drink I suppose…' Brandon smiled engagingly '…and as we stumbled back to halls we fell in with a girl. A young lady. She was hurrying along by herself in the dark and some of the chaps…' Brandon shrugged '…well, they made some false assumptions, I suppose.'

'Whereas you were instantly aware of her quality, of course.'

Brandon flashed her a grin. 'Of course! I persuaded the

others to leave her alone and then I escorted her back to her home. It was Emily. It turned out that she had been to an assembly in the town and had foolishly decided to return home alone and on foot when one chap became too pressing in his attentions.'

Juliana frowned. 'A dangerous undertaking. Why was she alone and friendless?'

Brandon sighed. 'Emily lives—lived—with her father and stepmother. Her father is a good sort of fellow, I suppose—' Juliana could see that he was struggling to be fair '—very upright and determined to do what is right. He is a shopkeeper. The stepmother is a die-away invalid who never had any interest in Emily from the start.'

'Poor Emily. So what happened when you started to pay court to her, Brandon?'

Brandon grinned. 'Credit to Plunkett—that's Em's father—he is no social climber. Solid middle class. He was horrified when I took an interest. He warned me off in the politest possible terms and forbade Em to see me again. He was sure my intentions were dishonourable.'

'And were they?'

Brandon looked indignant. 'No, never! I always wanted to marry Emily. But Plunkett would have none of it. He has a deep-rooted mistrust of the aristocracy and always intended Em for one of his colleagues. Even though I have no title he had me pegged as a no-good young wastrel. So we had to elope. Em is only nineteen, you see.'

'Oh, lord. You did not go to Gretna, Brandon?'

'No. There was a vicar of a parish close to Cambridge who was willing to marry us without asking too many awkward questions. For a fee, of course…'

'Of course.' Juliana wondered if the marriage had been legal since Emily was underage and did not have the consent of her parents. Probably not. That would put the cat among the pigeons.

'Emily was able to get away without suspicion, by pretending to be visiting a friend for the day. Then…she went back in the evening as though nothing had happened.' Brandon screwed up his face and took a deep pull on the brandy. 'I knew it was foolish, but we could not think what else to do. I could not afford to rent rooms for both of us and it was only going to be for a little while. Yet the longer it went on, the more difficult it became to tell the truth.'

'And I suppose that you continued to see each other when you could?'

Brandon shot her a shamefaced look. 'We would snatch meetings whenever we were able. Sometimes Emily even came to my rooms…'

He saw Juliana's look and spread his hands. 'I know I deserve all the opprobrium you can heap on me—'

'Steady,' Juliana said drily. 'I am sure you have berated yourself plenty of times.'

'Of course I have! I know there is no excuse.' Brandon put his head in his hands.

'And so Emily became pregnant, as is in the nature of things…'

'Yes, and of course Plunkett threw her out of the house. He was not interested in her explanations, the marriage lines, anything that might have mitigated the sin in his eyes. He told her he never wanted to see her again.' Brandon's face was haggard. 'She came to me in the greatest distress and I…well, what could I do? I was obliged to take rooms for us and live beyond my income, and then the baby arrived and Emily was ill and I resolved to leave

Cambridge and persuade Martin to buy me a commission.'

'Did you want to join the army?'

'Not particularly, but it would have enabled me to keep Emily and Henry, and perhaps for them to follow the drum with me…' He shook his head. 'I know I was living on dreams. Martin was furious that I had abandoned my studies and run into debt, and he refused point blank to buy the commission, saying that I was not cut out for an army career.'

'Why did you not simply tell him the truth?'

'I knew it would come out in the end,' Brandon said. 'I suppose I did not wish to disappoint Martin and I knew he would be sadly disillusioned by me when he knew the truth.'

'Why? You are not ashamed of Emily, are you?'

Brandon's head came up sharply. 'Of course not! But I deeply regret the way I have behaved.'

There was a sharp rap at the main door. At the same time, the house started to echo with the angry wails of a baby who was hungry and was determined that everyone should know it.

The door burst open. Segsbury tottered in, looking more distraught than Juliana had ever seen him.

'Mr Martin Davencourt is here, madam. Shall I show him in?'

Juliana swept past him and into the hall. The high roof seemed to reverberate with Henry's cries. Martin was standing inside the door, looking puzzled and irritated in equal measure. He swung around when he saw Juliana.

'Lady Juliana, I apologise for disturbing you at this hour, but I wondered if you might know where I could find Brandon? He is not at his club and a gentleman by the name of Plunkett has appeared on my doorstep making the most extraordinary claims.'

There was another angry roar from Henry. Martin frowned. 'What the devil—?'

Juliana smiled. 'Your arrival is most timely, Mr Davencourt. Brandon...' She drew a shrinking Brandon forward. 'Why do you not take your brother into the drawing-room and explain matters to him? You will find the brandy decanter on the sideboard should you need it.'

And with a bright smile she propelled the Davencourt brothers through the doorway and shut the door very firmly behind them.

Brandon called the following morning and spent the day in Portman Square with his wife and son. He had been intending to move them to Laverstock Gardens, but Emily had developed a slight chill and it was agreed that she should stay with Juliana until she was recovered. Juliana had no objection; Emily seemed a sweet girl and was hopelessly in love with Brandon, whilst baby Henry was a delightful child with a hearty appetite, as Juliana's ears could attest. Meanwhile she and Beatrix fended off the variety of callers who dropped into the house on the flimsiest of pretexts, having already heard the gossip about Brandon and Emily. One of the earliest callers was Serena Alcott, who expressed her disapproval at Brandon's behaviour and was sent away with a flea in her ear by Beatrix.

Brandon had also brought a written message from Martin. When Juliana had a private moment she unfolded the letter and scanned the scrawled lines written in Martin's strong hand. It looked as though he had been in a tearing hurry and Juliana thought that if he had all the business of Brandon's marriage to sort out, an irate father-in-law to placate and all his other responsibilities as well, it was no wonder.

The letter was couched in formal terms; Martin thanked her for her kindness in helping Emily and Brandon and hoped that the addition to her household would not prove too inconvenient. Juliana smiled wryly as Henry's squalls for more food mingled with the raised voice of Beatrix Tallant as she despatched yet another curious visitor from the premises.

At the bottom of Martin's note was an added message. He would call that evening, as soon as he was able, and he looked forward to speaking to her. Juliana's heart, which she had thought impervious to love and which had proved so very far from it, did an errant flip of anticipation.

By the time that evening came, she was practically pacing the carpet, unable to concentrate. Brandon had returned home and Beatrix was sitting with Emily, whose fever had got a little worse. It was a humid night and Juliana had opened the long windows leading out on to the terrace, but no breath of wind stirred the drapes. In the end she went out to pace on the terrace rather than in the house, and whilst she was there she had the good idea of going to the icehouse and fetching some ice for a cold compress for Emily. She took a candle from the sideboard, and went out into the dark.

The icehouse was located at the end of the garden, set into a bank and sheltered by a stand of trees that gave additional shade during the hot summer days. The Marquis had had it built some fifteen years before and Juliana had always thought it rather an indulgence to have her own icehouse when there was a perfectly good one for public use in St James's Park. Nevertheless, it was small and convenient, and she put her candle down to unlock the door, making sure that she propped it open carefully with a small stone. She picked up the ice bucket that was waiting inside the doorway, went along the entrance passage, and down the steps to the ice well. She was just rummaging around amongst the layers of straw, revelling in the chill of the icehouse after the humid night outside, when her candle flame flickered in a draught and there was the unmistakable sound of the outer door closing above.

Martin had waited for ten minutes in the drawing room before venturing out on to the terrace to see if Juliana was out there. He had found himself intolerably impatient to see her, and not simply to discuss his brother's situation. It had been as he was leaning against the balustrade that he had seen a light flicker away down the garden and had gone to investigate. The garden, fragrant, cool and moonlit, had been delightful and the chill of the icehouse was even more so. He went along the corridor to the top of the steps. He could see Juliana's face, upturned to him, illuminated by the light of the candle. She looked very appealing. Her hair was slightly rumpled and there was a cobweb tangled in her curls. She was wearing a plain gown in russet brown with a rich cream shawl about her shoulders and the simple clothes made her look very young.

'What on earth are you doing down here?' Martin demanded.

Juliana looked irritated. 'Good evening to you too, Mr

Davencourt! What do you mean—what am I doing here? It is my icehouse.'

'Yes, but what need could you have for ice at this time of night?'

Juliana sighed sharply. 'It is for Emily's fever. I thought that a cold compress would be just the thing for her.' She picked up her skirts and came across the cobbles to the bottom of the steps. 'What are you doing here, Mr Davencourt?'

'I came to find you, of course. I waited a while and when you did not appear I went out on to the terrace. Then I saw your light—'

'And came in and closed the door. That was not very clever of you. You have locked us in.'

Martin frowned. 'I did not close the door.'

'No, it swung closed behind you because you moved the stone as you came in. I heard the door latch. The stone was there to prevent the door locking us in.'

Martin gave an exasperated sigh. 'How was I to know that? There is clearly a design fault in any door that cannot be opened from the inside.'

Juliana shot him a look.

'Yes, I might have known that you would be preoccupied by the mechanical aspects of the situation.' She put her candle down on the small ledge beside the steps. 'I, on the other hand, could not be more appalled to be trapped in here with you. I doubt this cellar is big enough for the two of us without us coming to blows.'

Martin smothered a grin. He looked around. He could appreciate her point, for in a purely practical sense they did not have much space. The ice well was very small. It was about ten foot deep and built solidly of brick, with a vaulted roof. The cold was already beginning to seep into his bones.

'It is rather intimate,' he said.

'Well, you may acquit me of deliberately trapping you in here,' Juliana said crossly, 'just in case you were flattering yourself with that thought.'

Martin gave her a slow smile. He was utterly delighted to be trapped with her. 'Actually, I think it might be rather useful…'

Juliana looked up sharply. 'Useful in what way?'

'I need to talk to you and at least this way you cannot run away again. Though I suppose it will not take long for your servants to guess where we are.' He looked at her. 'After all, someone must know where you have gone.'

Juliana gave a frustrated sigh. 'Unfortunately, no one knows. Aunt Beatrix is upstairs with Emily and I did not tell anyone I was coming here. The servants will very likely assume that I have gone out with you.'

She scooted up the stairs and Martin heard her footsteps tap impatiently along the entrance corridor. She was rattling the bars on the door and shouting. Martin folded his arms and smiled to himself as he awaited her return. There was a note of anxiety in her voice, and Martin thought he knew why. She was afraid of what he might say to her and even more anxious not to betray her own feelings. Martin knew that she was not indifferent to him—she had admitted as much in the past—but this overwhelming sense of need was new to them both. He had to step very carefully. He had no wish to frighten her.

She was coming back down the corridor. The candle in her hand wavered and she squinted at him against the flame.

'That did no good at all. There are so many noisy people shouting in London at night that no one pays attention.'

She looked at him. 'I do not suppose that you are carrying a lock pick?'

Martin laughed. 'I am afraid not. It is not something that I generally carry with me.'

Juliana sighed. 'Never mind. If no one thinks to look here before, they will come in the morning. They always collect the ice early.'

Martin looked at her. She sounded matter of fact, but Martin thought that there was a slight quiver in her voice. He tried to speak reassuringly.

'If we sit by the entrance, someone may see the light and come to find us. It will not be so cold there either, for it is a humid night.'

After a moment, Juliana nodded. She preceded him down the corridor, candle in hand. They closed the inner door and sat down on the stone step just inside the ice-house entrance. It was an odd view. The garden was laid out in front of them in squares of moonlight and shadow, black and silver. They could hear the breeze in the tree-tops and even see the lights of the house far up the lawn, but they could not get out. The barred door with its solid latch stood between them and freedom.

Juliana shifted on the stone seat and placed the candle on the threshold in front of them. Her shoulders slumped a little. After a moment, Martin squatted down beside her.

'You said that I would be the last person you would wish to be trapped with,' he said. 'Who would you like to have locked in here with you?'

'Oh!' Juliana looked up and smiled a little. 'Apart from a locksmith, you mean? The Duke of Wellington, perhaps.

At least we could pass the time in interesting conversation.'

'You may talk to me,' Martin said. 'I can be interesting when I try.'

Juliana cast him a fleeting look. 'You had better sit down then.'

Martin sat. The step was small and his body was pressed against hers. His thigh brushed hers and when he moved, his sleeve touched the side of her breast. Juliana appeared not to notice at all. Martin took a breath and fixed his thoughts firmly on conversation.

'What would you like to talk about?'

'Let us avoid all delicate topics. That rules out most things…' Juliana paused. 'I have it! Your work.'

Martin gave her an amused look. 'I scarce think that that would interest you.'

'Try,' Juliana said succinctly.

'Very well. At the moment I am canvassing support to be elected to Parliament at the next sitting. Henry Grey Bennet has enrolled my help with the bill to abolish the use of climbing boys in the practice of sweeping chimneys. It is a barbaric and wretched business.'

'Particularly as it is not even necessary. I understand that there are machines in development that are quite as efficient.' Juliana shuddered. 'I cannot abide such cruelty.'

Martin was surprised. 'Have you read up on such things?'

'Of course not!' Juliana looked amused. 'But I observe. I turned one sweep out of the house for his ridiculous cruelty to his climbing boys and gave them some money so that they should not suffer from the loss of work…' Juliana voice trailed away. 'What are you looking at me

like that for, Mr Davencourt? It was scarcely a philan-
thropic gesture!'

Martin did not argue, although he thought that that was
exactly what it was. He wondered suddenly how many
acts of careless generosity Juliana had actually committed—whilst pretending to indifference.

'I suppose that your brother talks of such matters,' he
said carefully.

'Yes, Joss is quite a political animal at heart these
days,' Juliana said. 'And the Ashwicks have always been
interested in social reform. I suspect you are all a bunch
of radicals at heart!'

Martin smiled. 'That is what I was discussing with your
brother and Adam Ashwick that night at Crowns. We need
all the support that we can muster in the Lords.'

'But Joss does not have a seat in the Lords.'

'No, but he is influential. As is Ashwick. I was keen to
enlist their support. The bill has powerful enemies who
may well talk it down, Lauderdale amongst them.'

Juliana wriggled crossly. 'Oh, the Earl of Lauderdale is
one of those facetious gentlemen who are so entertained
by their own wit that they cannot see that others detest
them! I do believe he should be forced up a chimney
himself!'

'A pleasant thought,' Martin said. He watched the play
of light over Juliana's animated face. 'Are you interested
in politics?'

'Not particularly, thank you. But this is quite interesting
because it is a cause that you all support.' Juliana flashed
him a mocking look. 'You are surprised, are you not? I
realise that you think me a simpleton.'

'No, never that.' Martin spoke quickly, sincerely. 'I

have the greatest respect for your intelligence, Lady Juliana. I merely thought that you would not be interested.'

He saw the slight smile that curved her lips. 'I rather like the thought that I have surprised you.' Their gazes met and trembled on the edge of something else, something deeper. Martin saw Juliana swallow hard and then she looked away.

'Now you can tell me about your experiences in the diplomatic world, Mr Davencourt,' she said. Her voice was light.

Martin clamped down hard on his frustration. He knew she was trying to keep him at arm's length, to keep him talking. She would do almost anything to deflect him from intimacy. But they had a long night ahead of them. He would lead her there by slow degrees. He had the time. And one thing was for sure. She would not escape.

Martin talked and whilst he talked he watched her; watched the reflection of the candlelight in her eyes and her smile and the shadows that came and went in her expressive face. When he had told her something of his experiences in Europe she asked him about Davencourt. That used up another fifteen minutes. When he tried to ask Juliana something in return, she turned the conversation back to him. Martin smiled to himself and waited.

When the conversation finally slowed between them, Juliana said, 'I should have asked about Mr Plunkett. Is Emily's father reconciled to the match now?'

'I have managed to smooth him over,' Martin said. He gave her a wry smile. 'Plunkett is an upright citizen, terrified of scandal, fearful of anything outside his small sphere of experience. He is deeply disapproving of Brandon and Emily, and I cannot say that the way they have

behaved has done anything to help their case. However…'
Martin sighed.

'However, having such a pillar of the community for
an elder brother must surely have reassured Mr Plunkett
that Brandon is not all bad?' Juliana said slyly.

Martin laughed. 'Maybe, maybe not. Plunkett distrusts
all politicians. He believes that we are only in it for self-
aggrandisement.'

'For shame! Where can he have got that idea from?'

Martin cast her a look of amusement. 'Your cynicism
is as bracing as ever, Lady Juliana. But I am sure you
will be glad to know that he is reconciled to the match
and is even prepared, albeit belatedly, to give his consent.'

'So there need be no awkward questions about illegal-
ity?'

'I hope not.'

He felt Juliana relax beside him. 'Oh, thank goodness!
For although I know that Brandon would have married
Emily again tomorrow if necessary—with her father's
consent this time—I am very glad that she need not suffer
any of the scandal and slander that might have ensued if
the marriage were illegal.'

Martin was watching her face. 'You have always felt
such matters very keenly.'

'Well, of course! Emily is the sweetest creature and for
her to be labelled a fallen woman would have been quite
absurd! Yet that is what would have happened to her if
the gossips had got hold of the story. A runaway match,
an infant out of wedlock… Even now they would have a
field day if the whole came out, and Emily would be the
one whose reputation would suffer. It is the woman who
always does!'

'We have spoken of this before. I know that you feel

very strongly about such things and I can see exactly what you mean.'

Juliana turned her face away. 'So will you give the farm at Davencourt to Brandon? He wishes to settle down and breed horses, you know. I am persuaded that he would make a very good job of it.'

'I see that he has told you everything.' Martin felt resignedly amused. His siblings' tenacious attachment to Juliana no longer rankled. 'Yes, that is to be Brandon's and he had better breed a Derby winner within five years to give me a return on my investment!' He sobered. 'I have suggested that Brandon and Emily remove to Davencourt as soon as Emily is recovered from her chill, but in the meantime I am most grateful to you for giving them a home.'

'I suppose that there can be no difficulty now that Aunt Beatrix is in residence here,' Juliana said.

'I imagine not.' Martin looked at her downbent head. 'The real point, however, is that you were kind enough to take them in, Lady Juliana. I am most grateful to you.'

Juliana shrugged. 'I could not have turned them away.'

'Some people would have, I am sure. Just accept my thanks.'

'Rather than your censure?' Juliana smiled at him and Martin felt his heart contract. 'It makes a change, I suppose. Which reminds me—how are Kitty and Clara?'

'They are very well.' Martin's eyes twinkled. 'Mr Ashwick promises to become something of a visitor in Laverstock Gardens, I think. He has already called twice, sent flowers and taken Kitty out driving.'

Juliana looked up. 'I am glad. I thought that Kitty and Edward seemed to take to each other's company very well.'

'Indeed.' Martin looked concerned. 'You do not mind? Mr Ashwick has always been one of your beaux.'

Juliana laughed. 'Oh, Edward is one of my dearest friends, but I do not have any other designs on him! I should be delighted if he and Kitty were to make a match of it. She is very shy, but Edward is the kindliest man I know and I am sure he would be good for her.'

'And as he lives in the country, Kitty would not need to stay in town when she clearly detests it.'

Juliana smiled. 'Did she tell you that?'

'Yes. In the end.' Martin laughed. 'She confessed the whole of her plan to be banished back to Davencourt.'

'Oh, dear. No doubt you were not amused.'

'Not particularly. What concerned me, however, was the fact that she had ever thought it would be a viable idea.' Martin ran his hand through his hair. 'I do not believe I shall ever understand the way my siblings' minds work. I used to believe that it was just the girls I could not understand, but after this fiasco with Brandon I am resigned to the fact that none of them wish to confide in me.'

Juliana moved a little closer. Martin felt her softness pressing against him and shifted slightly. By slow degrees they were moving closer to personal subjects. On to dangerous ground…

'I do believe that they will trust you after this.' Juliana sounded as though she wanted to comfort him, and Martin was touched. 'They did not know you very well before, but now that they realise you are not an ogre—'

'An ogre!' Martin said. His tone softened. 'I do believe I may have to be an ogre with Clara if she insists on pursuing Fleet.'

'She will not marry him.' Juliana's voice was softly confident. 'I spoke to her at the musicale.'

'I saw you. Thank you, Juliana.'

'You are very welcome. But could you not turn the matter to your advantage? With Fleet as a brother-in-law you could be truly influential.'

Martin laughed. 'Tempting as that is, I cannot let it sway me.'

'No, I thought not. You are too principled.'

'Not principled enough for Mrs Alcott, it would seem.'

Juliana looked up sharply. 'What can you mean?'

'Only that she is not prepared to tolerate a relative who is in trade and she told me so earlier in no uncertain terms. When I pointed out that no one had asked her to lower her standards by marrying in to the family, she flounced off in a huff.'

Juliana smothered a giggle. 'How unchivalrous of you, Martin.'

'I know.' Martin sounded self-satisfied.

Juliana made a slight gesture. 'Serena has led a sheltered life. One must make allowances.'

'I can make allowances for many things,' Martin said, the steel coming into his tone, 'but not for snobbery.'

Juliana looked at him. 'I always knew that Serena was...conscious of her rank as the niece of a Marquis.'

'Conscious of her rank! That is putting it mildly, I assure you. She behaved like an outraged Archduchess!'

'Oh, dear. And Aunt Beatrix is dreadful at stirring things up. I suspect she put Serena up to it this morning. Serena called here before she came to see you, you know.'

'Then I am obliged to Lady Beatrix. She saved me from a difficult situation. I never had any intention of letting the matter go so far and I was horrified that I appeared to have committed myself to an offer.'

'You should be more careful,' Juliana said. Her shoulders were shaking and after a moment Martin saw that her eyes were bright with mirth. 'I suppose that I should commiserate with you, all the same. Now you will have to start all over again in your search for a wife.'

'It seems I must. I shall try not to make such a fool of myself this time, however.' Martin paused. 'Perhaps I shall not have to look very far, either.'

The silence in the icehouse was suddenly intense. Juliana fidgeted with her skirt and did not look at him and Martin was frustrated that their position next to each other on the step did not allow him to see her face clearly. He leaned forward at the same time that Juliana turned her head and looked directly at him.

'Why are you staring?' she enquired. Her voice was quite steady.

Martin allowed his gaze to travel over her in comprehensive appraisal. 'I beg your pardon. I suppose I am more accustomed to seeing you in silks than in a plain gown.'

Juliana twitched her brows. 'How singular that you should notice, Mr Davencourt. I thought that you were seldom aware of what a lady was wearing.'

'I am aware of you, I assure you.'

Juliana cleared her throat and looked away. Martin had the distinct impression that she was searching about for yet another change of subject. 'Yes, well…it would hardly be appropriate for me to come rootling about in the ice house in a ball gown, would it?'

'I suppose not. Why did you not send your butler in the first place?'

'Because I had the idea and immediately put it into action. Giving order to servants is so time consuming, do you not find? By the time I had rung for Segsbury and given him instructions I could have been in and out of here with the ice.' She gave him a darkling stare. 'I would have been had you not intervened.'

Martin sighed. 'I do not believe that it will profit us to discuss that once again.'

Juliana sighed sharply. 'I suppose not. How long have we been here, do you think?'

'About an hour and a half, I suppose. The night is young.'

There was a breath of wind through the bars of the door, setting the cobwebs shivering. The candle went out. Martin heard Juliana catch a sharp breath. In the dark, all his senses seemed suddenly heightened. His whole perception of their situation changed. Previously he had managed to hold his thoughts at bay by concentrating fiercely on their conversation and on the various problems of Brandon, Kitty and Clara. Now he was aware of Juliana's breathing, quick now with an edge of panic. He put out a hand and located hers. After a moment she clung to him.

'Are you afraid of the dark?' He kept his voice extremely gentle.

'No. Not precisely.' Juliana sounded different. The clear-cut edge, the habitual authority, had gone from her voice. She sounded uncertain, vulnerable. 'That is, I do not like the dark, but it is more the bats that I am afraid of. I do not wish to sound missish, but I dislike the idea of them flying around my head when I cannot see them.'

Martin laughed and squeezed her hand. 'That sounds

perfectly reasonable to me. I'll wager that you have never been missish in your life, Juliana.'

'No, I do not think so. Papa did not encourage it and as I have been so much on my own, it is a luxury I have not been able to indulge in.'

It had not occurred to Martin that Juliana had been alone. He had known, of course, that she had been widowed a long time before she had run away with Clive Massingham, but he had thought—assumed, he realised now—that she had not lacked masculine company during that time. Certainly he had presumed that in the years since Massingham's death she had had any number of lovers. Yet from the way she spoke it sounded as though she had spent a great deal of her time on her own, if not actually lonely. Either these men had been ephemeral entertainment or…or the roll call of lovers had not existed at all. Martin felt his heart miss a beat. Yet did it matter to him any more? He was no longer sure that it did. Not now that Juliana was his. And she *was* his, no matter what she said or how she struggled against fate. Martin felt her body against his and felt a huge, powerful urge to claim and possess her, to make good his stake in the face of the world.

The darkness was wrapping them in an intimate embrace. Pale slivers of moonlight scattered the floor. Martin could smell the faint, sweet scent of lilies that seemed to be emanating from Juliana's skin and her hair… His senses tightened. That scent of lilies was incredibly distracting. Cool, pale, soft… He wanted to bury his face in a pile of them and inhale the perfume. He wanted to press his face to Juliana's bare skin and do the same…

Martin shifted sharply. The movement brought him hard up against Juliana's side, for the step was hardly wide enough for complicated manoeuvres. It was the reverse of what he had intended. For a moment he felt the yielding softness of her breast against his arm and he jumped as though scalded.

'Are you feeling quite well, Mr Davencourt?' Juliana's voice held nothing but an enquiring courtesy. Martin gritted his teeth.

'I… Yes, I am very well, thank you.'

'Are *you* afraid of the dark?'

'No. Certainly not.'

'There is no need to feel ashamed. Everyone has their weakness, you know.'

Martin knew. He also knew exactly what his weakness was at that moment. She was sitting right next to him.

'Are you cold?' Juliana continued, sounding concerned. 'The icehouse, as its name implies, is not designed to hold the heat.'

Martin tried to wrench his mind away from the fundamentals of attraction and concentrate on conversation. Unfortunately, a conversation about his physical wellbeing was not helpful for it tended to focus the mind on his state of discomfort. He did not feel cold. Parts of him felt very hot indeed…one might almost say burning.

'I am not cold, thank you, Lady Juliana. Are you? You may have my jacket if you require it.'

As soon as he had spoken the words, Martin reflected that taking his clothes off was not in the least helpful. Once he had started he might not stop, and then he would start on Juliana's clothes as well…

'I am quite warm at the moment and I should not wish to deprive you of your jacket.' Juliana sounded matter of fact. 'I have my shawl and it is quite thick.' She laughed. 'How polite we are being to each other this evening, Mr

Davencourt! It just goes to show that we may manage it when we try.'

'Even so,' Martin said, 'we should try to conserve our bodily warmth in case the temperature drops. If I were to put my arm about you, Lady Juliana, would you object?'

There was another pause. 'I believe that might be quite acceptable,' Juliana said. She moved slightly so that Martin could free the arm trapped between their bodies and slip it about her shoulders. After a moment she leaned closer into the curve of his body, resting her head against shoulder.

'That is very comfortable,' she said, giving a tiny yawn. 'Thank you, Mr Davencourt.'

They were silent for several moments although Martin's silence was very active. During it he registered the soft pressure of her body against his, the brush of her hair against his cheek, that infuriatingly tantalising scent of lilies, the warmth of her hand as it slid confidingly across his chest and came to rest on his waist, the fact that her mouth was only a couple of inches below his and if he chose to tilt her chin up...

'It is a pity that you do not have a companion,' he said at random. 'Then there would be someone to raise the alarm if you went missing.'

Juliana raised her head slightly. 'I do not think it a pity at all.' She sounded slightly sleepy. 'Why should I be obliged to tolerate the company of some tiresome poor relation day in day out, just in case I should one day disappear and need someone to find me?'

Martin laughed. 'Put like that, I do see your point.'

'You have a house full of relatives. Do you not find that too much sometimes?'

Martin hesitated. 'Not really. I enjoy the company.'

'And you are a man. You have a far greater freedom to do as you please.'

Martin reflected ruefully that just at that moment he had absolutely no freedom to do as he pleased, although the only thing standing between him and the pursuit of pleasure was his own self-control. Someone should give him a medal for such single-minded restraint.

He cleared his throat. 'Juliana, I want to apologise for what I said to you about keeping away from Kitty and Clara. I realise I must have sounded very pompous. I am sorry.'

There was a pause. 'You were dreadfully pompous,' Juliana said. 'I suppose that now that Aunt Beatrix is here it is acceptable for Kitty and Clara to call.'

'It has nothing to do with Lady Beatrix.' Martin stopped. He knew he sounded quite fierce. 'At least, I suppose in a way it does.'

'Of course it does! You would not permit them to call when I lived here alone. I do believe you considered it a house of ill repute! Now that Aunt Beatrix is here she has the most reputable visitors calling at all hours.' She sounded cross. 'She has almost made me respectable again! It is dreadfully vexing.'

Martin smiled. 'Lady Juliana, this has nothing to do with Lady Beatrix, and everything to do with my own folly. You have been very kind to Kitty and Clara—and to Brandon, too—and that in itself should have been enough to make you a most welcome acquaintance. Unfortunately, I was arrogant and a fool, and was not prepared to fly in the face of convention, for which I apologise.'

He felt Juliana move slightly. He could hear the smile in her voice. 'Your apology is accepted, sir, but only if you promise to stop apologising to me. It is very wearying.'

Martin squeezed her hand again. 'Pray do not jest. This is very important to me, Juliana. I want you to believe that I am doing this because I realise that I have been prejudiced. It is not because of Lady Beatrix, or your sudden respectability, or any other factor.'

He saw the moonlight reflect in Juliana's eyes. They were very wide and dark. 'You cannot suddenly believe me to be good, where previously you thought me quite the reverse.'

'I don't.' Martin frowned. 'I see I am explaining myself very badly. It is simple. Previously I was a judgemental fool. And now—'

'Now?'

'Now I do not care. I know what I want.'

Something came out of the dark and brushed softly against his face. He jumped. Juliana gave a little squeak and burrowed closer.

'Was that…a bat?' She sounded breathless.

Martin tightened his arm about her. 'I believe so. Are you feeling nervous?'

'I…yes, a little.'

Martin allowed himself the briefest of reassuring strokes of her hair. It twined softly about his fingers. He found it difficult to untangle himself and, after a second, did not try.

'They will not hurt you. Even if they flew right into your face they are quite harmless.'

'I would rather not put that to the test.' Juliana sounded as though she was trying to be calm and not quite managing it. Martin felt a tremor go through her. After a second he put his other arm about her and turned her gently into his arms. He half-expected her to resist, but instead she wriggled a little closer. Her breasts were pressing against his chest and the soft pressure was exquisite torture. He felt her breath feather across his cheek with the lightest of touches.

It was enough to push him over the edge.

Juliana had always been afraid of enclosed spaces, ever since Joss had locked her in the cellar when she had been five years old. In the intervening time she had almost forgotten her fears, but the combination of the dark, the small space pressing in on her and the presence of small flying mammals had been sufficient to make her very nervous indeed that evening. Nervous to the point where she was actually glad that Martin Davencourt was there in the dark with her.

They had managed to be civil enough to each other and it had been quite a pleasant relief. For a little while she had almost felt safe, thinking that perhaps Martin did not intend to pick up where he had left off the previous day. But then she had seen the expression in his eyes, the intent concentration that told her that she was not going to escape so lightly. Her stomach had been tied in knots ever since. And then the bats had struck. She had turned into Martin's arms easily, instinctively, and then both of them were swept away.

Martin's kiss was so light and tantalising that Juliana's heart jumped and she put a hand out to pull him closer. Her fingers slid across the smooth material of his jacket and she grasped his lapel, clutching at it both to steady herself and to draw him to her.

'Please…'

Martin responded to the entreaty in her voice, kissing

her hard and with a deliberation that made the desire flare up within her. Juliana felt as though she had been waiting a very long time for that kiss. She kissed him back almost savagely, until she was gasping for breath.

Martin's lips left her, pressing tiny kisses down her throat to the hollow at the base. Juliana could feel the tickle of his hair like soft feathers against her neck. It was incredibly difficult to think coherently. She wrapped her arms about him and he tipped her back against the curve of his arm, trapping her against his body. Their position on the step was frustrating in the extreme, for they could not get close enough to each other. In the end, Martin solved the problem by pulling her down with him on to the flagstone floor. The floor was cold and hard, but Juliana barely noticed. She felt Martin's hands slide down her back, moulding her yielding curves against the hard length of him. He kissed her again, his tongue touching her bottom lip and sliding into her mouth. Juliana gave a little gasp as the shock coursed through her.

She felt his hand curve around her breast and his thumb skim the nipple through the thin silk of her dress. Then the warmth of his hand was against her bare skin and Juliana's stomach squirmed with anticipation and desire.

Martin slid her bodice down and Juliana took her arms from about his neck and put out a hand to halt his. Suddenly it seemed vitally important that he should not think her wanton. 'No…'

'Why not?' His soft whisper tickled her ear. She knew he could sense her need for him, just as she knew how much he wanted her. 'I thought you did not care who saw you? At Brookes's dinner and at the gaming hall…'

Juliana bit her lip. 'All those times did not matter.'

'And this does?' Juliana heard the smile in Martin's voice. 'I am glad...'

He was kissing her again, deeply, insistently. It stole Juliana's breath and the last of her scruples. She ran her hands over his back and felt the muscles straining against the constricting material of his jacket. His body felt warm and strong and oh so delicious against hers. Juliana had almost forgotten what it felt like...

Martin was kissing the hollow of her throat, his tongue sending shivers of sensation rippling all the way down to Juliana's toes. He eased her dress from one shoulder and nipped the skin there, so that Juliana cried out with a mixture of longing and desperation, arching up as he traced the line of her collarbone with his lips and tongue. This time when he tugged the bodice of her gown down she made no demur, squirming with pleasure when she felt the silky warmth of his hand on her breast, gasping as he lowered his head to take a small, careful bite, almost screaming aloud as he moved his tongue over her skin with tiny licks and nips until the heat and excitement building in the pit of her stomach was almost too much to bear.

She rolled over and almost hit her head on the wall. 'Martin, this is hardly the time and place—'

Martin was evidently returning to his senses as well. He wrapped his arms about her and pulled her close, cushioning her against the coldness of the flagstones with his body. After a moment Juliana stopped resisting and allowed him to draw her up to sit on the step beside him once more. She turned her head against his shoulder. 'Do not apologise, Martin,' she said warningly. 'I would have to banish you if you say that you are sorry.'

Martin pressed his lips against her hair. 'I would not

dream of it. Apart from anything else, I am not sorry. I enjoyed it.'

Juliana gave him a sideways look. 'Oh.'

'Please do not tell me that you did not enjoy it too. Apart from the damage to my self-esteem, I would then be obliged to start apologising all over again for my poor technique.'

Juliana tried not to laugh. She narrowed her gaze on him. 'Whether I enjoyed it or not is beside the point. I am only now coming to terms with becoming respectable again and I have no intention of allowing you to spoil everything.'

Martin raised his brows. 'How could I do that? Is kissing not respectable?'

'Certainly not. How can you even ask? A single lady, even a widow, must be careful of her reputation. It is quite out of the question.' Juliana moved away a little. 'That is why I had not kissed anyone—excluding you—for almost three years.'

She felt the shock go through Martin. 'You have not kissed anyone for three years?'

'Almost three years. Must you keep repeating everything I say? It makes you sound very slow.'

'Yes, but...*three years*, Juliana?'

Juliana smiled slowly. 'I told you before that you had made a lot of assumptions about me, Martin.'

Martin ran his hand through his hair. 'But in that case you cannot have... I mean...all those lovers...'

Juliana frowned at him. 'Now you are just being coarse, Martin. A gentleman does not question a lady on such matters.'

'No, but Andrew Brookes...and Jasper Colling...'

'I told you before that I had not been Andrew Brookes's mistress. As for Colling, you must think I have no taste.'

Martin tightened his arms about her. 'Pray stop making fun of me, Juliana! What exactly are you telling me?'

Juliana looked him in the eye. 'As you are so persistent, Mr Davencourt, I am telling you that I have slept with only two men in my entire life, and I have married them both. And if you are wondering why my reputation is quite the reverse, it is because I am damned if I will accept the judgement of society and behave like a meek little widow just because people expect it of me, or make them free of that information just so that they will not condemn me!' She broke off and clapped a hand to her mouth. 'Devil take it! I cannot believe that I have told you that!'

Martin was laughing softly. 'Juliana, I believe that you have just demolished your bad reputation once and for all.'

Juliana glared at him. 'Pray forget that I ever said it!'

'I do not believe that I can do that. Nor do I want to.'

Juliana struggled away from his embrace. 'Of course not. All men like to think their women innocent—or relatively so.' She got to her feet. This was burningly important to her. She moved as far away from him as possible, standing with her back to the barred door, holding on to it for support.

'Think about this, Martin. It is not simply sexual immorality that sets a woman beyond society's boundaries. In your relief to excuse me, remember all the rest. The wild parties, the foolish pranks, the gambling to excess, the sheer, wanton selfishness of my behaviour...' She spun away from him and went across to the top of the steps, turning back to fix him with her gaze. 'Remember what you said to me when you discovered the escapade in Hyde Park! You know nothing! When I was barely eighteen I almost ruined the family with my reckless gambling. Joss saved me by taking the blame then, just as he saved me three years ago when I tried to blackmail a former friend out of spite and jealousy. In your hurry to think me virtuous, remember that I had a wild affair with Clive Massingham before I married him. I was besotted with him.' Her face crumpled for a moment and she put it in her hands. 'I have made enough mistakes to last several lifetimes and then I have crowned my folly by playing the part of the outrageous widow because I had too much pride to say that I was sorry and creep meekly back into the fold.'

Martin stood up, but he made no move towards her. He had not taken his eyes from her as she spoke. 'I do not understand why you are trying to make me think badly of you,' he said quietly.

Juliana looked up. 'Because sometimes I hate myself and I want you to hate me too.'

'You cannot make me do that.'

Juliana's smile was full of self-mockery. 'I know. It is most trying. You are a man who holds tenaciously to his opinions. Now that you have decided to like me I fear that I am stuck with it. Matters were so much easier when you detested me.'

A faint smile touched Martin's lips. He moved a little closer to her. 'I never detested you, Juliana.'

Juliana's look was almost derisive. 'No? Well, I disliked you heartily, Martin. You are too good for me. You make me want to live up to your standards.' She threw a hand out. 'Look at me! I have my house invaded by a maiden aunt whom previously I would have sent packing, I give refuge to a runaway bride and her baby, I hand out

advice free of charge to your sisters and your brother...
Whatever next? I shall probably open an orphanage!'

Martin smiled tenderly. 'You should not think that the
change is all in one direction, Juliana. Look at me. I was
the most stubborn, prejudiced fool—a man who holds tenaciously to his opinions, as you so rightly said—but you
have changed me. You have made me see that such obstinacy is not always a good thing. I have been blind.'

He came across and took her in his arms. 'Do not try
to make me see you differently,' he said, against her lips.
'All I can see is you, and you are—'

'Yes?'

'Lovely.'

His mouth was on hers again for one long, dazzling,
breathtaking kiss.

Then there were shouts from outside and the flare of
lights. Martin let her go. Beatrix Tallant was standing outside the door and had evidently had the presence of mind
to bring Segsbury, a lantern and several large blankets
with her. The butler unlocked the icehouse door and Juliana stumbled through, almost falling into her aunt's
arms. Martin took one of the blankets and wrapped it
about Juliana.

'Let me take you inside.'

Juliana struggled out of his grip. Now that they were
rescued she was not sure what she felt. Shock, bewilderment and a wonderful elation struggled within her.

'I am perfectly all right, Mr Davencourt.' Her voice
trembled slightly. 'Please... I need time to think...'

Martin stood back. 'Very well, Lady Juliana. I will bid
you goodnight. I have to go out of Town tomorrow, but
I shall be back shortly and I will see you then.'

It sounded like a promise. Juliana did not answer, except to bid him goodnight in return, and Segsbury escorted Martin up the steps to the terrace and out to the door.

Juliana and Beatrix followed more slowly, Juliana pulling the blanket close about her to quell her shivering.

'I hope that you are all right, my dear,' Beatrix said, a bright look in her amber eyes. 'I left you as long as I thought you needed. Did he make love to you?'

Juliana glared, shaking herself out of her confusion. 'You sound like the madam of a bawdy house, Aunt Trix!'

Beatrix laughed. 'The man is head over heels in love with you, Juliana. Take him and be grateful.'

Juliana shivered. It was not that easy. A part of her was overwhelmed that Martin should love her and another part was deeply afraid.

'I cannot marry again, Aunt Trix.' She tried to carry on but her voice broke. 'I cannot...'

Beatrix took her hand in a warm clasp. 'Because of Myfleet? You loved him a great deal—'

'It is not that I am still in love with him,' Juliana said. She steadied herself with a hand on the terrace balustrade. 'But when I lost him my heart broke, and if that were to happen again...' She shook her head. 'I could not bear it, Aunt Trix. Never again.'

Chapter Eleven

'I see that you have acquired a chaperon,' Joss said to his sister in an amused undertone when they met the following night in Lady Knighton's ballroom. 'At your age too, Jul'

Juliana gave him a hard stare. 'Only because you and Amy refused to have Aunt Trix to stay. What was I to do—turn her away as well?'

Joss laughed. 'I would not have put it past you.'

Juliana turned her shoulder. 'Well, I could not do it. What was all that nonsense about me being in greater need of the company than the two of you? I never heard such bare-faced lies.'

'Surely it is true?' Joss raised a brow. 'Confess it—you have enjoyed having someone to go around with. I hear that you have even been seen out during the day!'

'Yes, we went to a concert yesterday and to some tedious exhibition at the museum today. Lud, I was afraid that I might fall asleep where I stood!'

'How long does Beatrix intend to stay?'

'I have no notion. She plans to visit Ashby Tallant before she goes on her travels again. She has been abroad for the best part of the last twenty years, you know, Joss.'

'Was she not aware that there was a war in Europe?'

'Oh, the war-torn continent is far too tame for her! Aunt Beatrix has been to Egypt and Indochina and to Japan.'

'No wonder that one recalcitrant niece is no match for her, then!'

'Perhaps she should turn her attention to Clara Davencourt,' Juliana said, with a laugh. 'Aunt Beatrix, of all people, might be able to make an impression there.'

'I hear that you are the only one Clara attends to,' Joss said. 'Though you have your work cut out, Ju! No sooner has Fleet been vanquished than Clara turns her attention to Amy's brother Richard. She seems mightily taken with him.'

Juliana clapped a hand to her mouth. 'The little minx! I warned her against him. He is the most inveterate gambler—'

'But tall, fair and handsome with it. And he is looking for a rich bride.'

Juliana scanned the floor, noticing with a slight smile that Edward Ashwick was sitting next to Kitty Davencourt. The chair beside them was empty; Clara had apparently not taken up her usual place on a rout chair, but was dancing, and in time to the music as well. She was laughing up into Richard Bainbridge's face, and chatting nineteen to the dozen. Juliana frowned.

'I will have to speak to her again. She has the most dreadful penchant for unsuitable men. Why are you laughing?'

Joss straightened his face. 'No reason, Ju. And I agree with you. Clara Davencourt cannot marry Richard.'

'What does Amy think?'

Joss's smile vanished. 'Oh, Amy is quite set against Richard marrying anyone.'

'I can understand that. She need only look at what her

father did to her mother through his appalling gambling to see the misery that might be the lot of Richard's bride.'

Joss gave her a shadowed smile. 'That is perceptive of you, Ju. Yes, Amy fears for the fate of any young lady whom Richard might marry, but I am not so sure. After all—look at me. I did not find it too difficult to reform my own gambling habits, and though I still play, I am not in thrall to the cards. The same thing might happen to Richard were he to settle down.'

Juliana tucked her hand through his arm. 'Ah, but you are like me, Joss. We both played only to alleviate our boredom. I do believe that Richard Bainbridge, like his father before him, plays because he cannot help himself. It is an obsession for him.'

Joss let it go. 'Have you stopped playing then, Ju?' he enquired lightly.

Juliana grimaced. 'With my lack of funds, how could I help it?'

'A shortage of money has never stopped you before,' Joss observed. 'I hear that Papa has redeemed your necklace.'

'Yes, is that not unfortunate? It is the ugliest thing.'

'And that he has summoned you to Ashby Tallant.'

'Yes.' Juliana's smile faded. 'I do not wish to go.'

'I wish you would, Ju.' Joss's face was serious. 'I am certain that Papa wishes to be reconciled with you. He is stiff-necked and difficult, but he is doing his best—'

'It is too late, Joss,' Juliana said.

'A pity. I mentioned to Davencourt that you were thinking of travelling that way and he offered his escort.' Joss's eyes twinkled. 'Apparently he is planning to visit his godfather at Ashby Hall. Now are you tempted?'

'Even less so!' Juliana snapped. She felt panicky. The thought of the intimacy of travelling with Martin Davencourt made her most nervous. The last time that they had been in an enclosed space together she had lost her heart and almost lost her head as well.

'I would rather that you took me there yourself! Why must you throw me into Martin's company, Joss?'

Joss looked amused. 'I beg your pardon. I thought only to be helpful.'

'Well, it was not helpful at all! I am trying to avoid Martin—Mr Davencourt—at the moment.'

'Why on earth should you do that?'

'Because…' Juliana failed to meet her brother's gaze.

'Because you like him too well and you are afraid of what might happen?'

'Because I like him too well and I am trying to cure myself of this affliction!' Juliana snapped.

'In God's name, why, Juliana?' Joss raised his brows. 'Why do you not just accept your fate?' He glanced across at Amy and smiled a little. 'I did.'

'I seem to recall that you struggled hard enough, in all conscience,' Juliana said. 'Several times I pointed out that you were in love with Amy and you denied it.'

'So now our roles are reversed and I can provide the same service for you. You are in love with Martin Davencourt and I think—no, I am certain—that he is in love with you. So where is the difficulty? What are you afraid of, Juliana?'

'I would have thought that that was manifestly obvious,' Juliana snapped. 'My matrimonial record is of the worst. Besides, you know perfectly well that a man like Martin Davencourt cannot marry a lady with my reputation. You know it, he knows it, I know it. You must see that there is nothing for us. So I am trying to put some distance between myself and Martin Davencourt before it is too late and my surprisingly inexperienced heart is broken again.'

Joss looked at Amy again. 'It does not work like that, Ju. The harder you try to ignore your feelings, the more acute they will become.'

'Thank you for that insight. You are so helpful tonight.'

'Besides, surely it is Davencourt's decision whom he marries? Stop trying to make that decision for him.'

'I am not! I am merely trying to prevent his choice falling on me, at which I should be obliged to reject him and we may all be miserable.'

'Then accept him.' Joss shrugged. 'It seems perfectly obvious to me.'

Juliana glared at him. 'And of course you are the expert, Joss! How long did it take you to acknowledge your feelings for Amy?'

'Too long. But I got there in the end. Which is why I thought that you could benefit from my experience.'

'Thank you, but you know that we all have to make our own mistakes.' Juliana sighed. 'You had best take me back to Aunt Beatrix. A chaperon is just what I need at the moment!'

The following day saw Juliana, Joss, Amy and Beatrix Tallant setting out for the family home. Beatrix had decreed that it was time for her to visit her brother, Joss had concluded his long-delayed business in London, and Juliana had grudgingly agreed to accompany them in order to get her duty visit to her father over with.

They found the Marquis in improved health, but still confined to bed and grumbling at his doctors. Propped up on his pillows, he offered his daughter a leathery cheek to kiss and she dutifully obliged. She thought that he seemed older—withered somehow—and shrunken against the pristine white of his bedclothes. The bedroom windows were open to banish the sour smell of the sickroom, but Juliana felt a sudden clench of fear. Her father had been a constant in her life, no matter how difficult their relationship, and if she were to lose him now she was not at all sure how she would feel.

However the Marquis clearly had no intention of departing this life before he was good and ready. His amber eyes were still as sharp as ever, and so was his tongue. He gestured his daughter to a chair by the side of the bed, and focussed his gaze upon her.

'I heard that Sir Henry Lees's godson offered you his escort, Juliana. Lees and I play a game of chess every so often. Two old codgers together.' The Marquis looked thoughtful. 'Martin Davencourt, eh? Is he your latest? Or is he too much of a gentleman to try anything havey-cavey?'

Juliana laughed. 'Oh, Mr Davencourt is the perfect gentleman, Papa. And no—he and I are not…involved.'

The Marquis laughed. 'Don't have a very high opinion of men, do you, Juliana? After that disaster with Massingham I do believe you have given them all the go by.'

'Your information is always impeccable, sir,' Juliana said lightly. It had always perplexed her that her father had such a strong intelligence network when he was in poor health and confined to the country.

'I've been hearing interesting things about you, Juliana.' The Marquis peered from under his thatch of hair. 'Now that you share a home with your Aunt Beatrix, I hear that you have given up your old cronies and have befriended Amy and Annis Ashwick, and that you visit the opera and the theatre…' The Marquis nodded. 'Glad to hear it, girl.'

'Pray do not let it excite you too much, sir,' Juliana said. 'I am sure it is only a phase I am going through.'

The Marquis laughed. 'Your respectable phase, eh? Still got that damned odd sense of humour, haven't you? Just like me.'

Juliana shivered in the draught from the open window. 'I should hardly think so, sir,' she said coldly. 'I understood that I had inherited nothing from you.'

There was an awkward pause. The Marquis shifted on his bed. 'Inheritance was what I wished to speak to you about. Thought to give you another chance. Shan't be around for much longer, so I have been speaking to the lawyers.' He shifted irritably against the pillows. 'Most of the stuff is entailed, of course, for Joss to keep up this old mausoleum.'

'Of course,' Juliana said. 'Poor Joss.'

'However...' The Marquis wheezed slightly. 'I have cleared your debts this one last time and I have let it be known that I am settling one hundred and fifty thousand pounds on you.'

Juliana's head spun with the sudden shock of it all.

'One hundred and fifty thousand pounds,' she said faintly.

'Aye. Not a lot if you run through it all at cards.' Her father looked at her sardonically. 'Enough to tempt some suitors, though.'

Juliana frowned. 'I beg your pardon, sir?'

The Marquis sighed. 'Seemed to me that the only time you have been happy is when you were married to Myfleet, my dear. So I thought to give you a dowry and tempt some suitors.' He looked at her. 'That is the only stipulation on the money, Juliana. You are to marry within three months of your thirtieth birthday. Get the matter settled quickly.'

Juliana was silent whilst a thousand thoughts battled for supremacy in her head. She felt hot and shaken. Her father was seeking to buy her a husband. He thought that she should be married off, but he did not believe that there was any way of her finding a man to marry her unless he was bought and paid for...

She stood up and went over to the window, gulping down the cool, calming air. The words were almost bursting from her but she held them back by sheer discipline. Eventually, when she felt a little calmer she said carefully, 'Forgive me if I am slow, but I do believe I need clarification, sir. You have made it known to the world that I will have a fortune of one hundred and fifty thousand pounds if I marry within three months of my thirtieth birthday?'

The Marquis plucked irritably at his sheets. 'Aye, that's so. But marriage to a man of honour, mind you, not any old riff-raff. It is your birthday next week, is it not?'

Juliana bit her lip. 'It is. However, I regret that there is no man...' her voice faltered for this bit was untrue '...there is no man that I esteem sufficiently enough to want to marry him.'

The Marquis looked slightly confused. 'No one you want to marry? But you have three months to find him. Besides, with the money as inducement—'

'The money is no inducement to me,' Juliana said politely, 'and if it is inducement to my suitors then I want nothing of them.'

A frown touched the Marquis's brow. 'Now it is I who am uncertain. Are you rejecting my offer, my dear?'

'Yes,' Juliana said. She came across to the bed and sat down next to him, so that the spotted mirror above the mantel reflected their images side by side. 'I will only marry for love, Papa. The reason that I was happy with

Edwin Myfleet was because we loved each other. It is the only reason good enough to tempt me into marriage.'

Her father made a dismissive gesture. 'Marrying for love! I do believe that is where you go wrong, Juliana.'

'You married for dynastic reasons,' Juliana pointed out quietly, 'and that did not work out very well, did it?'

She carried on bravely when her father would have interrupted.

'I do believe that you underestimate love, sir. Look at me. I have the Tallant auburn hair. My face is the same shape as yours, cast from the same mould. You yourself have said that I have your sense of humour. Yet for all my thirty years you have never believed that I was your child. You never loved me. Oh—' she made a slight gesture '—you did not say the words aloud, but everyone knew. They all knew you thought I was not your own and so could not care for me.'

'I '

'And maybe I am not.' Juliana turned on him, suddenly fierce. 'Maybe, despite all the similarities I imagine I see, you were correct and I am the child of one of my mother's lovers. You must believe that, Papa, for that is what you have been punishing me for these thirty years past.' She stood up. Her voice broke a little. 'But should that have mattered? It was never my fault! I would have given every one of those hundred and fifty thousand pounds for just one word of affection or approval from you, but I never had them. In the end I gave up trying. So I freely admit that I have done almost all the things that have gained me your disapproval in the past thirty years. And now it is too late, Papa. We cannot settle our differences with money now.'

'Juliana, wait!' the Marquis said.

Juliana shook her head. She came back to the bed and

bent to kiss his cheek. 'Excuse me, Papa. I am going back to London. I never cared for the country and I wish I had never come. Now I wish you good health and…' she smiled '…many more years in your dish.'

It was fresh outside after the stuffiness of the sickroom. Juliana was so angry that she did not want to talk to either Joss or Amy, but she did not immediately want to return to London either. Leaving the carriage drawn up in front of the portico, she took the path through the wilderness garden down towards the river. Pushing aside the fronds of willow, she slipped into the green darkness beside the riverbank, sat down on the grass and drew her knees up to her chest as she had done as a child. She felt entirely miserable. A single tear tracked down her cheek and she rubbed it away, resting her forehead on her knees as she hugged herself tightly. One hundred and fifty thousand pounds. So much money. In his own way her father had made her a very generous offer. Yet it just left her feeling hollow and sad, for what was the money when compared to all the love and cherishing that he had been incapable of giving? There was so much that she could have said— so many angry words welling up inside her—but in the end she had repressed them, thinking that there was no point. Not now, after all this time.

Buy yourself a husband… Had she come to that then, that she needed to bribe a good man to overlook her past and make her an offer? Her father clearly thought so. The idea was intolerable, and yet in her heart she believed it herself. She had told Joss that she could never marry again; that no honourable man could overlook her poor reputation. The thought hurt her.

She felt torn. Part of her was glad—glad that she need not make herself vulnerable again, glad that she need not trust a man and put herself in his power by doing so. It was the part that had always pushed people away since the fiasco of her love affair with Clive Massingham. It was the part of her that rejected Martin Davencourt at the same time as wanting him fiercely.

There was another side as well; the little girl who had wanted her father's approval still wanted to be thought lovable. Juliana scrunched herself up tighter still, then slowly relaxed with a sigh, raising her head and brushing the hair back from her face.

There was a sound behind her, a twig breaking, the crack sharp above the quiet run of the river. Juliana spun around.

Martin Davencourt was standing in the shelter of one of the willow trees. He did not speak. Juliana opened her mouth to say something, then closed it again. She could not begin to imagine what he could read in her face. She felt the hot colour come into her cheeks, as though she had been caught out in some misdemeanour, but she could not pull her gaze away from his. She scrambled to her feet.

Martin moved then, crossing the space between them in two strides. His arms went around her, he pulled her close, and then he was kissing her with a violence that Juliana found terrifying and yet utterly tender.

After a long time, she freed herself a little from his embrace.

'Martin...' When she spoke his name her voice held a mixture of wonderment and reproach.

Martin looked dazed. He shook his head slightly. 'Juliana—are you all right?'

Juliana freed herself. 'Of course. I came down here for a little quiet before I return to London...'

She tried to tidy her hair, but the trembling of her fingers and the slightly shaken undertone to her voice gave the lie to her apparent indifference. Martin trapped her fingers in his and raised her hand to his lips. Juliana looked at him and quickly away. There was such a look of tenderness in his eyes that it brought a lump to her throat.

'Martin,' she said again, and this time there was entreaty in her voice.

'Why were you crying?' Martin said.

Juliana freed herself and turned away. 'Oh, it is nothing. My father has offered me a fortune and I have turned him down. I was wondering what sort of a fool I had been.'

Martin smiled. 'Why was he offering you a fortune?'

Juliana felt cold. She wanted to confide in him, but could think of nothing more demeaning than telling Martin Davencourt that her father was offering her money to lure a husband.

'Oh, let us not speak of it! It is too dreary. I must be getting back to London.'

Martin did not move out of the way. 'It must have been very miserable to make you cry.'

'Not particularly!' Juliana fixed a bright smile on her face. She was sure it—and she—must look ghastly and unconvincing. 'I am forever crying at the drop of a hat, you know! It is one of my talents and most useful.'

Martin looked sceptical. Looking at him, Juliana wished heartily that there was just one ounce of superficiality in his make up. Then she thought that she probably had enough for two people, which rather brought her back to the beginning again. They were utterly incompatible and she simply must not think of them together.

'Then if we are not to talk of your fortune, may we

speak of what is happening between us?' Martin said. 'The other night in the icehouse…'

Juliana cast him a look from under her lashes. 'There is nothing to talk about. Sudden attraction is not unusual, Martin, and it dies as quickly as it begins. I should know. These things just do happen sometimes.'

'Nonsense.' Martin's blue gaze narrowed with bad temper. Contrarily, Juliana found it extremely attractive. She could feel herself slipping helplessly ever more deeply in love and struggled fiercely against the emotion.

'They do not just happen to me,' Martin said. 'Nor to you, from what you said to me the other night, so do not pretend.'

Juliana felt trapped. 'I know what I said.'

'Well, then.' Martin folded his arms. 'Juliana, if you persist in being so superficial and keeping me at arm's length, I shall have to find another way.'

Juliana pressed her hands helplessly together. 'But I *am* superficial. I keep telling you this. Why do you not listen to me?'

'You are certainly damnably obstinate. Anyone who can kiss like that and pretend that it does not mean anything…'

Juliana pushed her hair willy-nilly under her bonnet. She was desperate to get away. Any more of this and she would almost certainly cave in, admit she loved him and come out with all kinds of embarrassing and hopeless nonsense. She had to get rid of him. Now, before she was completely undone.

'I am sorry, Martin, but I do not wish to pursue this. It means nothing to me.'

Because she had not been able to watch him as she spoke, she completely missed the murderous blue light that came into Martin's eyes. The only warning she had was a moment of absolute stillness, before he took the hat from her fidgeting fingers and tossed it carelessly aside into the grass. His hands bit into her arms as he turned her to face him but when he spoke, his voice was very gentle, at odds with the expression in his eyes.

'Juliana, you try my patience too far. Don't *ever* pretend to me again. You trembled when I kissed you and I refuse to believe that this means nothing to you...' His fingers, featherlight, traced a line from the corner of her eyebrow, to her cheekbone and down to the curve of her jaw. His thumb brushed her bottom lip. His touch was warm against her skin. Juliana shivered. She could not help herself and she saw the flash of satisfaction in Martin's eyes.

'You see? And this is just the beginning...' He paused, his gaze intent on her mouth. Juliana felt hot and faint and deeply disturbed all at the same time. She squirmed, trying to free herself, but Martin held her fast.

'Remember that you are indifferent to me so you have nothing to fear,' he said. His mouth was very close to hers now. 'Nothing at all...'

When he kissed her Juliana's first feeling was relief, followed swiftly by a searing desire that left her weak with need. She felt her body soften against him, felt him release her only so that he could put his arms about her and draw her to him. She leaned against him, trembling, desirous, grateful. Martin lifted his mouth from hers.

'Absolutely indifferent,' he said, and she could hear the laughter in his voice. He kissed her again, parting her lips, his tongue tangling with hers. Juliana made a little sound of capitulation deep in her throat. She dragged herself away, hands against his chest, her breathing ragged, her entire body aching for his touch.

'Martin, you have proved your point.'

'Not to my satisfaction.'

He pulled her back into his arms. After a long interval he let her go and stepped back, but she could feel the control he was exercising and see the blaze at the back of his eyes.

'*Now* I have proved it to my satisfaction.'

He turned back towards the curtain of willows.

'Where are you going?' Juliana demanded in bewilderment.

Martin paused, holding the willow strands aside. 'I am going to ask your father's permission to pay my addresses to you.'

'I will not marry you!'

Martin gave her a look. 'I am not asking you—yet.'

'When you do—'

'When I do, you will agree.'

Juliana was practically bursting with indignation. 'When you do—'

But Martin had already gone.

The Marquis of Tallant had risen from his sickbed and was taking a glass of wine with his son in the library when Martin Davencourt was announced. Martin came in, bowed to them both, and Joss took one look at his friend's face before putting his glass down and moving towards the door.

'I suspect that your business with my father is serious, Davencourt. I will leave you to discuss matters. You will find me in the drawing room if you wish to talk later.'

Martin put a hand up. 'Please do not leave on my account, Tallant. I am happy to speak before you both.' He turned back to the Marquis. 'My lord, I have come to ask for the hand of your daughter in marriage.'

'You wish to marry Juliana?' the Marquis said. He

flashed a look at Joss. 'Have you spoken to her this morning, Mr Davencourt?'

'Yes, my lord.' Martin looked slightly puzzled. 'I saw her just now and I apprised her of my intention of asking your permission to pay my addresses to her.'

'I see,' the Marquis said slowly. 'What did she say?'

Martin gave him a rueful grin. 'That I could ask you all I wished, but that she would never give her consent.'

Joss choked on a laugh. His father gave him a disapproving look.

'I beg your pardon, sir,' Joss said, 'but that is so like Juliana. I am just grateful that it is Davencourt who wishes to marry her and that he will not be discouraged by such a show of unwillingness!'

Martin sketched a bow. 'Thank you, Tallant. You are, of course, quite correct that my affections are steadfast. My lord—' he glanced at the Marquis '—if you would grant me permission—'

'A moment, Mr Davencourt,' the Marquis said. 'Did my daughter mention to you about her fortune?'

Martin frowned. 'She said only that you had offered her a fortune, my lord, and that she had refused it.' A tinge of colour came into his face as the implication of the Marquis's words sank in. 'I do not wish to marry her for her money, my lord! I do not need to and I am no fortune-hunter—'

'Peace, Davencourt,' the Marquis said humorously. 'There is no need to call me out! I never suspected it of you. I am indebted to you—and grateful—that you wish to marry Juliana.'

Martin bowed, the relief clear on his face. 'The happiness is all mine, my lord.'

'My daughter plans to return to London immediately,'

the Marquis continued. 'I imagine that you will wish to return also—and persuade her of your affections?'

'I will.'

'I should be glad, however,' the Marquis said slowly, 'for the wedding to take place here at Ashby Tallant.' He held out a hand, and after a second Martin gripped it. 'Bring my daughter back to me, Davencourt,' the Marquis said softly. 'That is all I ask.'

After Martin had gone out, Joss reached for the bottle of canary on the sideboard and silently refilled his father's glass, raising his own in a salute.

'He is exactly the right husband for Juliana, sir.'

'I know it. She is fortunate. At last.' The Marquis sighed. 'Do you think that she will accept him?'

'Without a doubt. She loves him. And Davencourt is not a man to be easily dissuaded once he sets his mind to a particular course.'

The Marquis nodded and sat down with a little grunt in his chair. 'He seems a sound sort of a man. Friend of yours, isn't he, Joss?'

'Yes, sir. Though I am not sure if you view that as a recommendation.'

The Marquis gave a short bark of laughter. 'He will do. He will do very well.' He sighed. 'So Juliana refuses her inheritance yet still finds herself a husband. The Lord moves in mysterious ways sometimes, does he not, Joss?'

Joss laughed. 'And he moves very quickly,' he said. 'Very quickly indeed.'

Juliana was exhausted by the time that she reached London, and not well pleased to find that Sir Jasper Colling had just arrived and was in the hall, admiring his reflection in the silver dish on the top of the side table. When Juliana came in he straightened up quickly and smoothed his hair back. He came across and kissed her hand, looking at her with odious familiarity. Juliana was hard pressed not to run upstairs and scrub the kiss off her hand at once. She could not believe that she had once found his company enjoyable.

'Juliana.' He gave her a perfunctory bow. 'How are you?'

'I am very well, thank you, Jasper.' Juliana sighed. 'Would you care to come into the library for a moment?'

Colling followed her in and sat down, flicking his coat-tails out of the way.

'We had not seen you for an age, so I thought to call and see how you were. I hear you have been to Ashby Tallant.'

'I am just returned, so I cannot spare more than a few moments.' Juliana gave him a close look. 'So you had heard that I have been home?' A suspicion grabbed her. 'Surely that cannot be why you are here, Jasper? What have you heard?'

Colling smiled, showing his yellow teeth. 'Can't deny I have heard a rumour… So the old man's come through with the money at last, hasn't he? I knew he'd never cast you off for good. Blood is always thicker than water.'

Juliana sighed sharply. She should have thought of this, should have realised that her father would already have set his plan in motion by leaking news of her inheritance to the gossip-mongers of the *ton*. Clearly he had expected her to accept his conditions and even though she had not, now she would be fending off every fortune-hunter from here to Edinburgh.

She inclined her head politely. 'What is your point, Jasper?'

Colling did not appear put out.

'Here's the thing, Juliana. We marry, split the money

and go our separate ways. Can't say fairer than that. I'll not trouble you—I realised a while ago that you weren't interested in me. Think you're probably frigid. Massingham always said—'

'Spare me what you and Massingham discussed in your cups. Do I have this aright? You would like to marry me for my money, split the hundred and fifty thousand pounds and each of us to behave as we please?'

'That's the thing! Perfect, eh?'

Juliana got up. 'Here is some advance gossip, Jasper, setting you ahead of the pack. In a few more days everyone will hear that I have rejected my father's offer, and then I will not appear such a tempting subject.' She eyed his red, angry face with satisfaction. 'Had you not thought of that? Yes, it is true. I have rejected the hundred and fifty thousand pounds.'

Colling struggled to his feet. 'In God's name, why, Juliana?'

'I did not like my father's terms.'

Colling glared. 'You are insanely proud. I would do anything for one hundred and fifty thousand pounds.'

'Indeed.' Juliana smiled pleasantly. 'You have just proved it, have you not, Jasper? Good evening.'

She told Segsbury to turn away all other callers and went rather wearily to bed, falling into a deep sleep of complete exhaustion.

The following morning matters did not look any brighter, and after breakfast Juliana retired to the library. She wished that Beatrix was there, and that Amy and Joss had not left town. Now that she had had some time to think, she wanted someone to talk to. Once again the house felt lonely. She was just debating whether she dared risk leaving the house to take refuge with Annis and Adam, when Segsbury announced Edward Ashwick.

'Mr Ashwick is here to see you, Lady Juliana. I appreciate that you are not receiving callers, but I thought that you might wish to make an exception.'

Juliana put aside the book that she had not been reading and went out into the hall. She held out her hands to greet Edward.

'Eddie! How lovely to see you.'

Edward Ashwick was looking decidedly uneasy. He came forward, turning his hat in his hands and leant over to give her a quick peck on the cheek.

'Juliana. How are you?'

'I am very well,' Juliana said, smiling. 'But you, Eddie…what can be the matter? You look quite glum.'

'Not at all!' Edward said, adopting a falsely cheerful expression that paradoxically made him look even more miserable. 'I came… I wanted… That is, I have heard about your father's offer.'

'Oh, I see,' Juliana said, her smile fading. She gestured to him to follow her into the library.

'I wanted to tell you,' Edward said, rather desperately, 'that you must not feel you have to accept any offer just to fulfil his criteria. That is, I would not wish you to think that you should marry any cad in order to receive the money.'

'Thank you,' Juliana said, starting to smile again as she thought of Jasper Colling. 'There is no danger of me doing that.'

'No, of course.' Edward looked embarrassed. 'Didn't mean to imply that you would marry a fortune-hunter, my dear, just to get your hands on the money. I know you better than that. Nor would I wish you to think that I am hunting a fortune myself, but—' He broke off, frowning.

'But?' Juliana prompted.

'But I heard some cock-and-bull tale that you had rejected your father's wishes and would therefore lose everything you have.' Edward's shoulders slumped dejectedly. 'Dearest Juliana, I have told you before that I would deem it an honour for you to be my wife. Please, Juliana. I am most anxious for you to regain your father's good opinion and your rightful place in the world.'

Juliana sighed. She sat down and gestured him to do the same. Edward was watching her with a slightly anxious, puppyish devotion. Juliana smiled at him.

'Eddie, dear, I am so very grateful for your offer. You are the kindest man alive, but…'

'But you mean to refuse me.'

'I do. I cannot let you sacrifice yourself just to redeem me. That would be most unjust.'

A frown crinkled Edward's brow. 'But your debts! It is all wrong that you should be cut adrift like this! If the Marquis refuses to help you then you must let me offer you the protection of my name…'

'Eddie,' Juliana said quietly, 'you are all that is honourable, but I cannot accept your proposal.'

'Why not?'

'There are several reasons.' Juliana smiled. 'For a while now I have thought that you have been proposing to me out of habit rather than real feeling—'

'Devil a bit! I am devoted to you, Juliana. Everyone knows that.' Edward blushed angrily.

'Examine your heart, my dear.' Juliana shook her head. 'I believe that for many years you have been entirely constant in your affections and I have known that and have taken the most shameless advantage of you, asking you to squire me about, taking you for granted…'

'Well…' Edward looked at her out of the corner of his eye, as if uncertain whether to agree or not.

'Admit that your feelings for me have changed a little of late,' Juliana pursued. 'They have, haven't they? Do you not love me with a brother's affection now rather than that of a potential husband? For that is how I care for you. I love you very dearly, Edward—I esteem you very highly, but I could never marry you. You are like a brother to me.'

A tinge of colour crept into Edward's cheek. 'Well…I suppose…'

'You may admit it. I am not about to jump down your throat.'

Edward sighed. 'It is true that at first you dazzled me, Juliana. I have been fond of you for such a very long time…'

'But recently there has been another who is in your mind,' Juliana said gently. 'I should never wish to come between you and Kitty, Edward, not when you are beginning to love her. I will always remember your kindness to me, but I will not take advantage of it. Besides, I would have been the very worst sort of wife for a country vicar!'

Edward looked agonised. 'But what will you do, Juliana?'

'I do not know yet. Sell my jewellery and some of the furniture to pay my debts, I suppose, then see how I may live once all the bills are settled. I know that Joss would help me, but I do not wish to put him in so awkward a position with our father.' Juliana shrugged. 'I shall think of something.'

'You know that you are always welcome to stay at Eynhallow if you wish. I am sure that Adam and Annis would say the same.'

'I am sure they would. They are very kind. However,

I have no intention of turning into one of those desperate people who foist themselves on friends and family the whole year round in order to stave off penury.' Juliana shuddered. 'I could not bear to be thought of as the house guest from hell.'

Edward laughed. 'You will not have to work for a living?'

'I should hope not!' Juliana frowned. 'Can you imagine it? Who would employ me? I am scarce qualified to be a governess or teacher and people would only employ me to have the freakish pleasure of boasting of it to their friends!'

'Perhaps the Marquis will reconsider.'

'You should not bank upon it. I will not.' Juliana laughed. 'My father's temperament is not of the most flexible kind.' She put out a hand and rang the bell. 'And now that our business is concluded so amicably, Edward, will you join me in a drink? You may then tell me all about your budding romance with Kitty Davencourt. I should like to take the credit for introducing the two of you, I think. Perhaps if I have no money in future I could set up as a matchmaker!'

'Mr Davencourt is here to see you, madam,' Segsbury said at five o'clock that afternoon. 'He asks that you would see him. He says that it is most urgent.'

Despite the fact that she had been half-expecting Martin—and half-hoping that he would not call—Juliana panicked. She had been thinking about Martin's declaration on and off since she left Ashby Tallant and none of her thoughts had been helpful. She knew she loved him. She also knew she could not marry him.

'Pray tell Mr Davencourt that I am not at home,' she said.

'Mr Davencourt says that he will wait until you decide that you *are* at home, madam.'

Juliana pursed her lips. 'Oh, very well! Show him in.' She saw Martin's tall figure behind Segsbury in the doorway. 'Oh, it appears that he is in already. Thank you, Segsbury. Good afternoon, Mr Davencourt.'

Juliana's heart was beating a little quickly. Martin was looking exceptionally handsome and rather severe, and she had the feeling that he would not be deflected.

'Good afternoon, Lady Juliana.'

Segsbury closed the door. Martin came across to her. Looking up at him, Juliana felt her throat dry.

'Am I too late?' Martin said.

Juliana stared. 'I beg your pardon?'

'I understand that you are in need of a husband. Fairness might prompt you to accept the first offer.'

Juliana smiled faintly. 'The first offer came from Sir Jasper Colling, sir. Would you have wished me to accept?'

Martin stepped closer. 'Certainly not. And the second?'

'From Edward. Poor Ned, he was so torn between his old loyalty and his new love.'

Martin took the final step that brought her to his side. 'What did you say to him?'

'I thanked him. And sent him back to Kitty.'

Martin's smile was tender. He took her hands in his. 'And the third?'

Juliana bit her lip. 'I am not sure that I wish to receive a third.'

A smile crept into Martin's eyes. 'Still running away, Juliana? But you cannot deny me. I have the advantage over your other suitors.'

'You do?'

'Of course. You agreed to marry me when you were only fourteen. Surely you remember?'

Juliana frowned, then her brow cleared and she laughed. 'Oh, yes! I was prattling on that I might never get a husband, and you—'

'And I said that if you were in need of a husband when you reached the age of thirty, I would marry you myself.'

'Not a particularly elegant a proposal,' Juliana said, smiling. 'Still, it was chivalrous of you, Martin, and I do apologise for laughing you out of court.'

Martin pulled her a little closer. 'Are you laughing now?'

'No, but you are under a misapprehension.' Juliana felt a little panicky. 'I have to tell you that I am not looking to marry.'

Martin frowned. 'I had heard that the contrary was the case. That you need to marry, and soon.'

'Then you have been listening to gossip, sir.' Juliana tried to free her hands and Martin let her go, but he did not move away. He was watching her face, a slight frown in his eyes.

'It is true that my father offered the inducement of one hundred and fifty thousand pounds to persuade me to take a husband,' Juliana said, avoiding his gaze, 'or to pay a man to overlook my reputation and take me, whichever way you care to look at it.'

She saw the grim lines settle about Martin's mouth. 'That is insulting to you, Juliana. I do not care to think of it in that way.'

'Then you will be pleased to learn that I have turned down my father's offer. I was not to be bought and I did not care to give myself to a man who would only take me if the bribe were great enough. So—' Juliana turned her shoulder '—you may be easy, Martin. I am not in need of a husband, but…' she moderated her tone slightly '…I thank you for your kindness.'

Martin was still looking at her intently.

'Now it is you who are under a misapprehension, Juliana. I am not offering through kindness. I am offering because I wish to marry you.' He took her hands again, his own warm and strong. 'Juliana, I am happy to hear that you rejected your father's proposition. I would not seek to alter your opinion of that. The only matter on which I wish you to change your mind is your refusal of my suit. I want to marry you.'

'But there is no necessity!' Juliana frowned. 'Have you not understood what I am telling you?'

'Perfectly. It is you who has not understood me. I want you. I want to marry you. Must this be so difficult?'

Juliana took a deep breath. 'I am sorry, but I have no desire to remarry.' She peeped at him from under her lashes. 'I have been thinking, however…' Her words came out in a rush. 'I would be happy to be your mistress—'

She broke off. Martin's eyes had darkened to a furious blue glitter. 'What did you say?'

Juliana quailed. This time she withdrew from him completely and took refuge behind the escritoire. 'I said that I would be happy to be your mistress.'

'Thank you,' Martin said, impeccably polite, 'but that position is not on offer. I made you a proposal of marriage sixteen years ago and you agreed. It is not acceptable to try to wriggle out of it.'

Juliana stared at him. 'But I am not a suitable wife.'

Martin gave a sharp sigh. 'Is that what this is about? Please spare me the self-pity, Juliana. You are entirely suitable—'

'No, I am not!' Juliana wailed. 'Oh, Martin, I would be the most inappropriate wife for a Member of Parliament!

Surely you can see it would do your career no good at all?'

'Rubbish.'

'What, to have a wife who has disported herself immodestly with half of London? Martin, be serious.'

'Juliana, I have told you that I care nothing for the past and only for our future.'

'Your colleagues will never accept me.'

'They will if you accept the one hundred and fifty thousand pounds,' Martin said cynically. He smiled at her, a smile so warm and certain that Juliana trembled. 'Stop looking for excuses, my love.'

'But surely you can see the truth of what I am saying.'

'Just at the moment,' Martin said in a furious undertone, 'all I can see is your damned obstinacy and your wilful blindness. And...' his voice softened as his gaze swept over her face '...I can see that sulky, sensuous mouth of yours. I swear I shall run mad if I do not kiss you now.'

'Now?'

'Immediately. At once.' Martin strode around the desk and took her in his arms. Cool, gentle, the kiss made Juliana tingle down to her toes. He let her go.

'So, do you still refuse?'

'Yes,' Juliana said, with spirit. 'The fact that you wish to kiss me does not mean that I would be a suitable wife.'

'To hell with that. Your concept of suitability and mine are clearly far apart.' Martin ran a hand through his hair. 'It is true that I was once stupid enough to believe you unsuitable. However, it seems ironic that now I have changed my mind, you are the one telling me you are not an appropriate wife.'

'I believe that your judgement is unduly influenced by

other factors at the moment, sir,' Juliana said. 'You are not of sound mind.'

Martin glowered. 'Come here.'

'Why?'

'So that I may kiss you again. I wish to suffer more undue influence.'

'Is this your means of persuasion? If so, I must say you are wasting your time—'

'Save your breath.'

Martin kissed her again. Juliana trembled.

'It is quite persuasive,' she said, when at last she could breathe again.

Martin's eyes were blazing. 'I love you, Juliana. Will you marry me?'

Juliana looked at him. 'Martin, I—'

'Do you love me?'

'Yes, but I still cannot marry you.' Juliana freed herself and moved away. 'I do not want to marry ever again. That was why I said that I was happy to be your mistress.'

Martin's eyes narrowed. 'Please do not raise that again. It is marriage or nothing. Why do you not wish to marry me, Juliana?'

Juliana moved away from him. She had known that she would have to explain to him in the end, for it was only fair that if she refused Martin's suit she gave him the real reason. Nevertheless, it was very difficult. Her voice was muffled.

'The only other man I ever truly loved was Edwin Myfleet, and when he was taken from me it broke my heart. I never want that to happen again.'

Martin rubbed a hand across his forehead. 'But if you love me already you will not stop simply because you refuse to marry me!'

Juliana bit her lip. 'No, but I can avoid making it worse!

If I married you I would be in danger of loving you more and more with each passing day.'

Martin smiled tenderly. 'I should hope so.'

'There! You see!' Juliana flung out a hand helplessly. 'You are already doing it!'

'Doing what?'

'Making me love you more. I wish that you would stop.'

Martin pulled her close to him again. 'Juliana, this is foolish. I am strong and healthy and I have no intention of dying and leaving you as Myfleet did.'

Juliana shook her head. 'How can you possibly know that, Martin?' The tears came into her eyes. 'I *hated* Edwin for leaving me—*hated* him! I have never forgiven him! I loved him so much and he abandoned me, and I thought that I would die with the grief of it! How could he do that to me? To leave me when I needed him so...'

Her voice broke on a sob and she buried her face in Martin's shoulder.

For a while he just stroked her hair whilst the sobs shook her body. She felt frail in his arms, a broken butterfly. His heart was full of love and pity. Eventually, when her crying had ceased, he held her a little away from him and looked down at her woebegone face.

'Is that what this has all been about, Juliana? This business of not letting people get close to you?'

Juliana looked at him. 'Partly. After Myfleet died I thought that perhaps I could recapture that happiness with Clive Massingham. I thought I was desperately in love with him, but now I see it for the counterfeit it was. And when Massingham proved false I resolved never to risk such hurt again. So I played a few games, always keeping my suitors at arm's length.'

'Not just men. People who could have befriended you, like Amy and Annis Ashwick and even your own family.'

Juliana shrugged awkwardly. 'I was jealous of Amy. The only person I ever cared for was Joss. He was the only person who had ever shown me loyalty. When he married I was furious—and envious of his happiness. But it is true that I rebuffed Amy's offers of friendship, and Annis, too.' She wrapped her arms about herself and moved away a little. 'It was easier to stay at a distance. I dare say I could even have become reconciled with my father had I tried a little harder a little sooner. I did not want to love anyone any more.'

'Then you started to let people close.'

Juliana nodded dolefully. 'Yes… First Clara and Kitty and Brandon, then Aunt Trix and Amy, and even my father, just a little. And then you. You were the most dangerous of all because I wanted you from the first and once I had come to love you…' she shook her head '…then I was completely undone.'

Martin stepped closer to her. 'I shall not go away, you know, Juliana. I will not meekly accept a rebuff and leave you. Not when I know that you care for me.'

Juliana sighed. She could feel her resistance weakening in the face of such certainty. She did not really want to resist.

'But, Martin, if I lost you—'

'Hush. You will not. Never.'

Juliana was in his arms again and she could feel her fears receding, trembling on the edge of being vanquished. She made one last effort.

'I shall never change into a sweet little respectable wife, you know. Even when I am old I shall be one of those elderly people who delight in being a nuisance to their relatives, like Beatrix.'

Martin smiled. 'I look forward to being there to see it,' he said, as he bent to kiss her.

Chapter Twelve

Juliana Davencourt sat in front of her mirror and stared long and hard at the reflection in the glass. For some reason she had expected herself to look different in some way, as though becoming Martin's wife would have wrought a visible change. She could not quite comprehend what had happened that morning. She repeated it in her head, as though it would make it seem more real. She was now Lady Juliana Davencourt. Martin's *wife*.

She had sworn never to marry again. She had loved Edwin Myfleet with all her heart and Clive Massingham with a desperate passion, but what she felt for Martin was more than this—love and passion and tenderness and belonging, all wrapped up like the most extraordinary present and given to her. She felt dreadfully undeserving and amazingly content. Even her estrangement from her father had not been able to withstand the onslaught of happiness. When Martin had gently suggested that they might be married at Ashby Tallant, Juliana had grudgingly agreed. That morning, when her father had led her into the chapel to marry Martin with Beatrix, Joss and Amy the only witnesses, she had felt her heart would burst.

Juliana smiled at her reflection. Perhaps there was a

difference. Her eyes sparkled and her lips were curved into a smile, and it was happiness that lit that spark within her. And anticipation. For soon Martin would join her and she felt ridiculously nervous, like a first-time bride.

Juliana stood up and walked restlessly across to the window, pulling back the heavy curtain to look out over the park. In the last glow of the July twilight the meadow stretched away down to where the river ran, sinuous and dark beneath the stars. She had seldom seen Ashby Tallant looking more beautiful. The window was open and a faint breeze stirred the bed hangings and set the candle flames flickering.

There was the sound of voices from the adjoining room; Martin dismissing his valet. Juliana's mouth suddenly went dry. Now...

The door opened and Martin came through, closing the door softly behind him, pausing to look at her as she stood at the end of the bed in her simple white nightdress. Her hair had been fastened back in one fat copper plait and Juliana saw Martin smile with sweet tenderness as his gaze lingered on it.

'You look about eighteen with your hair like that, my love.' He put down his candle on the nightstand. 'Come here.'

Juliana walked slowly towards him in her bare feet. Her heart was beating in her throat and she felt a little dizzy. She reached Martin and put a hand against his chest, feeling the smooth silkiness of his dressing gown beneath her fingers.

'Martin, I am...quite frightened...'

Martin smiled into her eyes. 'Yes, you look terrified. There is no need to be afraid, my sweet.'

He kissed her very softly, his lips just brushing hers

with the lightest of touches. Juliana gave a little sigh. 'Mmm. That is very nice...'

'You see...' she felt Martin smile against her mouth '...there is not the slightest need to be frightened.'

This time he kissed her more deeply, touching his tongue to her bottom lip, sliding it into her mouth. His hands tightened a little on her waist, warm through the thin nightdress. The sweet sensations sent all of Juliana's senses into a spin. She held on to the lapels of his dressing gown and pulled him closer until her breasts were pressed against his chest and the slippery silk was crushed between them. Her legs trembled.

'Martin—' She drew away a little. 'I am not sure that I can stand for much longer...'

'Good.' Martin's voice was a little rough. He scooped her up and placed her gently in the centre of the big bed, then came to sit beside her. His hands went to her plait and he started to unravel it very gently. Juliana's gaze clung to his face. His expression was intent. Slowly, very slowly, he leaned over and kissed her again, his fingers tangling in her hair. He smelled warm and masculine and very, very appealing. Juliana wriggled with suppressed desire. She slid her hands inside the dressing robe and pushed it away impatiently, running her hands over his chest, digging her fingers into the smooth bare skin of his shoulders.

Martin groaned. His hand came up to touch her breast through the fabric of her nightgown, stroking gently. With infinite care he tugged on the ribbons and eased the garment away from her, trailing soft kisses from her collarbone down over the curve of her breast as he did so. Juliana felt as though she was drowning in sensation, tense with intolerable need. The touch of his mouth against her breasts was exquisite torment, teasing her, driving her deeper into the spiral of sensual awareness.

'I love you, Juliana…'

The words brought her eyes open to stare up into Martin's face in wonder and acceptance. She saw the concentrated desire in his eyes and felt her stomach clench with shock and excitement and frantic wanting.

When she felt his weight come down on top of her, hard and urgent, she felt nothing but gladness. She parted for him with a gasp of mingled relief and desperation, and felt him move inside her, gentle and insistent, fierce and sweet, bringing endless pleasure. She cried out and she thought he did, too, and when the last tremors had faded away he wrapped her close in his arms, cradling her to him.

The nightmares left her then; Edwin dying and breaking her heart, Massingham leaving her to face all her fears alone. She felt utterly safe and utterly loved, and she turned her face against Martin's neck and clumsily kissed the hollow of his throat.

'I love you too,' Juliana whispered, burrowing closer still.

Martin made a sound of sleepy contentment and pulled her into the crook of his arm. A moment later he stirred slightly, pressing his lips to her hair.

'Juliana, why are you laughing?'

Juliana ran her hand lightly across his chest. 'I am laughing at you, my love. I used to think that you were so serious, so controlled—'

She gasped as Martin tumbled her beneath him. There was a blaze of heat in his eyes. 'And now?'

Juliana's laughter stilled. 'Now I know how wrong I was,' she whispered as he bent to kiss her again.

* * *

After dinner the following evening, Juliana excused herself from the family and went out alone into the gardens. They let her go without comment, exchanging smiles to see the quiet happiness in her eyes. Martin kissed her lightly and told her that if she was not back within the half-hour he would come to look for her.

Juliana walked without purpose in the twilight, inhaling the sharp scent of the yew trees and revelling in the caress of the breeze on her face. Her steps were airy and her mind empty and light. All her senses seemed alive. This was the first time that she had been happy at Ashby Tallant—happy without reservation. But even now time was short, for they were to return to London within a few days and Juliana was looking forward to seeing Kitty and Clara again, and furthering her acquaintance with her new family. A part of her had wanted them at the wedding, but it had been arranged so quickly and so quietly that there had been no time. She hoped that they would forgive her and be pleased to have her as a sister.

She wandered past the lake and turned back towards the terrace. From the open windows she could hear the sound of piano music, laughter and voices. Her steps quickened at the thought of rejoining Martin and taking her place in the lighted room. Her mind had already skipped ahead to the night that was before them, and she was experiencing a *frisson* of excited anticipation, when she felt a shiver that was not so much excitement as fear. She looked about. Just for a second she had been sure that someone was watching her.

There was an ancient oak to the right of the terrace, its trunk huge and thick and its branches sweeping almost to the ground. Behind it the laurel bushes whispered secretively in the wind. Juliana quickened her pace, suddenly anxious to be inside. It was very dark here. Dark and somehow cold.

Someone moved on the path in front of her. Moved and spoke. It was a voice she recognised but she had never thought to hear it again.

'Good evening, Juliana,' Clive Massingham said. 'I have been waiting for you.'

Chapter Thirteen

'Massingham,' Juliana said flatly.

Clive Massingham stepped out of the shadows of the laurel and into the full moonlight. It fell full on that well-remembered face; the handsome features coarser now, the eyes narrow and full of suspicion, the fleshy mouth with its bitter twist. Juliana wondered that she could ever have loved him. It seemed impossible. She thought that she had come so far, yet here she was at the beginning again. A dull misery settled on her heart.

'I thought that I had seen you,' she said tonelessly. 'Outside Emma Wren's house one night, and again at a ball one night. Then I thought I must have been imagining things…'

'Dreaming of me?' Massingham laughed. 'Yet you do not seem particularly pleased to see me, my love.'

Juliana pressed her hands together. 'I am not. Of course I am not. I thought that you were dead.'

'You do not seem shocked to find that I am not.'

Juliana shifted slightly. She realised that she was shocked, but she was not remotely surprised.

'It is just the sort of thing that you would do, Massingham. I always had the strangest feeling that I was not rid of you.'

'Why would you want to be?'

Massingham sounded genuinely hurt and Juliana realised that his conceit was so great that he had seriously expected her to fall into his arms with tears of joy. She spoke coldly.

'There are so many reasons. Where do I start?'

'Is it because of your new husband?' Massingham jerked his head towards the lighted windows of the hall. 'Done well for yourself this time, Juliana, I'll say that for you. A fine, upright man rather than—'

'Rather than an adventurer like you?'

Massingham's face darkened. She saw the bitterness twist his features again. 'There was a time when you rather enjoyed my company, Juliana. We lived by our wits, you and I, and it suited us both.'

Juliana locked her shaking fingers together tightly. 'That was before you used your wits to rob me of all our money and then abandoned me on my own in Venice.' She looked at him. 'They told me you had died in the debtor's prison.'

Massingham laughed again. 'That was where some of your precious money went, my dear. It was easy enough to purchase my freedom—and a new identity. I found it liberating.'

'It liberated me, too,' Juliana said steadily. 'From my infatuation with you. Lord, what a fool I was, to prize excitement so high! And it never really was exciting, was it, Clive? Rather it was desperate and demeaning and rather sad. You were never faithful to me and you never cared about me. I wish you had not come back.'

'Are you are in love with Davencourt?' A jeering note had come into Massingham's voice now. 'The little lady rakehell turns respectable after all and marries a dull old stick.'

'I believe you mean a man of honour and integrity.' Juliana's voice strengthened. 'Yes, I do love Martin with all my heart. He has all the qualities which you so conspicuously lack.'

'And I thank the lord for it.' Massingham thrust his hands into his pockets. He sounded decidedly cheerful. 'Well, this changes things a little, but not for the worse. I was afraid that I might have to pretend that I had missed you. At least we may make a business transaction, you and I, and need not put ourselves to the trouble of pretending to an affection we do not feel.'

Juliana stared. 'What do you mean, a business transaction?'

'Come now, my dear. You may have turned respectable, but have your wits gone begging?' Massingham grinned. 'Surely you do not expect me to go meekly away and keep quiet whilst you live out an idyll of love?' He laughed mirthlessly. 'A rich idyll.'

'Oh, I see.' The light dawned on Juliana. 'Yes, I suppose that it was naïve of me to assume that you would be here if you did not want something.'

'Of course.'

'Money, I suppose?'

'Of course,' Massingham said again. 'I hear you have rather a lot of it now and so does Davencourt. God knows why he married you. You can have nothing in common. I have yet to learn that you take any interest in politics.' He appraised her thoughtfully. 'I suppose he wanted you. You're still a damned good-looking woman, even if you're as cold as ice. Let us hope he isn't as disappointed as I was.'

Juliana clenched her fists. 'You have a fine way of persuading me to pay you off, Clive.'

'Well…' Massingham shrugged. 'You're in no position to complain, are you, my love? After all, you are *my* wife. A word from me, and all is undone.'

Juliana bit her lip so hard she tasted blood. His wife. That was something she did not want to think about at the moment, for she was afraid that once she did her world would break apart and she could never put it back together again.

She took a deep breath. 'What exactly do you want?'

Massingham laughed. 'I would like to say that all I wanted was for you to pay me to go away. Unfortunately for us both, it is more lucrative to be your husband than it is to blackmail you, my love.' He waited, but when she did not speak, he added, 'I want the one hundred and fifty thousand pounds that your father is settling on you, Juliana. That is why I am about to return from the dead—as your husband.'

Juliana went cold. 'Papa will never pay if he knows that that money is going to you! There is no one that he detests more!'

Massingham's lip curled. 'All the more reason why he should be *made* to pay,' he snarled. 'And of course he will. The old man is a realist, unlike you, my sweet. He understands that it is money that makes the world go round, not old-fashioned sentiment!'

'But—'

'This is what is going to happen,' Massingham said in a voice that chilled her. 'I shall announce my return from the dead and come to claim my wife with all haste and affection.' The sneer in his voice was very pronounced. 'Your father will pay up to minimise the scandal. If you even thought of objecting, Juliana, I should be obliged to

broadcast all the intimate details of our affair and elope-
ment to the *ton* and drag your name through the dirt so
thoroughly that this time you would never recover. Your
past indiscretions would be as nothing to this, my pet, and
I would drag Davencourt down with you, too.' He smiled.
'It is fortunate that you have had such a quiet wedding
this time, for this way we may get rid of Davencourt with
no one the wiser. Best say your fond farewells to him, my
sweet. I wish to claim you and my place in society.'

'You mean that you wish to claim the money,' Juliana
said, her voice shaking. 'You care nothing for anything
else.'

'Not quite true. I care for revenge.' Massingham
smiled. 'Which is why, my sweet Juliana, even in the
unlikely event of your father being prepared to match the
money and pay me off, I would not be prepared to go. I
want you all to suffer. You, your father, Davencourt... It
gives me immense satisfaction.'

'I truly believe that you are sick, Clive,' Juliana said
shakily. 'Twisted with envy and bitterness—'

'Sick of poverty and having no real place in the world,'
Massingham said. 'That is all. Now, I want you to tell
Davencourt that I am returned and he is dismissed. No
arguments, no tears or promises. You are legally my wife,
not his, and that is all there is to be said.'

'He will never accept it,' Juliana said. 'He will not simply leave me.'

'He will if you tell him that you have always been in
love with me and that as I am returned, your legal husband, you want to come back to me.'

'I cannot do that!'

'Yes, you can!' Massingham put his face close to hers.
'You can if you do not want Davencourt's career in ruins.
Think of the effect on him if I start to spread the scandal.

The bigamous husband... Would he be considered an unsound fool or just a laughing-stock?' He made a derisive noise. 'Would you do that to him, Juliana? Both of you would be utterly ruined, not to mention the prospects of those pretty little sisters of his...'

Juliana caught her breath. Up until now her mind had been full of her own predicament and the effect that it would have on Martin. She had not had the time to think more broadly, but now she could see what Massingham was getting at. This did not simply affect her. It did not only involve Martin. It embraced the whole of the Davencourt family.

She thought that very probably it would not affect Kitty's prospects of marriage, for Edward Ashwick was head over ears in love with her and was tenacious in his affections. Clara was a different matter, however, and then there were all the younger girls to be considered... They would never have the chance of making a good match if the family was disgraced. She could never bring that upon them all.

'I will tell him at once,' she said, through dry lips. 'But you must give me a little time to sort matters out. A day? I will meet you again tomorrow night.'

'Then we will talk again.' There was satisfaction in Massingham's voice. She could tell that he thought she had already given in. 'Poor Davencourt. Losing his dearly beloved wife—' there was heavy sarcasm in his voice '—I could almost sympathise with him.'

Juliana went inside, ignored the light flowing from the half-open drawing-room door and made blindly for the stairs. Once inside her room, she locked the door and lay down on the big bed, staring blindly at the ceiling.

It seemed inconceivable. Even when she had thought

she had glimpsed Clive Massingham in London she had
dismissed it as her mind playing tricks. Yet it had been
no illusion. And now Massingham was back and she was
in the most dire straits imaginable.

She sat bolt upright. Massingham was her husband and
nothing could change that. She was legally bound to him
and there was no escape. Her marriage to Martin was
false; meaningless. Thank God that it had been a quiet
affair with only the family present. As far as the rest of
the world was concerned this was just a house party. They
could hush the matter up, swear everyone to secrecy. Martin could go back to London and take up his parliamentary
career, his siblings would be untouched by scandal and in
a few weeks Juliana could announce to the startled world
that the husband she had thought dead had returned...

She buried her head in her hands. It was not that simple,
even in practical terms. Firstly there was the prospect of
her father refusing to pay the hundred and fifty thousand
pounds. She could quite easily see the intransigent old
man washing his hands of her this time, and who could
blame him? To give a huge sum of money to the man
who had run off with his wife and then years later married
his daughter was asking too much of him. The tentative
steps she and her father had taken towards reconciliation
would be crushed forever. Yet if the Marquis did not pay,
Massingham would produce every vengeful, disgusting
story that he could manufacture about her, and worse still,
her mother, and then the Marquis would be broken. That
would be too much for the frail old man to take.

Juliana gave an involuntary sob, and bit her lip vi-
ciously to regain her self-control. That misery was bad
enough but it was as nothing compared to the desolation
of losing Martin. She loved him so desperately—they had
been so happy for a short while. Yet what could they do?

She was Massingham's wife and that made her Martin's mistress. No more, no less. They could not live together openly for the scandal would ruin his career and destroy his sisters' lives. He had to let her go.

Juliana stared dry-eyed into the darkness. She knew Martin and she knew that that would be the difficult part. Massingham had suggested that she lie to Martin, deceive him. She knew she could never do that. He was an honourable man and he deserved honesty in return. Besides, he would never believe her if she told him she loved Massingham, not him. He would know it was a lie.

Juliana grimaced. If she told him the absolute truth, he would never let her go. Something terrible would be bound to happen. He would insist on her divorcing Massingham, or even worse, he would challenge Massingham to a duel and either way the scandal would come out and everyone would be ruined anyway. Martin would never desert her. She knew that in her soul. It was what set him apart from a man like Clive Massingham, what made his love true against Massingham's counterfeit, what made her love him all the more.

It was what would make her tell him the whole truth.

She slid off the bed.

The house was quiet, though the door to the drawing room was still open and there was the sound of laughter and voices from within. She remembered what she had said to Martin only the day before when they had been walking together in the gardens: *I could not be happier than I am here and now...*

Juliana took a deep breath. These people were her family and there could be no concealment, especially if they were all to stick together in the story that they told to the outside world.

Just for a second, when she stood in the shadow of the

drawing-room door, they all turned their smiling faces towards her and she thought that she would remember that moment forever. Just for a moment they were frozen in happiness, and then she saw their faces change and their smiles start to fade as they took in her appearance and someone—Amy?—said, 'Juliana? What has happened?'

But Juliana was looking at Martin, who had already got to his feet and started to come towards her across the room, a frown in those blue eyes as he took in her evident distress.

'Excuse me, everyone,' Juliana said steadily. She did not take her eyes from Martin's face for a second. 'I need to speak with Martin. I am sorry, but I have something to tell him. And then I think I need to talk to you all too.'

Martin's arms were about her so tightly that Juliana thought her ribs might crack, though she made no word of protest. His face was buried in her hair and he kept repeating:

'I will not let you go. I will not let you go. Never...'

Juliana freed herself a little. They were in the empty drawing room and it was very late. She had told Martin everything and they had argued themselves to a standstill, with Juliana trying to impress upon him the importance of keeping the whole matter secret and Martin insisting that the only thing that mattered was that they should be together and hang the consequences. It was what Juliana had known he would say. It was what she had wanted him to say in her heart of hearts—the ultimate proof that he loved her above all things—and yet now it terrified her.

She brushed the tangled hair back from her face and sat back on the sofa. 'Martin, we have been over this so many times, my dear. There is no alternative. I am Massingham's wife, no matter how little either of us want that to be the case.' She saw the look on his face, the distaste and stubborn refusal to accept the truth. He took a sharp turn about the room.

'Are you sure?' he said suddenly. 'Are you certain that the marriage was legal?'

Juliana stared and then she started to laugh. 'Oh, Martin, would you truly prefer that I had lived in sin with him than that we were legally wed?'

'Infinitely.' Martin came across to her and knelt by her side. 'It would not have been your fault and, even if it was, it does not matter one whit to me. What matters is for us to be married. Officially, I mean, for in my heart I could not feel more married to you. Juliana—'

Juliana looked away. She could not bear the hope in his voice, in his eyes, nor the fact that she had to dash it.

'The marriage to Massingham was legal,' she said flatly. 'It was performed by an English pastor in Venice. I have the marriage lines. I am sorry, Martin. I would prefer it, too, but I am afraid it is not so.'

The light went out of Martin's face like a candle being extinguished. He ran a hand through his hair.

'Then if that is the case, you must divorce him instead.'

Juliana made a desperate gesture. 'Martin, we have spoken of this. You do not know the man! He will spread the most vile scandals about me and then you will be utterly ruined.'

'It does not matter. I will still have Davencourt—and you.'

'And the girls?' Juliana said. 'How will they feel to be branded the sisters-in-law of the most notorious bigamist in London?'

There was a silence. 'They will have to accept it,' Martin said.

'Oh, Martin, you cannot do that to them! You know you cannot.'

Martin came back to her. 'It is either that or I put a bullet through him. Take your choice.'

Juliana shook her head. 'That is no solution, tempting as it is! We are not thinking clearly.'

'I will not leave you,' Martin said again. His jaw was set in so stubborn a line that it almost made Juliana smile. 'Supposing there is a child, Juliana? I could not countenance for Massingham to claim it as his, or for you to be obliged to raise it alone.'

Juliana had not thought of this and the pain the thought engendered ripped through her. To bear Martin's child, yet to be forever separated from him, seemed intolerable. Not to bear his child when she so desperately wanted it seemed almost as bad. Her agonised gaze clung to his.

'Our child? Oh, Martin, do not even think of it...'

'I must. Can you deny the possibility?'

Juliana closed her eyes. 'No, I cannot, of course. Not yet. But at least we will know in a little while.'

'That is not good enough. It is simply another reason why I will not let you face this alone.'

Juliana put her head in her hands. Her thoughts were scrambling around like rats in a trap. 'I cannot think straight any more. Let us sleep on this and talk again in the morning.'

'I cannot sleep.' Martin's face softened. 'But you look exhausted, my love. You must go to bed.'

'Not without you,' Juliana said. She looked at him. There was a split-second of tension between them. 'I shall not sleep without you there.'

Martin put out a hand and pulled her to her feet. He kissed her with all the pent-up love, longing and desperation that was between them. Juliana wanted the kiss to go on forever, but he let her go and she felt chilled. She scanned his face.

'Come, let us go to bed. Matters may seem clearer in the morning.'

The house was in darkness and silence. They climbed the stairs hand in hand, but when they reached the landing, Martin made to go into his dressing room.

'I should leave you to sleep alone.'

Juliana smiled tremulously. She put up a hand to touch his face, feeling the stubble rough against her palm, the hard line of his jaw beneath her fingers.

'I thought that you said you would not leave me? Are you to renege on your promise so soon?'

Martin groaned. He turned his mouth against her palm. 'Juliana, God knows, I want you. I love you so much. But...I should not touch you now.'

'Then Massingham has already won,' Juliana said tiredly, 'and there is no more to be said.'

She turned away, but Martin caught her arm. He flung her bedroom door open with a crash, propelled her over the threshold and kicked the door closed behind them. Hattie, who was warming Juliana's nightdress before the fire, looked up, startled.

'Leave us, please,' Martin said tersely, and Juliana smiled that, even in his anger and grief, Martin was polite to the servants.

The door had barely closed behind the maid when Martin crushed her to him, his mouth taking hers hard. He had one hand on the small of her back, holding her against him, and the other went to the neck of her gown. He pulled it down, freeing her breasts, baring her to his gaze.

Juliana gasped. The driving urgency and desperation in Martin transmitted itself to her and turned her wild. Misery and desolation burned up in a violent storm. Martin divested himself of his clothes quickly, kicking them aside, shrugging out of his shirt with impatient movements. He performed a like service for her, tossing her gown to the floor and pulling her down beside him on the bed. He licked the warm hollow between her breasts and her whole body shuddered as he touched his tongue to her nipple, biting down gently. His lips traced a path across her stomach and it tightened with excitement and fierce anticipation, her legs parting helplessly beneath the sweet onslaught of his kisses. He came back to her mouth to kiss her again deeply until she moaned and pulled him to her, careless with wanting. She wrapped her arms about him, relishing the feel of the muscles of his naked back hard under her questing fingers. They rolled over and tumbled off the bed and on to the floor, where the fire cast its heated glow over the polished boards. Juliana started to struggle up, but Martin held her down, her shoulders against the bare wood, his weight trapping her lower body and holding her fast. He was on her and inside her, caressing her breasts, calling out her name, and the darkness washed over Juliana, building in waves, holding her helplessly on the brink of ecstasy until she tumbled over the edge.

It felt so right for Martin to make love to her. It had to be right.

But then the emotion broke and Juliana turned her face away and cried and cried until she could cry no more. And although Martin took her back to bed and held her and comforted her, she knew it could never be the same, and for the second time in her life, her heart was breaking, and she knew that Martin's was breaking, too.

Chapter Fourteen

The family met after breakfast and talked all day, but still could reach no solution. The Marquis was all for paying Massingham off and Juliana's broken heart took another blow to see her father offer to pay the full one hundred and fifty thousand pounds without hesitation to the man he hated above all things. The Marquis's face was lined and old, and when she went across to kiss him, she could feel his tears wet against her cheek and almost cried again herself.

'My first choice of action would be to put a bullet in him,' Joss said cheerfully. 'A duel. Quick, efficient. Martin, what do you think?'

Martin nodded. 'Decidedly. No other option comes close.' He laughed, the grim lines of his face lightening briefly. 'I had already come up with that suggestion. The difficulty is that it does not meet with Juliana's approval.'

'If anyone is entitled to shoot Clive Massingham, then it is me,' Juliana said, trying to match Joss's cheerfulness. 'However, we have to consider the repercussions. For any of us to end up in prison for murder would scarce be a sensible course of action.'

'Get rid of the body,' Joss said briefly. 'No one would miss him and the man deserves it anyway.'

There was a silence.

'It is tempting,' Juliana said at last, 'but I cannot agree. Surely we do not condone murder?'

'Generally not,' Amy said thoughtfully, 'but I could stretch a point in this case.'

Juliana sighed. 'Perhaps you are right. I do not know. I do not know anything any more.'

Amy took her hand in a comforting clasp. 'When did you say that you would meet with him again?'

'Tonight,' Juliana checked the clock. 'In an hour's time. In the summerhouse by the lake. Oh, what shall we do?'

There was a pause. Joss and Martin exchanged a look. 'Go and meet him,' Martin said, sounding as though there was a bad taste in his mouth. 'And play for time. We need more time to think—or at least to fashion a plan.'

Joss nodded. 'Tell him that you have not had the chance to talk to Martin but that you will do it tonight. Tell him that your feelings are in turmoil at his reappearance. Martin and I will be close by and, if matters turn sour, we come out—'

'I think it would be worse if you showed your faces,' Juliana said with a shiver, 'for how would that end? Best to leave it to me. I can manage Massingham. He has not changed much.'

She saw the look that Martin gave her and she felt cold, as though his love for her was unravelling where she stood. With Massingham dead, all her indiscretions might have been left in the past, where they belonged. But with Massingham alive, the wedge was already driven between them. Even now, they were moving further and further apart.

* * *

Massingham did not come.

Juliana waited in the summerhouse whilst the moon rose over the lake and the breeze rippled across its surface and made her shiver with a combination of cold and nervousness. After an hour, Martin came out of his hiding place amongst the trees and took her back inside. Neither of them spoke at all, and that night, Juliana slept alone.

The following morning, everyone looked jaded and tired at the breakfast table, as though none of them had slept. Forcing down a cup of tea and a piece of toast and honey, Juliana reflected that she simply could not bear to spend another day of uncertainty, wondering why Massingham had not come last night, whether he was deliberately trying to make them all suffer by prolonging the ordeal, and what would happen next. When the butler came in with a letter for her, she was almost certain that it must be from him and took it with a word of thanks and a heavy heart.

She looked at it closely. It did not look like Massingham's writing, but she could not be sure. She slid her knife under the seal and looked at the signature.

Martin was watching her. 'Is it from him?'

'No,' Juliana said slowly. 'It is signed by someone called Marianne.'

There was a clatter as the Marquis dropped his knife and a footman came forward to retrieve it. Juliana looked at him. His face was paper white and Beatrix put out a hand to him. Juliana saw Amy shoot Joss a questioning look. She frowned.

'What is it? Have I—?'

The door opened and the butler came in again.

'Mr Creevey, the parish constable, is here, my lord. He

apologises for the earliness of the hour but said that his business was most urgent. Shall I ask him to wait?'

The Marquis threw his napkin down. 'We will all see Mr Creevey now, Edgar. Show him into the blue drawing room.'

They all filed into the drawing room and Edgar ushered the Constable in. Mr Creevey, a naturally cadaverous man, was looking very shaken. He seemed even more disturbed to find that he was obliged to impart his news in front of the ladies, and was only slightly re-assured when the Marquis gave him his full permission to proceed.

'My apologies for the disturbance, my lord, but I thought to apprise you of this at once. A shocking thing has occurred, my lord, quite shocking! We have never had a murder in Ashby Tallant in all my years here!' The constable looked as though he was taking it as a personal insult. 'And a stranger as well!'

Juliana cast Martin a sharp look. He looked back at her, and shook his head very slightly. Juliana looked at Joss. He gave her the ghost of a grin and raised his shoulders in a tiny shrug.

'A murder,' the Marquis said slowly. 'You find us agog, Mr Creevey. Who is the unfortunate victim?'

'A gentleman staying at the Feathers, my lord. A stranger from London, apparently.'

'Better that than a local man or woman,' Lady Beatrix opined, at her most patrician. 'Trust a stranger to have the indelicacy to get himself murdered on our doorstep!'

'Shockingly poor behaviour,' the Marquis said. 'I hope that you have the matter in hand, Mr Creevey?'

The constable nodded gloomily. 'Seems an open-and-shut case, my lord. The gentleman—' he consulted his notebook '—a Mr Masham, according to his papers, was staying at the Feathers. Just passing through, on his way back to London, apparently. Did you know him, my lord?'

The Marquis shook his head slowly. 'Never met him, Creevey,' he said.

'Just so, my lord. Unlikely you would have done, I suppose.' Mr Creevey shook his head. 'Mr Masham was not travelling alone. It seems there was a lady with him.'

He shook his head again at the immorality of man in general and Mr Masham in particular. 'Quietly spoken lady, so Cavanagh at the Feathers said. Older, no Covent Garden doxy. But you never can tell. It's the quiet ones you have to watch.'

Martin put his hand over Juliana's where she was tightly gripping the material of the sofa. She made a conscious effort to relax her fingers. She had no idea where this was tending, but she was absolutely certain that the victim was Clive Massingham. The question was how…

'What happened, man?' The Marquis's voice was quite steady.

'Well, sir…' The constable shot a nervous look in the ladies' direction. 'Seems there was some hanky panky, if you know what I mean.'

The Marquis looked down his nose. 'Barely. You will have to be more precise, I fear, Creevey.'

Mr Creevey blushed. 'Some amorous indulgence, my lord. Between the lady and the gentleman.'

'Ah.'

'Only it seems to have gone wrong.' The Constable riffled through the pages of his notebook a little nervously. 'The corpse—Mr Masham, I should say—was found stark naked, my lord, gagged, spread-eagled and tied to the four corners of his bed. There was a pot of feathers on the mantelpiece, and an—'

'Sufficient detail, I think, Creevey.' The Marquis's voice was dry. 'Dare one ask the cause of death?'

'Suffocation, my lord. The gag…' Mr Creevey look awkward. 'Very tight, it was, my lord. And the poor gentleman with his eyes starting out of his head in an effort to break free and breathe. But the bonds were fastened too well, see, and—'

'Yes, thank you, Creevey,' the Marquis cut him off ruthlessly. 'I believe we have the picture now. An open-and-shut case, you said. And his companion? The lady?'

Creevey sighed. 'Gone, my lord. Cool as you please. Took the gentleman's coach and horses last night and said that Mr Masham wanted to be left undisturbed as he had some papers to work on. She said that he would be hiring a horse to follow her up to London, and Cavanagh let her go, never guessing…' Creevey shrugged. 'This morning he goes to see if the gentleman wants breakfast and finds this!'

Joss spoke quietly. 'Do you think there is any chance of finding her, Creevey?'

'None, my lord. Cavanagh did not even know her name and he thought her hair was brown. Someone else thought she had fair hair. No one can describe her properly, she was so self-effacing. Like I said, it is always the quiet ones…'

'Well, thank you Creevey,' Joss said, catching his father's eye and standing up to usher the constable to the door. 'I am sure that you will let us know if anything further transpires.'

'Of course, my lord.' Creevey took his dismissal politely. He bowed awkwardly. 'Excuse me, ladies.'

The door closed. They all waited until they heard the sound of Edgar closing the front door.

'Killed by his own vice,' Lady Beatrix said at last, and

there was unmistakeable satisfaction in her voice. 'How poetic. How tidy.'

Juliana slumped against Martin, shock and relief coursing through her veins, making her light-headed. 'I cannot believe it!' Her voice fell to a whisper. 'I cannot believe he is dead…' She could feel the warmth and reassurance of Martin's body and pressed herself closer to him. 'The co-incidence—'

'It is no co-incidence.' The Marquis's voice was harsh. 'Where is your letter, Juliana?'

Juliana frowned. She had almost forgotten the letter in her astonishment at Creevey's news. 'It is here. But—'

'I suggest that you read it.' The Marquis levered himself to his feet with difficulty. 'If there is anything that you wish to tell us, you will find the rest of us in the breakfast room.'

He went out, leaning heavily on Beatrix's arm and after a moment Amy and Joss followed. Martin made to go out with the others, but Juliana put a hand out and caught his sleeve. 'No… Martin, please stay with me.' She met his eyes and saw the smile in them as he returned to her side, and her frozen heart started to melt. Perhaps it was going to be all right.

She unfolded the letter and started to read.

My dear Juliana,

This was never intended to be a confession, but should you ever need it to stand as one then I leave that to your discretion. Clive Massingham may have told you that he assumed a new identity in Italy and I doubt that the truth will ever come out. I hope not. It would serve no purpose. He is dead now and by the time you receive this I too shall be gone.

Massingham sought me out in Italy a few months ago. It was more than twenty years since he had left me, but he assumed that I would be pleased—happy, even—to make his acquaintance once again. He was mistaken, but then Massingham always did have an inflated opinion of his own attractions. It is a common fault in that type of man, I find. But I digress.

I was on the point of throwing him out of my house when he started to speak of you—how he had eloped with you, married you and abandoned you in Venice two years before. He seemed inordinately proud of his appalling behaviour.

At first I could not believe what I was hearing. To cause such pain to a child of mine…I think my grief was all the greater because I had never done anything at all for you myself, and then this man was telling me so proudly of all the unspeakable wickedness he had inflicted upon you… I think perhaps that I went a little mad then, for if I had had some weapon to hand I would certainly have despatched him to his maker there and then. I had no idea how much time had passed, or how I must have appeared, yet when my anger cleared I realised that he was still talking and had absolutely no idea of what I was feeling.

When he suggested that we should return to England, he and I, and convince your father to make our fortunes by paying us both to go away, I needed little persuasion. It was not for the reasons that Massingham imagined, arrogant fool that he was. I knew he intended more trouble for you and *that* I could not permit. Whatever was between your father and myself was dead and buried long ago, but Massingham had done you enough harm—too much harm—already, and could not be permitted to cause trouble again.

We came first to London, where he made discreet enquiries into your whereabouts and your situation. He was delighted to discover that you were being courted by Martin Davencourt, for he could see the potential profit in the situation. I do believe that what he intended at first was simple blackmail, but when he heard of your father's plan to endow you with a fortune he was cock-a-hoop. He planned to reappear as your husband, claim the fortune, and then split it with me. I believe that he apprised you of this when he came to see you two days ago. Naturally he saw it as a means for us both to revenge ourselves on your father—and to make a pretty penny into the bargain. Strangely he never doubted that my aim was the same as his, and that was his mistake.

The rest was easy. On the night that he was to come back to see you, I lured him to his chamber. As I say, it was easy. Massingham had a boundlessly good opinion of his own attractions and I am still a passably good-looking woman... He suspected nothing until the moment I pressed the gag into his mouth with rather more force than was necessary for a love game. I will spare you the unpleasant details of his death, but I fear he suffered quite a lot. Such is the lot of the evil extortioner.

Dear Juliana, I was never there to give you anything as a child, and no doubt there will be those who will say that what I have done for you now is somewhat unorthodox, even for a mother. Nevertheless I shall pray for your happiness with your good man. Marry him again at once, with all speed, and never let him go. That is the only piece of advice

that I shall ever give you, but it is from the heart. I wish you all the luck in the world. Your mother,
Marianne

'Juliana?' Martin said, but when he saw her face he simply gathered her into his arms without another word.

It was later in the day, when all the talking was done, that Juliana went up into the attic. She pulled aside the cloth that cloaked the Marchioness of Tallant's picture and stared at the pretty, painted face. The eyes were definitely the same as hers; emerald green with specks of gold and with the same bright, unquenchable spirit. Oh, yes, Marianne Tallant was unorthodox, amoral even... There were those who would have to condemn her if they ever knew what she had done. Then there were those like her husband the Marquis, who would keep his silence even to the grave, and those like her daughter who would know that in her own, strange fashion her mother had loved her and set her free...

Juliana smiled a little sadly and pulled the cloth back across the painting. She knew that none of them would ever meet Marianne Tallant again.

It was the following day that Juliana and Martin went down to the river. They made their way down through the water meadows and pushed aside the screen of willows and slipped into the green darkness. Today the river ran softly. Here Martin had spread his books and papers on the bank, drawn his sketches and made his models. Here she had lain in the warm grass and chattered about balls and parties and the London Season whilst his pencil had whispered across the paper and he had let her talk at will. She could almost see the ghost of them sitting there, almost here the echo of their words down the years.

If you are still in want of a husband when you are thirty years of age I shall be glad to marry you myself.

If I am unmarried at thirty I would be happy to accept your offer.

Juliana smiled slightly. Time had a strange way of moving in circles. Slow, unpredictable sometimes, but finally the circle was closed. That morning they had married again with the Marquis and Beatrix, Amy and Joss, as witnesses again and this time it was for good.

Wordlessly Martin put out a hand and drew her into the crook of his arm. Juliana leaned her head against his shoulder. His breath stirred her hair.

'Is all well, Juliana?'

Juliana turned in his arms and pressed her cheek against his. She rubbed it gently, then slid her hands round to the back of his neck so that she could pull his head down and kiss her husband. 'It is well,' she said, smiling. 'It is very well indeed.'

* * * * *

If you enjoyed what you just read,
then we've got an offer you can't resist!

Take 2 bestselling love stories FREE!

Plus get a FREE surprise gift!

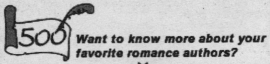

COMING NEXT MONTH FROM

HARLEQUIN HISTORICALS®

- ## THE LAST CHAMPION
  by **Deborah Hale,** author of BEAUTY AND THE BARON
  Though once betrothed, Armand Flambard and
  Dominie De Montford were now on opposite sides of the
  civil war raging in England. But when Dominie found herself
  in dire straits, Armand was the only man who could help her.
  Would they be able to put aside the pain of the past and find
  a love worth waiting for?
  HH #703 ISBN# 29303-8 $5.25 U.S./$6.25 CAN.

- ## THE ENGAGEMENT
  by **Kate Bridges,** author of THE SURGEON
  After his brother jilted Dr. Virginia Waters at the altar, mounted
  police officer Zack Bullock did the decent thing and offered a marriage of convenience…but then broke off the engagement when vil-
  lains threatened Virginia's life. And to make matters worse, Zack's
  commanding officer ordered him to act as the tempestuous beauty's
  bodyguard.…
  HH #704 ISBN# 29304-6 $5.25 U.S./$6.25 CAN.

- ## THE DUKE'S MISTRESS
  by **Ann Elizabeth Cree,** author of MY LADY'S PRISONER
  Three years ago Lady Isabelle Milborne had participated in
  a wager that had ruined Justin, the Duke of Westmore. Now Justin
  would stop at nothing to see justice served, but would he be content
  to have Belle as his mistress for just the Season, or would he need
  her in his life forever?
  HH #705 ISBN# 29305-4 $5.25 U.S./$6.25 CAN.

- ## HIGH COUNTRY HERO
  by **Lynna Banning,** author of THE SCOUT
  Bounty hunter Cordell Lawson needed a doctor to treat a wounded
  person stranded in an isolated cabin, and Sage Martin West was
  his only hope. As Sage and Cordell traveled to the victim, their
  attraction was nearly impossible to deny. Could the impulsive boun
  hunter and the sensible, cautious doctor overcome their differences
  and find a lasting love?
  HH #706 ISBN# 29306-2 $5.25 U.S./$6.25 CAN.

KEEP AN EYE OUT FOR ALL FOUR
OF THESE TERRIFIC NEW TITLES

HHCNMO